FORGET TOMORROW

PINTIP DUNN

ENTANGLED PUBLISHING, LLC

PINTIP
DUNN

FORGET TOMORROW

Entangled Publishing, LLC
2614 South Timberline Road
Suite 109
Fort Collins, CO 80525

Entangled Teen is an imprint of Entangled Publishing, LLC.

Visit our website at www.entangledpublishing.com.

Edited by Liz Pelletier
Cover design by L.J. Anderson
Interior design by Jeremy Howland

Print ISBN 978-1-63375-238-2
Ebook ISBN 978-1-63375-240-5

Manufactured in the United States of America

First Edition November 2015

10 9 8 7 6 5 4 3 2 1

For my sister Lana

1

"The next leaf that falls will be red," my six-year-old sister Jessa announces. An instant later, a crimson leaf flutters through the air like the tail feather of a cardinal.

Jessa grabs it and tucks it into the pocket of her school uniform, a silver mesh jumpsuit that is a smaller version of mine. Crunchy leaves blanket the square, the only burst of color in Eden City's landscape. Behind our patch of a park, bullet trains shoot by in electromagnetic vacuum tubes, and metal and glass buildings vie for every inch of pavement. Their gleaming spirals do more than scrape the sky—they punch right through it.

"Now orange," Jessa says. A leaf the color of overripe squash tumbles from the tree. "Brown." Sure enough, brown as mud and just as dead.

"You going for some kind of record?" I ask.

She turns to me and grins, and I forget all about to-morrow and what is about to happen. My senses fill with my sister. The voice that lilts like music. The way her hair curves around her chin. Her eyes as warm and irresistible as roasted chestnuts.

I can almost feel the patches of dry skin on her elbows, where she refuses to apply lotion. And then, the moment passes. Knowledge seeps through me, the way a person gains consciousness after a dream. Tomorrow, I turn seventeen. I will become, by the ComA's decree, an official adult. I will receive my memory from the future.

Sometimes, I feel as if I've been waiting all my life to turn seventeen. I measure my days not by my experiences but by the time remaining until I receive my memory, *the* memory, the one that's supposed to give meaning to my life.

They tell me I won't feel so alone then. I'll know, without a shred of doubt, that somewhere in another spacetime exists a future version of me, one who turns out all right. I'll know who I'm supposed to be. And I'll never feel lost again.

Too bad I had to live through seventeen years of filler first.

"Yellow." Jessa returns to her game, and a yellow leaf detaches from a branch. "Orange."

Ten times, fifteen times, twenty, she correctly predicts the color of the next leaf to fall. I clap and cheer, even though I've seen this show, or something like it, dozens of times before.

And then I notice him. A guy wearing my school's uniform, sitting on a curved metal bench thirty feet away. Watching us.

The back of my neck prickles. He can't possibly hear

us. He's too far away. But he's looking. Why is he looking? Maybe he has super-sensitive hearing. Maybe the wind has picked up our words and carried them to him.

How could I be so stupid? I never let Jessa stop in the park. I always march her straight home after school, just like my mother orders. But today, I wanted—I needed—the sun, if only for a few minutes.

I place a hand on my sister's arm, and she stills. "We need to leave. Now." My tone implies the rest of the sentence: before the guy reports your psychic abilities to the authorities.

Jessa doesn't even nod. She knows the drill. She drops into step beside me, and we head for the train station on the other side of the square. Out of the corner of my eye, I see him stand up and follow us. I bite my lip so hard I taste blood. What now? Make a run for it? Talk to him and attempt damage control?

His face comes into view. He has closely cropped blond hair and a ridiculously charming grin, but that's not why my knees go weak.

It's my classmate, Logan Russell, swim team captain and owner of what my best friend Marisa calls the best pecs in this spacetime. Harmless. Sure, he has the nerve to smile at me after ignoring me for five years, but he's no threat to Jessa's well-being.

When we were kids, his brother Mikey made a racquetball hover above the court. Without touching it. ComA whisked him away, and he hasn't been seen since. Logan's not about to report my sister to anyone.

"Calla, wait up," he says, as if it's been days instead of years since we sat next to each other in the T-minus five classroom.

I stop walking, and Jessa clutches my hand. I give her three squeezes to let her know we're safe. "My friends call me 'Callie,'" I tell Logan. "But if you don't already know that, maybe you should use my birthday."

"All right, then." Coming to a stop in front of us, he jams his hands in his pockets. "You must be nervous, October Twenty-eight. About tomorrow, I mean."

I lift my eyebrow. "How would you have the first clue what my feelings are?"

"We used to be friends."

"Right," I say. "I still remember the time you peed your pants on our way to the Outdoor Core."

He meets my gaze head on. "Ditto for the part where you splashed us both with water from the fountain so no one else would know."

He remembers? I look away, but it's too late. I can smell the protein pellets we made a pact never to eat, feel the touch on my shoulder when Amy Willows compared my hair to straw.

"Forget her," the twelve-year-old Logan had whispered, as the credits rolled on the documentary on farming methods before the Technology Boom. "Scarecrows are the coolest ever."

I had gone home and daydreamed I'd received the memory from my future self, and in it Logan Russell was my husband. Of course, that was before I learned the older girls waited until a boy received his future memory before deciding if he was a good match. Who cares if Logan has dimples, if his future doesn't show sufficient credits to provide for his family? He may have a swimmer's physique today, but it might very well melt into fat twenty years from now.

By the time I figured out my crush was premature, it didn't matter. The boy of my dreams had already stopped talking to me.

I cross my arms. "What do you want, October Twenty-six?"

Instead of responding, he moves behind Jessa. She's taken the leaves from her jumpsuit and is twisting them around each other to make them look like the petals of a flower. Logan sinks down beside her, helping her tie off the "bud" with a sturdy stem.

Jessa beams as if he's given her a rainbow on a plate. So he makes my sister smile. It's going to take more than a measly stem to compensate for five years of silence.

They fool around with the leaves—making more "roses," combining them into a bouquet—for what seems like forever. And then Logan holds one of the roses up to me. "I got my memory yesterday."

My arms and mouth drop at the same time. Of course he did. I'd just used his school name. How could I forget?

Logan's birthday is two days before mine. It's why we sat next to each other all those years. That's how the school orders us—not by last name or height or grades, but by the time remaining until we receive our future memory.

I notice the hourglass insignia, half an inch wide, tattooed on the inside of his wrist. Everyone who's received a future memory has one. Underneath the tattoo, a computer chip containing your future memory is implanted, where it can be scanned by prospective employers, loan officers, even would-be parents-in-law.

In Eden City, your future memory is your biggest recommendation. More than your grades, more than your credit history. Because your memory is more than a predictor. It's a guarantee.

"Congratulations," I say. "To whom am I speaking? A future ComA official? Professional swimmer? Maybe I should get your autograph now, while I still have the chance."

Logan gets to his feet and brushes the dirt from his pants. "I did see myself as a gold-star swimmer. But there was something else, too. Something…unexpected."

"What do you mean?"

He takes a step closer. I'd forgotten his eyes are green. They're the green of grass before summer, a sheen caught somewhere between vibrant and dull, as if the color can't decide whether to thrive in the sun or wither in its heat.

"It wasn't like how we were taught, Callie. My memory didn't answer my questions. I don't feel at peace or aligned with the world. I just feel confused."

I lick my lips. "Maybe you didn't follow the rules. Maybe your future self messed up and sent the wrong memory."

I can't believe I said that. We spend our entire childhood learning how to choose the proper memory, one that will get us through the difficult times. And here I am, telling another person he screwed up the only test that matters. I didn't think I had it in me.

"Maybe," he says, but we both know it's not true. Logan is smart, too smart to be beat by me in the T-minus seven spelling bee, and too smart to mess this up.

And then I get it. "You're kidding. In the future, you're

the best swimmer the country has ever seen. Right?"

Something I can't identify passes over his face. And then he says, "Right. I have so many medals, I need to build an addition to my house in order to display them."

He wasn't kidding, something inside me yells. *He's trying to tell you something.*

But if Logan's one of the anomalies I've heard rumors about—the ones who receive a bad memory, or worse, no memory at all—I don't want to know about it. We haven't been friends for half a decade. I'm not going to worry about him just because he's deemed me worthy of his attention again.

Suddenly, I can't wait for the conversation to end. I reach for Jessa's hand and connect with her elbow. "Sorry," I say to Logan, "but we need to get going."

Jessa hands him the bouquet of leaves, and I tug her away. We are almost out of earshot when he calls, "Callie? Happy Memory's Eve. May the joy of the future sustain you through the trials of the present."

It's the standard salutation, spoken the day before everyone's seventeenth birthday. In the past, Logan's address would have filled my cheeks with warmth, but this time his words only send a chill creeping up my spine.

We walk into the house to the smell of chocolate cake. My mother's in the eating area, her dark brown hair twisted into a bun, still wearing her uniform with the ComA insignia stitched across the pocket. She's a bot supervisor at one of the agencies, but she gets paid by the Committee of Agencies, or ComA, the governmental entity that runs our nation.

We drop our school bags and run. I hug my mother from behind as Jessa attacks her legs. "Mom! You're home!"

My mother turns. Powdered sugar clings to her cheek, and chocolate frosting darkens one eyebrow. The red light that normally blinks on our Meal Assembler is off. Actual ingredients—packets of flour, a small carton of milk, *real* eggs—lay strewn across the eating table.

I raise my eyebrows. "Mom, are you cooking? Manually?"

"It's not every day my daughter turns seventeen. I thought I'd try making a cake, in honor of my future Manual Chef."

"But how did you…" My voice trails off as I spot the small rectangular machine on the floor. It has a glass door with knobs along one side, two metal racks, and a coil that turns red when it's hot.

An oven. My mother bought me a functioning oven.

My hand shoots to my mouth. "Mom, this must have cost a hundred credits! What if…what if my memory doesn't show me as a successful chef?"

"It wasn't easy to find, I'll give you that." She takes off the rag around her waist and shakes it. A cloud of flour puffs into the air. "But I have complete faith in you. Happy Memory's Eve, dear heart."

She hoists Jessa onto her hip and pulls me into a hug so that we are in a circle of her arms, the way it's always been. Just the three of us.

I have few memories of my father. He is not so much a gaping hole in my life as he is a shadow who lurks around the corner, just out of reach. I used to pester my mom for details, but tonight, on the eve of my seventeenth birthday, the heavy knowledge of him is enough.

My mother begins to clear the ingredients off the table, the bare, gleaming skin of her wrist catching the light that emanates from the walls. She doesn't have a tattoo. Future memories didn't arrive systematically until a few years ago, and my mother wasn't lucky enough to receive one.

Maybe if she had, she wouldn't have lost her job. My mother used to be a medical aide, but as more and more applicants came with memory chips showing futures as competent diagnosticians, it had only been a matter of time before she got downgraded to bot supervisor. "You can hardly blame them," she had said with a shrug. "Why take a risk when you can bet on a sure thing?"

We sit down to a dinner usually reserved for the New Year. Everything has the slightly plastic taste of food prepared in the Meal Assembler, but the spread itself is unrivaled by the best manual cooking establishments. A whole roast chicken, its skin golden brown and crispy. Mashed potatoes fluffy with butter. Sugar snap peas sautéed with cloves of garlic.

We don't talk through most of dinner—can't talk, our mouths are so full. Jessa savors the snap peas like they are candy, nibbling at the ends and rolling them around her mouth before sucking the entire pods down.

"We should have invited that boy to dinner," she says, a snap pea dangling from her mouth. "We've got so much food."

Mom's hand stills on the serving spoon. "What boy?" she pries.

"Just one of my classmates." I feel my cheeks growing red and then remind myself that I have no reason to be embarrassed. I don't like Logan anymore. I help myself to more dark meat. "We ran into him at the park. It was no big deal."

"Why were you even there in the first place?"

The chicken suddenly feels dry in my mouth. I messed up. I know that. But I couldn't bear to be stuck inside today. I needed to feel the sun's warmth on my face, to look at the leaves and imagine my future.

"We only talked to him for a minute, Mom. Jessa was calling out the color of the leaves before they fell, and I wanted to make sure he didn't hear—"

"Wait a minute. She was doing what?"

Uh oh. Wrong answer. "It's no big deal—"

"How many times?"

"About twenty," I admit.

My mother pulls the necklace from under her shirt, where it normally resides, and rubs the cross between her fingers. We're not supposed to wear religious symbols in public. It's not that religion is illegal. Just...unnecessary. The traditions of the pre-Boom era gave their believers comfort, hope, and reassurance—in short, everything that future memory provides us now. The only difference is we actually have proof that the future exists. When we do pray, it's not to any god, but to Fate herself and the predetermined course she's set.

But my mom can be excused for clinging to one of the old faiths. She never got her glimpse of the future, after all.

"Calla Ann Stone." She grips the cross. "I depend on

you to keep your sister safe. That means you do not allow her to speak to strangers. You do not stop in a park on your way home from school. And you do not display her abilities for anyone to see."

I look at my hands. "I'm sorry, Mom. It was just this once. Jessa is safe, I promise. Logan's own brother was taken by ComA. He would never tell on her."

At least, I don't think he would. Why *did* he talk to me today? For all I know, he was spying on Jessa. Maybe he's working for ComA now. Maybe his report will be the one that sends my sister away.

Or maybe it has nothing to do with Jessa. Maybe the falling leaves reminded him of another time, when we used to be friends. My mind drifts to an old book of poems Mom gave me for my twelfth birthday. Pressed in between the pages, next to a poem by Emily Brontë, is a crumbling red leaf. The first leaf Logan ever gave me. A small piece of my heart, one I didn't even know still existed, knocks against my chest.

"You were lucky." My mother strides to the counter and snaps up the cake stand. "Next time might not work out so well."

She plunks the stand on the eating table and lifts the dome. The chocolate cake is higher on one side than the other, the frosting glopped on and messy. Each mark of the handmade-ness reproaches me. See how hard your mother worked? This is how you repay her?

"There's not going to be a next time," I say. "I'm sorry."

"Don't apologize to me. Think how you would feel if you never saw your sister again."

The chocolate cake swims before my eyes. This is so

unfair. I would never let them take Jessa away from us. My mother knows this. I just wanted to see the sun. The world is not over.

"That's not going to happen," I say.

"You don't know that."

"I will! You'll see. I'll get my memory tomorrow, and in it we'll be happy and safe and together forever. Then you won't be able to yell at me anymore!" I leap to my feet, and my arm knocks the stand. It tips onto the floor, breaking the cake into a hundred different pieces.

Jessa cries out and runs from the room. I'd forgotten she was still here.

My mom sighs and moves around the table to put her hand on my shoulder. The tension melts away, leaving behind our shared guilt for arguing in front of Jessa.

"Which do you want? Clean up this mess, or talk to your sister?"

"I'll talk to Jessa." I usually leave the hard stuff to Mom, but I can't bear to sift through the chocolate cake, hunting for the few parts I can salvage.

Mom squeezes my shoulder. "Okay."

I turn to leave and see the eating table with its empty plates and balled-up napkins, crumbs layering the floor like an overturned flowerbox. "I'm sorry about the cake, Mom."

"I love you, dear heart," my mother says, which isn't a reply but answers everything that matters.

Jessa is curled on the bed, her purple stuffed dog, Princess, tucked under her chin. Her walls have been dimmed, so the only illumination comes from the moonlight slithering through the blinds.

"Knock, knock," I say at the door.

She mumbles something, and I walk into the room. Sitting on the bed, I rub her back between the shoulder blades. Where do I start? Mom's so much better at this than me, but since she took an extra shift at work, I've had to pinch hit for her more and more.

I used to worry I wouldn't say the right thing. When I told Mom, she blew the bangs off her forehead. "You think I know what I'm doing? I make it up as I go along."

So I gave my sister a bowl of ice cream when Alice Bitterman told her they were no longer friends. And when Jessa said she was afraid of the monsters under her bed? I gave her a toy Taser and told her to shoot them.

Maybe it's not the best parenting in the world, but I'm not a parent.

Jessa turns her head, and in the glow of the walls, I see tears in her eyes. My heart twists. I would give up every bite of my dinner to take the sadness away. But it's too late. The food lodges in my stomach, heavy and dense.

"I don't want to leave," she says. "I want to stay here, with you and Mom."

I gather her in my arms. Her knees poke into my ribs, and her head doesn't quite fit under my chin. Princess tumbles to the floor. "You're not going anywhere. I promise."

"But Mom said—"

"She's scared. People say all kinds of things when

they're scared."

She sticks a knuckle into her mouth and gnaws. We weaned her from the thumb-sucking years ago, but old habits die hard. "You don't get scared."

If she only knew. I'm scared of everything. Heights. Small, enclosed places. I'm scared no one will ever love me the way my father loved my mother. I'm scared tomorrow won't give me the answers I've been waiting for.

"That's not true," I say out loud. "I'm scared of one thing."

"What?"

"The tickle monster!" I attack. She shrieks and squirms away, her head flinging out. I wince as her face almost smacks the metal headboard. But this is what I want. A laugh that jerks her entire body. Screams that come from the pit of her belly.

After a full twenty seconds, I stop. Jessa flops across her pillow, her arms dangling over the edge. If only I could wipe out the topic so easily.

"What do they want me for?" she says, when her breathing slows. "I'm only six."

I sigh. Should've tickled her longer. "I'm not sure. The scientists think psychic abilities are the cutting edge of technology. They want to study them so they can learn."

She sits up and swings her legs over the bed. "Learn what?"

"Learn more, I guess."

I look at her scrawny legs, the knees scabbed over from falling off her hovercraft. She's right. This is ridiculous. Jessa's talent is a parlor trick, nothing more. She can see a couple of minutes into the future, but she's never been able to tell me anything really important—how I'll do on a big test, say, or when I'll get my first kiss.

Jessa's frown relaxes as she snuggles into her pillow. "Well, tell them, okay? Tell them I don't know anything, and then they'll leave us alone."

"Sure thing, Jessa."

She closes her eyes, and a few minutes later I hear her slow, even breathing. Standing up, I'm about to slip out when she calls, "Callie?"

I turn around. "Yes?"

"Can you stay with me? Not until I fall asleep. Can you stay with me all night long?"

It's the eve of my seventeenth birthday. I need to call Marisa, speculate with her one last time what my memory will be—if I'll see myself as a Manual Chef or have a different profession altogether.

It's been known to happen. Look at Rita Richards, in the class ahead of me. Never touched a keyboard in her life, but her memory showed her as an accomplished concert pianist. Now, she's off studying at the conservatory, all expenses paid.

And earlier this year, Tiana Rae showed up to school with bloodshot eyes when her memory revealed a future career as a teacher instead of a professional singer. Still, we all agreed it was better to find out now that it wasn't meant to be, rather than spend an entire life trying and failing.

Whatever the possibilities, one thing is clear: I need to be in my own bed tonight, alone with my thoughts. But Jessa won't notice if I leave ten minutes after she falls asleep. And tomorrow, she won't remember she asked me to stay.

"Okay." I cross back to her bed.

"Promise me you won't leave. Promise you'll stay forever."

"I promise." It's a lie, but a small one, so white it's practically translucent. I can't be concerned. This is it. The moment I've been waiting for all my life.

Tomorrow, everything changes.

2

Perched on a cliff overlooking a river, the steel and glass building rises out of the forest like a serpent shooting out of the surf, all curved lines and shiny scales.

I swallow hard as I exit the bullet train. The Future Memory Agency. The place where I'll receive my glimpse of the future. In cities all over North Amerie, there are similar buildings, regional agencies where the area's inhabitants can go to receive their memory. But since I live in Eden City, the nation's capitol, this agency is the nicest and biggest.

FuMA doesn't have the whole building, of course. Down, down in the bowels of the earth, in the basement floors of the structure, the scientists from the Technology Research Agency dissect the brains of their psychic subjects.

My stomach executes a slow back flip, the way it does every time someone even mentions the word "TechRA."

But I'm not going to that part of the building. I'm only here to get my future memory, and the scientists will have no reason to notice me. Or my sister.

At the entrance, I scan the ID embedded in my right wrist. By the end of the afternoon I'll have a matching chip, containing my future memory, implanted in my left wrist. A bot leads me to a conference room, where twenty or so kids talk to each other in small groups.

No Marisa yet. I press my back to the wall and try to look unconcerned.

My best friend and I have the same birthday. It probably has something to do with the fact that when Logan stopped talking to me, I scooted my chair farther and farther away from him, until I was practically sitting in the next student's lap. Lucky for me, that student was Marisa. Instead of being offended, she cracked a joke about how our teacher had talons for nails, and we've been friends ever since.

I pull my long brown braid onto the shoulder of my silver jumpsuit and fiddle with it. A few minutes later, Marisa saunters into the room, a pair of trapezoid spectacles perched on her nose. She doesn't actually need the spectacles for seeing, of course. Everyone fixes their eyes with lasers, but the latest fashion is to dress like our ancestors before the Technology Boom. So people wear fake plaster casts on their arms and legs and fake hearing aids as if they're earrings. I even see a guy across the room who has glued tiny metal strips to his teeth.

"October Twenty-eight!" Marisa swoops down on me. Out of all my friends, she's the only one who calls me by my school name, probably because we have the same one.

A couple of kids stare, and she shoots them each a salute. "So good to see you, October Twenty-eight. And you, too, October Twenty-eight."

They avert their eyes, as though she's gotten their names wrong. She hasn't, of course. On this Memory Day, everybody in the room has the same name.

Marisa turns back to me and weaves her hand through mine. "Are you ready for this?" she asks, serious for once.

"Scared out of my mind," I admit.

She grips my hand tighter. We both know how important this day is. It'll determine the track we'll enter, the careers we'll have. It will lay out the parameters for the rest of our lives.

"If only we didn't have our hearts set on artistic fields," she says lightly. "Too bad we don't want to go into bot maintenance. Plenty of job openings there."

I snicker. My best friend yearns to be a live actress, and she'll probably do it, too. With her big, brown eyes and her deep tawny skin, she commands attention wherever she goes. And she's got the talent to match her looks. She's had the lead in our school's live dramas the last four years and has been known to move the audience to tears with a single line.

"Oh, I can totally see you underneath bots all day," I say. "Grease on your nose, streaked through your hair. Who knows? You'll probably start a new trend."

At that moment, a woman in a FuMA uniform comes in and strides to the podium. Supposedly, all the different agencies have an equal say in ComA, but rumor has it FuMA's power is growing, as future memory becomes more and more important in our society.

The woman's hair is bright, artificial silver, cut close to her head. It's no longer than an inch anywhere. She's about my mother's age, but that's where the resemblance ends. My mother is a bot supervisor, while this woman's uniform is navy all the way through—navy blouse, navy jacket, navy skirt—the mark of a high-ranking official.

"Take a seat, everyone," she says. Marisa makes a beeline for the front row, and I trail after her. Once we're seated, the woman smiles, but her gray eyes remain flat.

"I am Chairwoman Dresden, head of the Future Memory Agency. Let me be the first to congratulate you on your entrance into adulthood. Later this morning your life will change for the better. For the first time, you will have direction and guidance from an indisputable and all-knowing source—the future."

Scattered applause breaks out across the room. The Chairwoman endures it with a tight smile. The clapping falters and then stops.

"As you know, the very first future memories arrived twenty years ago. They struck the lucky recipients like bolts of lightning—randomly and without warning—painting such a vivid picture of the future, they erased all doubts from the people's hearts. These select few turned into the most productive members of our society. And it isn't any wonder. Instead of second-guessing their decisions, they could put their passions and energies into endeavors they knew would succeed.

"Ten years ago, FuMA discovered these memories weren't arriving in a haphazard manner after all. Every citizen under ComA's jurisdiction receives a memory from his future self on his seventeenth birthday. We only needed to teach you to open your minds so that you could access those memories, a directive FuMA has met with resounding success."

Chairwoman Dresden pauses, as if expecting cheers. But the audience is no longer sure what's acceptable, and she is met with silence. She arches an eyebrow and continues.

"It is our hope this memory will serve as a beacon to you, guiding you through the treacherous waters of life. But do not ignore the dangers." She looks us each in the eye. I feel the cold metal of the chair through my jumpsuit when her gaze lands on me. "Some of you may take the future as given. You may be tempted to slack off, go wild, even break the law. You may, in essence, think of yourself as invincible. You would be wrong."

She steps out from behind the podium. Maybe she doesn't intend the movement to be threatening, but it makes my palms clammy with sweat.

"The memory you are about to receive is but a snippet of your future. It cannot tell the entire story. Make no mistake, future memory will not protect you from the laws of physics. It will not give you immunity from the directives of ComA. If you fling yourself off a cliff, you will be hurt. You may still go on to discover scientific breakthroughs, but you might be paralyzed from the waist down. If you break ComA's laws, you will be imprisoned. You may still become a famous singer, but you will record your music from the comfort of your cell."

The room stirs, and Marisa and I exchange a glance. It's not like Chairwoman Dresden has told us anything new. We've always known our memories are mere glimpses into our futures, but I've never heard it phrased quite so ominously before.

"On the flip side, all of you have doubtless heard gossip about someone who's managed to change his future. I'll tell you right now: do not waste your time. The hand of Fate is strong. We all know the parable of the man who traveled back in time to save his wife from drowning. He managed to pull her out of the water. But the next day, she fell down a flight of stairs and died anyway."

The Chairwoman doesn't speak for a full minute. And then she smiles. "But let's not dwell on the negative. Your bright, brilliant futures are upon you. In a few minutes, you will each be led into your rooms. Open your minds like you've been taught, and the memory will come to you. Once it does, you will proceed to Operations and have the black chip implanted in your wrist. Please report back to FuMA two days from now. People react differently to their future memories, and we want to make sure everything is progressing…smoothly."

She turns to leave and then pauses. "Should you be one of the rare individuals who do not receive a memory, please report to the Memory-less Division for further processing. That will be all. Good luck."

Guards in navy and white uniforms enter the room, and I wipe my palms on my pant legs. There's no way my memory's not coming. I can't even consider the possibility. I've been waiting too long for this day. I want this memory. I need it.

I say a quick prayer to the Fates. *Please, let me have a wonderful memory. Let today be the first day of the rest of my life—a good life, a happy one.*

One of the guards calls my name. Marisa squeezes my hand, and I look one last time into her eyes. Standing up, I follow the guard from the room. He leads me to where my destiny is waiting, where my present and future are about to collide.

3

Who knew Fate lived in a glass box? The floor is made from a dark tile so shiny I can see my reflection, and a thick pane of glass serves as the wall for the front of the room. Thin white sheets hang on the other three walls, someone's paltry attempt to give the room privacy.

I settle onto the reclining chair. Rows of cylindrical cushions, six inches thick, make up the seat and the back. It is more fashionable than it is comfortable. I slip a metal contraption onto my head. It looks like the protective gear we wear during the Fitness Core, with narrow strips and lots of venting, and it hooks into a machine sitting on the table.

The guard punches a few buttons on the machine. His name tag says "William," and he looks young, barely older than me. He has the prettiest hair color I've ever seen— deep russet-red threaded with bits of gold. I'm tempted to ask which salon he uses, but he snaps on some gloves and slides a small metal chip into the machine.

I take a shaky breath. The computer chip that will record my memory. The one that will later be implanted under my skin.

"Don't worry," he says. "It's painless, I promise."

I wet my lips. "How did you get this job? Did you see it in your future memory?"

He grins. "Nah. The future me is a child-care parent, with jam in my hair and a whole gaggle of children. But my girlfriend's memory showed her as the head of FuMA thirty years from now. She's currently the personal assistant to the Chairwoman, so I guess they thought they'd better be nice to me, in case she decides to marry me."

He reaches under the table, pulling out a tray of meditation aids. "What do you want? A candle, white noise, aroma oils?"

I look at the candle, half-melted on the tray. How many memories has that dripping wax induced? The thought disturbs me, like I'm sharing something intimate with those faceless people. The green bottle holding the aroma oil makes me think of my pre-Boom ancestors, breathing in the unsanitized air.

"What kind of white noise?" I ask.

"Birds chirping."

Really? That relaxes people? Too much cheeping makes me want to tase myself. "Maybe I'll skip them all."

William frowns. "Are you sure? Most people need something to help them achieve the sufficient state of openness."

"I aced the Meditation Core. And I've been practicing every morning for the last six months."

He shrugs and adjusts the contraption on my head. "Fine. Open your mind and focus on receiving your memory. I'll be right next door, monitoring you. Good luck."

Before I can say anything else, he walks out, leaving the door open behind him.

The door is not closed, locked, or barred. It is open. A door made of glass, swung open at an angle. Like my mind. Like my future.

A rush of something flows through me. I feel it everywhere—in my toes and elbows. Behind my ears. The tip of my nose. What on earth? Is it relief? Stress? Anticipation?

I shift against the cushions, and my concentration shatters. What if my memory doesn't come? Maybe I should've taken the candle. Panic shoots through me, and I dig my fingernails into my palms. No. I can't think that way. I've got to focus.

Okay. What else is open? The wide blue sky, opening up over the fields. The canned vegetables the Meal Assembler cracks open for dinner. The windows I fling open on a hot, summer day.

The memory from the future that flows into my ready, open mind.

Open, open, open.

I feel that something again, stronger this time. Oh, my. It's not my emotions—it's my memory. My *memory*. OPEN.

*I am walking down a hall. It has green linoleum floors,
with computer screens embedded in the tiles. The lighted
walls shine so brightly I can make out a partial shoe print
on the ground. The acrid smell of antiseptic burns my nose.*

*I turn a corner and skirt around the shattered remains
of a ceramic pot. A trail of soil leads like breadcrumbs to a
broken plant stalk and loose green leaves.*

*I walk down an identical hallway. And then another.
And another.*

*Finally, I stop in front of a door. A golden placard, with
snail spirals decorating each corner, bears the number 522.
I go inside. The sun shines through the window, the first
window I have seen in this place. A teddy bear with a red
bow sits on the windowsill; otherwise, everything is hospital
white. White walls, white blinds, white bed sheets.*

In the middle of the sheets lies Jessa.

*She is young, hardly older than she was when I saw
her yesterday. Her hair falls to her shoulders, tangled and
unbraided. Wires protrude from her body like they are
Medusa's snakes, winding every which way before ending
in one of several machines.*

*"Callie! You came!" My sister's lips curve in a beautiful
smile.*

*I am gripping something in my hand, something hard
and small and cylindrical. "Of course I came. How are they
treating you?"*

*Jessa wrinkles her nose. "The food is gross. And they
never let me play outside."*

*I flex my hand and roll an object along my palm. It's a
syringe, with clear liquid swimming in the barrel. A needle.
I am holding a needle.*

"When you leave, you can play as much as you like." I move the wires off her chest and place my hand squarely over her heart. "I love you, Jessa. You know that, don't you?"

She nods. Her heart thumps evenly against my palm, the strong, steady beat of the complete trust a child has for her older sister.

"Forgive me," I whisper.

Before she can react, I whip my arm through the air and plunge the needle straight into her heart. The clear liquid empties into my sister.

Jessa stares at me, eyes wide and mouth open.

Loud beeping fills the room. And then the heart rate monitor goes flat.

4

I can't breathe. I take huge gulps of air, but it doesn't help. I'm drowning. I'm drenched in sweat, and my sweat is drowning me. I jerk up, and someone pushes my head between my knees. My reflection stares up at me from the tile. I'm back in the memory room.

"Breathe," William says. "I didn't see that coming. Who was that girl?"

"My sister," I mumble.

"You killed your own sister? Mother of Fate. Who are you?"

Good question. Who am I? Criminal. Murderer. Sister-killer.

No. No. *No.* That was a dream, a hallucination. That wasn't my memory. Not my future.

But it was. I can tell from the nausea clenching my stomach. The phantom ache in my shoulder. The nightmare's not fading. It's just as real now as it was a few moments ago. Just as real and even more horrible.

Oh, my baby Jessa. The girl I swore to protect. What have I done?

I begin to shake, insistent twitchy motions that vibrate my shoulders and rattle my teeth. My hands clench, but the shaking only spreads.

"Calm down." William grabs a blanket from a shelf and throws it over me. "Relax a minute and don't move."

Like moving is an option. I'm not sure moving will ever be an option again.

I huddle under the blanket. It smells like laundry detergent. The stiff fibers brush against my skin, and sweat trickles into my eyes. I pull the blanket over my head until my world is nothing but deep, dark blackness.

William clears his throat. Pushing the blanket down, I see him ejecting the chip out of the machine. He crosses the room, pries my hand open, and places the chip in my palm. I stare at it blankly.

"I know you're in shock," he says. "But you need to listen to me very carefully. You've had an atypical memory, one where you commit a Class A felony. According to FuMA law, I have to arrest you."

"Arrest me?" I sit up straight, and the blanket falls to the floor. "But I haven't done anything wrong."

"You haven't, but you will. The law is clear. There are no second chances at FuMA. No innocent until the crime's actually committed." He walks to the door and looks at me. I see a kindness I didn't notice earlier. "In exactly one minute, I'm going to sound the alarm. You need to get out of here. Now."

My mind screams with questions. Why are you helping me? Who are you? Where do I go? But he's gone, and the clock's ticking.

Escape!

Half a second later, I'm on my feet and flying down the hallway. The clamor of voices reaches me as I wrench open a heavy door, but I don't look back. Right, then left, then left again, past the conference room door, and... yes! A crowd of people going about their business. Lots of girls in silver mesh jumpsuits, their hair flowing down their backs.

I slow to a walk and tuck my head down as I cross the floor. My black sneakers squeak on the tile, shooting my heart into my throat. Has he sounded the alarm yet? The sea of people in navy and black slacks flows around me unabated. Their footsteps tap the floor in the ordinary rhythm of employees, not the relentless, hard slaps of officers in pursuit.

I'm almost at the exit when I hear a male voice. "Callie? Is that you?"

Putting on a surge of speed, I burst out of the building and run for the woods. The bullet train would get me farther, faster, but if I get in a compartment, they'll lock it down and I'll be trapped. My best bet is to hide. If only I can get to the trees in time.

Twenty yards.

I hear thudding footsteps behind me. And they're getting louder. Which can only mean one thing: my pursuer is gaining on me, fast.

Ten yards.

Come on, Callie. Run!

I'm almost there. I just have to get to the woods, and then I've got a shot. There are twists and turns in there. A bush to crouch behind, a log to crawl into. Just a few more yards. You can hold them off, Callie. You've got to.

Five yards, four, three…

I hear the whistle of motion and brace myself to be tackled. Instead, someone brushes past me and then slows down, running next to me.

Next to me? What on earth?

I see a familiar blur of features—and then I hit the woods.

"Logan?" I almost trip over some exposed tree roots. "What are you doing here?"

He grins, and dimples pop out in his cheeks. The zipper of his jumpsuit is pulled down a couple of inches, and he smells like chlorine, as if he's come from an early morning swim practice. "Just being a good citizen, reporting to FuMA for my post-memory check-in."

"No, I mean, why are you chasing me? Do you work for FuMA?"

"Of course not. That's the last thing I would do." His tone makes me think of the boy who used to be my friend. The one whose hair stuck up in the back, who was my defender against all slights, real and imagined. "I called your name and you took off. I wanted to make sure you were okay."

Can I trust him? I glance over my shoulder. The steel and glass building looms behind me. Even as I'm looking, a siren pierces the air, sending a couple of birds squawking out of a tree. My heart stops. The alarm.

I make a gut decision. There's no time for anything else. "I'm in trouble, Logan."

"Don't tell me that's for you."

"They were going to arrest me. I ran."

His eyebrows crease together, like maybe he's sorry he followed a fugitive into the forest. "What did you do?"

"Nothing!" I shouldn't be indignant. In the future, I murder my sister. The sooner I accept that, the better. "Almost nothing. It was my memory."

"They're after you because of something you did in your memory?"

I nod. Underneath the droning of the siren, I hear the faint barking of dogs. Oh, Fates. Dogs are trained to follow a scent. My knees give out, and I stumble on the uneven ground.

Logan catches my arm and turns me to face him. "Your memory. How bad was it?"

I blink rapidly. I'm not going to cry. If I cry now, I might as well throw myself at the mercy of the hounds. "It was bad," I whisper. "Really bad."

"Okay," he says. "Follow me."

We wind deeper into the forest. If Logan's taking a marked path, I don't see it. Yet his stride is steady and sure, so he must know where he's going.

The trees become dense, and a canopy of leaves closes over our heads so that we jog in the shadows despite the bright morning sun. Rocks and vegetation litter the ground, and the air feels moist and cool. Every once in a while, I hear the bark of a dog, but it's so distant I start to relax. They won't put much effort into finding me. I'm just a girl. I have no real power. I pose no real threat.

Except, perhaps, to my little sister.

My breath hitches on a sob. Mom must be awake by now. She's probably sitting with Jessa at the eating table, looking at the clock as their peppermint tea cools. They'll worry if I don't come home. I should let them know what happened. But even if I could get a message to them, what would it say? *Sorry, Jessa, I'd love to come back and eat the toast you ordered for me, but it turns out I'm going to kill you in a few months' time.*

My face crumples, my eyes burning with dammed-up tears. I bring my hand to my mouth and bite down, hard. I can't do this right now. I *cannot* do this. A pack of dogs waits to haul me away. I've got to keep it together if I'm going to escape.

I drag my eyes to Logan's back. He has the classic swimmer's torso—broad shoulders and narrow waist. Through the blur of tears, I see his muscles flexing underneath the silver jumpsuit. That's good—think about his back. Think how Marisa would drool over this view.

Marisa. My breath catches again. She must've gotten her memory. She must've seen herself as a famous live actress. I'll never see her on stage. I'll never see her again.

I exhale, slowly. I can't think about her, either. I focus on clambering up the rocks in front of me. The ground slopes upward and the trees thin out here. I can see the sun again. It burns my ears, and sweat condenses on my forehead like the beads outside a glass of water. I feel like we've been hiking forever, but probably no more than ten minutes have passed.

"Where are we going?" I ask.

Logan looks over his shoulder, scanning the ground

below us. "You can't stay here. They're going to find you, no matter where you hide."

"Where do you suggest I go?"

We're climbing up, up, up. There's nothing here but a cliff that dead ends in empty space, with a roaring river below.

He squints at me under the unseasonably warm sun. And then, all of a sudden, I get it.

"No," I whisper. "I'm not jumping into the river. That's suicide."

"Not if you know where to jump. Not if you have a place to go."

What on earth is he jabbering about? "I don't, clearly."

"I do," he says.

He continues climbing. I follow, conscious of the space separating us. I made the snap decision to trust him, but maybe I was wrong. Maybe my judgment was clouded. I was scared, and I wanted to trust him again. But people change in five years. He might not be mentally sound. Because this idea he's proposing? It's crazy.

A memory flashes across my mind. I was eleven or twelve, and we were picnicking on the cliffs next to the glass and steel building, overlooking the river. Mom was nursing Jessa, so I crept right up to the edge, much closer than she normally allowed. I wanted to see the water crashing over the boulders, to imagine the majestic white foam spraying across my skin. Instead, I saw a woman climb onto the metal railing…and swan dive over the edge. She hung in the air for an infinitesimal moment, caught in the sun's rays as if by the flash of a camera. And then she smashed onto the boulders below.

I've had nightmares about falling to my death ever since. But I'm not about to tell Logan that.

We reach the top. The ground plateaus before dropping off in a cliff. Here, there's no metal railing to keep people back and safe. There's just hard-baked earth crumbled into dust and granular lumps.

Logan turns to me. "Listen, Callie. There's a safe haven in the wilderness. It's called Harmony, and it's a refuge for anyone who wants a new chance at life. People with psychic abilities who are hunted by TechRA. People like you who want to escape their futures."

My hands clench at my sides. "How do you know this?"

"My brother," he says. "After TechRA arrested him, my family became members of the Underground, the group that set up Harmony. In case they came after anyone else we knew."

I stare at him, a million questions on my tongue. But they all fade next to the very idea of Harmony. A place to start over, to pretend my memory never happened. Was it possible?

All I'd have to do is jump off this cliff. Leave behind everything I've ever known.

I shake my head, hard. "I don't know what I was thinking, running away. I can't escape my future. I'm a criminal."

"Will you listen to yourself? The only thing you've done is sit in an uncomfortable chair and receive a memory from the future. Nothing else has changed. You're still the same Callie you were this morning."

"You don't understand. My memory—"

"Hasn't happened yet!" He reaches out as if to grab my

shoulders, but he's too far away. "What if you can change your future? What if you made it physically impossible for your memory to happen? I'm thinking you've got a pretty good shot at doing that if you disappear from civilization."

"But the Chairwoman said that was impossible."

"She was lying," he says flatly. "Our entire socioeconomic system is built around future memories coming true, so of course she has to say that. It won't be easy, since all of Fate is working against you. It will take an enormous amount of willpower and strength, which most people don't have. But it's happened. I've seen it."

I stare at him. Is he right? I'm not sure of anything anymore. But this is the first flicker of hope I've had since receiving my memory. If I never see Jessa again, then I can't very well kill her, can I? Or will Fate lead me back to my sister, no matter what I do?

"Let's say there's even a small chance I'm right," he says. "Isn't it worth taking?"

Yes! A thousand times yes! Save Jessa's life? I'd move mountains for that chance…or jump into raging rivers full of boulders.

And yet I hesitate. "I'm not that strong," I whisper. "I can't even defy my teachers at school. How am I supposed to go up against Fate?"

He looks at me like he can see straight into my soul. "If anyone can, it's you."

I want, with every cell in my body, to believe him. But what does Logan Russell know? He hasn't talked to me for five years. "I can't fight Fate. But I know who can. FuMA. I'm going to let them arrest me. Lock me up, so that I *can't* fulfill my memory. Even if I want to."

He stills. "But then you would be in detainment. For the rest of your life."

You'll never see the sun again, a voice inside me whispers. *Never get married and have your own family. The inside of a cell will be your home for the rest of your days.*

I don't care. Tears drip onto my cheeks, and I swipe them away. This is my sister we're talking about. My sister.

"I can't imagine ever doing what my future self did." I swallow hard. "But it happened. So I can't guarantee I won't change my mind." I straighten my shoulders. "The safest thing for me to do is take the decision out of my hands. And FuMA's offering to do just that."

He closes the distance between us. "You can't turn yourself in, Callie. Think about what you're saying."

"Both you and the Chairwoman said it—the hand of Fate is strong. I have to take extreme measures in order to defeat it. What can be more extreme than going to detainment?"

He opens his mouth, but before he can say anything, I twist away and look down the hill. "They're coming."

A fast-moving pack of bloodhounds drag along a blur of guards in navy and white uniforms. They've just begun their ascent, but the dogs are galloping up the slope, as if they can't wait to rip me apart. I've got a minute, tops.

My hand closes around the black chip, and I pull it from my pocket. Without another thought, I throw it as hard as I can over the precipice. There. It's gone. Just because I'm turning myself in doesn't mean I have to tell them about Jessa. They don't need any more reason to investigate her.

I turn back to Logan. His eyes pierce me with an expression of deep, unspeakable regret. Does he actually care? Underneath the years of silence and betrayal, does a kernel of friendship still remain?

"I'm sorry, Callie."

There's so much I want to say. I'm going away, for a very long time. This is my last chance to reconcile our old hurts. The last time to feel a real, human connection.

My last chance for a kiss. Oh, how I want to lean forward and press my lips against his. I don't want to die having never kissed a boy.

But there's no time. The dogs' barks shatter the air like the rat-tat-tat of a machine gun. We hear the scuffle of feet against dirt. The officers will be on top of us at any moment.

"Go!" I shout at Logan. "Get out of here, before they arrest you, too."

He opens his mouth to say something, but I shake my head. "Don't. Don't make this any harder than it is."

With his eyebrows pulled together, Logan nods, gives my arm one last squeeze, and disappears over the other side of the hill.

This is it. My last few moments of freedom.

Turning, I raise my hands in surrender. I take a deep breath, savoring the openness of the mountain air. And then I walk straight toward the officers.

5

"You have the right to remain silent," an officer intones. "Nothing you do can save you, but anything you say may be used against you."

My wrists are wrenched behind me, and a jolt of electricity zaps my arms. The current marches across my skin like a row of fire ants. The officer slaps another set of cuffs around my ankles, and the ants intensify their attack along my legs. I grit my teeth, struggling not to whimper.

A dirty rag is stuffed in my mouth. My tongue retreats, searching for escape, but there's nowhere to go. I taste other people's saliva, and the bile rises in my throat. The gag blocks its only exit, however, so I'm forced to swallow the bile again.

"You will not be appointed an attorney," the officer says. "You will not be tried in a court of law. Your future memory serves as indictment, trial, and conviction."

They drag me down the hill, and my feet kick up billows of dust, which makes my eyes sting and water. I cough violently, but they don't remove the rag. The officers march me back into the building and into an elevator capsule. We exit on a floor very different from the one where I received my memory.

Everything is cement—walls and floors. The air doesn't move in here, as if it's trapped underground and has nowhere to go. The smell is two-parts urine and one-part excrement.

Hands jerk around my body, taking the cuffs from around my ankles and wrists. The electricity stops, and I spit out the rag, collapsing onto the floor of a narrow intake area.

Someone pokes me in the ribs. "Are you alive?" The fingers nudge me again, this time in the stomach. "Come now. Give me a twitch. You feel anything?"

I look into the face of a bulky female guard.

"Good," she says. "You survived the electro-cuffs."

She places a helmet on my head and hooks it to a machine with a bunch of digital screens. I brace myself for a shock of electricity. But nothing happens. Numbers appear on the screens: 89…37…107…234. They don't mean anything to me.

A few minutes later, the guard takes the helmet off and hauls me to my feet. She strips me naked and pushes me under a hot spray. I hunch over, covering myself, and hear her harsh laughter.

"You've got nothing I haven't seen, little girl."

I stay hunched over anyway. The needles of water stab my skin, and then the guard yanks me back out, dripping wet, and throws a yellow jumpsuit at me. It looks a lot like my school uniform, but it's made with coarser material. I barely have time to get my arms and legs through the holes before I'm thrust down a hall. The jumpsuit rubs against me with every move, the rough material sanding off skin cells, dead and live alike.

The guard tosses me into a cell, and then I am alone. For the first time in my life, I am truly and completely on my own.

The minutes stretch into hours. The gnawing in my stomach is my only marker of time.

At some point, a bowl of cloudy water is pushed through the slot in the door. I crawl over and sniff it. It smells like urine, but everything here smells like urine. A few hours in and my skin has already absorbed the odor.

Which is worse? To smell like urine or not even notice it? To be served suspect water or be so thirsty you lap it up anyway?

I drink the water. It tastes stale and chalky, and I wrinkle my nose.

Immediately, I think of my sister in the future memory, wrinkling her nose. The food's gross, she said. And they never let me play outside.

The entire memory rolls through my mind, from start to finish, each detail rich and nuanced. It's as if I were living it once again.

I slow the memory down, freezing each frame and analyzing it. There's got to be some clue in here, something to make me understand how I could do such a thing.

In the memory, Jessa's hair fell to her shoulders. When I left her yesterday, it only reached her chin. That means I have time. Not a lot, because her face looks the same. But a few months, at least. Maybe a year.

She was in a hospital bed. Maybe that means she'll get sick. Maybe my future self kills her to spare her unthinkable pain.

No. I pull up the image of her face, zooming in as if my mind's eye were the lens of a camera. Her cheeks are a little pale, but her eyes are alert. Her body, even lying down, radiates the kind of energy you only associate with the healthy.

I rotate the image, viewing it from various angles, but cannot find any evidence of illness. So, not sick. Why is she in a bed with wires sticking out of her head, then? Where is she?

My mind runs through the memory again, picking out snapshots—like the golden placard, with four snail scrolls decorating the corners. Every agency has its own insignia. FuMA, for example, has the hourglass. Who do the snail scrolls belong to?

I search through the rest of the memory, looking for clues. Green linoleum floors. The teddy bear with the red bow. White blinds and white sheets…

Wait a minute. My breath catches and the images melt from my mind. How am I doing this? This isn't…normal. The memory is playing across my mind as if it were a movie. I'm taking it apart, manipulating each piece as if my mind were a…*computer*. I shouldn't be able to do this.

My pulse scampers off in a million directions. What's going on here? This has never happened before. Is it because there's something weird about future memories? Or is there something weird about…me?

My heart pounds, and all of a sudden I can't get a full breath. *No. Just stop. I'm fine.* There's nothing wrong with me. I've never had an ounce of psychic tendency in my life. It's not about to start now.

My body's oversaturated with emotions, that's all. I can't think about it anymore.

I look around my cell instead. Mistake. There's nothing to see. Just a ten by ten room with black bars along one wall, blocks of concrete everywhere else. No windows. No sun.

Will I ever see the sun again? In this moment, I'm so glad I took Jessa to the park on October Twenty-seventh. Glad I felt the warm rays of the sun against my face and body. Glad I shared one last afternoon with my sister. I'm even glad I ran into Logan Russell because now, at least, I have someone back home to dream about. I imagine that's more than most detainees get.

The small bit of gratefulness fades, and I gasp at the air. Detainee. I'm in detainment. The craziness I tried to subdue comes galloping back. I gulp and wheeze, like an engine that won't start, but I can't fill my lungs. My heartbeat doubles and then triples. An ocean roars in my ears. Panic attack. I'm having a panic attack, and I have to stop it. Stop it. *Stop it!*

A red leaf. I pull my knees to my chest. My fingers turn numb, and I flex them, in and out, to return the flow of oxygen. *Autumn leaves fluttering through the air.* Think of the leaves.

My breathing slows a fraction. My heart no longer feels like it's going to pound out of my chest. And I lose myself to the past.

Just another wiggle. A shift in my seat, a slight push of my arms, and my desk squeaks an inch closer to the window. An inch closer to the sun.

From the outside, our school looks like a spacecraft—long and flat, with circular windows cut out from the sides. The building's won a bunch of awards. Too bad the architect didn't think how the students would feel inside: trapped.

"What are you doing?" the boy next to me asks. He's got the short hair all the boys in the younger classes have. We haven't had our Fitness Core yet, but he smells like the swimming pool.

I glance at the front of the room, where the T-minus five teacher, Mistress Astbury, writes out fractions on the air screen.

"I'm trying to see the leaves," I say to the boy.

"Why?"

I push my tongue against my top teeth, trying to figure out how to explain. "When they fall from the tree, they can land anywhere at all. They're not stuck inside like we are. I'm just trying to see where the leaves go."

He nods, as if what I've said makes sense. "I'm Logan."

My cheeks get hot, and I edge my desk closer to the window. Of course his name is Logan. It's always been Logan, since we started school eight years ago.

But I've never really spoken to him before. I know his birthday. I know he starts in the first swim lane during the Fitness Core. But this is the first time he's given me permission to use his real name.

"My name's Callie."

"I know. I've heard some of the girls calling you

that." His smile is hesitant, as if he's not sure he should be admitting that. "Maybe that's why you like the leaves. Because you're named after the calla lily."

I'm not, actually. My father was a scientist, and I'm named Calla Ann after Tanner Callahan, the man who received the very first future memory. But I don't correct Logan. My father thought the name was clever, but me? I kinda like the idea of being a flower. No one's ever called me that before.

No one's ever smiled at me like that, either. Part of me wants him to do it forever. The other part doesn't know what to do with my elbows.

I tuck my palms under my legs, leaning far back. For a moment my feet hover in the air, with the plastic chair balanced on its two back legs. The next moment the chair comes crashing down, and I'm sprawled on the floor.

Mistress Astbury swipes away the air screen and strides to where I'm lying. "October Twenty-eight! What is the meaning of this?"

I stand up and smooth out my silver jumpsuit, making sure the zipper is straight. My elbows throb from the fall, but I hold them at my sides in perfect ninety-degree angles, clasping my hands in front of me. "I apologize, Mistress. I wanted to look out the window. I guess I… stretched too far."

She crosses an arm over her waist, resting the other elbow on it. Fingernails sharpened to talon-like points tap against her cheek. "Since the window proves to be such a distraction, October Twenty-eight, we'd better move you to a less tempting location." Mistress points her finger to the opposite corner of the room. "Pack up your desk screen and sit over there for the rest of the day."

My heart sinks. The new seat is so far from the windows the light rays don't even reach it. No hope of seeing the sun, much less tracing the path of the falling leaves. "Mistress, I…" The words die off. Like I might if I have to sit in that corner.

"You'll do as I say, October Twenty-eight, or I'll report you to the head of EdA."

I obey. I have no choice. For the next hour, I fidget in my seat, turning again and again toward the too-far window. I don't relax until the Outdoor Core.

I run across the school's grassy field, breathing in air that isn't cooped up inside a building. Soaking up real, natural sunlight. Watching the leaves dance wildly in the breeze. I don't stop running until a horn blares across the field, signaling the end of the core.

I'm the last student off the field. Every step I take makes my body heavier, as if the gravity increases the closer I get to the classroom. By the time I get to my seat, I'm surprised I don't crash through the floor.

And then I see it. There, on the middle of my desk screen, is a bright red leaf. I pick it up and glance around the classroom.

Nothing. Girls try on each other's eye tints, boys battle each other on their desk screens, but no one waves or nods in my direction.

I look across the room, at the desk that was mine until this morning. At the boy who sat next to me but never said a word until today.

But Logan's not looking at me. He hunches over his desk, his fingers typing on his glass-topped desk.

I let out a shaky breath and sink into my chair. Logan didn't have anything to do with the leaf. It's not a present. Someone probably dropped it on my desk by accident. I should put it in the compost slot, so it can be recycled.

But I don't. I place the leaf on my lap, brushing my finger over the raised veins.

My desk screen vibrates once, and a new post pops onto my front page. "A leaf for a flower," the message reads. "To remind you of the sun."

It's unsigned, but this time when I look up, Logan's watching me. He gives me a smile so big and so brilliant, for a moment, I wonder if it can rival those golden rays.

6

"**O**ctober Twenty-eight. Hey, October Twenty-eight."

The voice pulls me from my sleep. I blink in the darkness. I've been dreaming of autumn leaves and sweet boys, and I don't want to go yet. I want to stay in a time when the most complicated thing in my life was sitting too far from the classroom window.

I roll over on the hard concrete, determined to escape back to my dream. But the voice won't let me. Worse, it's joined by a pair of hands, shaking my shoulders.

"Hey, October Twenty-eight. Wake up. You've got the rest of your life to sleep."

My eyes open. The walls in my cell are dimmed, and it's quiet, with none of the grunting, shuffling, and screeching I heard before. It must be nighttime, or at least what FuMA has decided is nighttime. We are like fish in an aquarium, our days and nights subject to the whims of our keeper.

They already control every other part of my life. They

don't have to disrupt the only thing that gives me peace. Sullenly, I turn to the guard who's preventing me from sleep.

And I bolt upright when I see it's not just any guard. His russet hair has turned black in the dim light, but his face is the same. William. The guard who administered my memory. "What are you doing here?"

He presses a finger to his lips. "I called in a favor from a friend. They're going to interrogate me, and we need to get our stories straight. Where's the black chip?"

"I got rid of it."

He nods. "Okay. Since there's no chip, they're going to grill me about your memory. What should I tell them?"

I rub my eyes, wiping away the last traces of sleep. "I'd like to leave my sister out of it." I have a very bad feeling I know exactly why Jessa was in that hospital bed. It has nothing to do with her getting sick, and everything to do with her psychic ability. "Let's give them the exact same scenario, but say it was a man I killed. My future husband. Probably because he was cheating on me."

William's brow furrows, as if he's taking mental notes. "What does this man look like?"

"Brown hair, brown eyes," I say, making it up on the fly. "Ski-jump nose. A mole on his chin. Crooked teeth he chose not to fix."

"Crooked teeth, got it." He glances over his shoulder, through the black bars. The hallway remains empty, but he stands to leave. "I can't stay. It's too risky."

"Wait!" I grab his arm, desperate for human contact. "I don't get it. Why did you help me in the first place?"

"A moment of weakness." He gives me a small smile

and gently disengages his arm. "I was there, you know. The monitors let me live your memory right along with you. I could tell how much you love your sister, and to have the memory end the way it did... Well, I felt sorry for you." He pats my shoulder. "I am sorry for you."

Thank you, I want to say. I feel sorry for me, too. But before my mouth can form the words, he is gone, like a ghost in a dream.

'm not sure I sleep for the rest of the night, but I jerk awake when my walls flicker on, the equivalent of a FuMA wake-up call.

My stomach growls, and I force down a few spoonfuls of the glop they passed off as my dinner the previous night. It tastes like wet sawdust and makes me want to turn my stomach inside out. Which kinda defeats the purpose of eating.

I empty my bladder into one of the two buckets in the corner. One for urine, one for feces. Lovely. And then I walk in circles around the cell. I want to think about my future memory, but I'm afraid my mind might turn into some weird replay device again. Useful, to be sure. But creepy. Really creepy.

I ponder, instead, the memory that William and I made up. A man with a ski-jump nose. Mole on the chin. Crooked teeth. I'm going to be ready when they come for me. I'll be able to recite this version of my future memory in my sleep.

There's only one problem. They never come. I circle

my cell 1028 times. I fill in details of my made-up memory, down to the fine black hair curling on my supposed husband's chest. My stomach begs for another serving of glop. And they still don't come.

I hook my arms through the black bars and peer into the hallway. My cell faces a concrete wall, and if I crane my neck to the left or right, I can see the pale flesh of a few arms in the same position as mine.

And I can certainly hear the other prisoners. Hooting, hollering, yelling out unfamiliar names.

I've been in detainment for over two days. No one has interrogated me, no one has informed me how long my sentence is. For all I know, they'll keep me here forever, without further explanation.

I don't feel like waiting any longer.

"I want to talk to Chairwoman Dresden," I call over the din.

For a moment, dead silence meets my statement. Then the chatter resumes.

"Well, I want to be waited on hand and foot," one girl yells.

"And I'd like my smart lens so I can watch movies from my cell!"

"I want a hot bath with rose petal water!"

"But I have no black chip." My words reverberate down the hallway and echo back to me. For the first time since they slapped the electro-cuffs around my wrists, I feel in control. Of myself and my emotions. Of my very fate. "They've locked me up in here, but they don't even know what my memory is."

Murmurs ripple down the row of cells. I can't tell if the

inmates are actually communicating with each other, or if they're talking to themselves. I don't even know if they're discussing me, or if my words have fallen on indifferent ears. But then a girl screeches, "They don't have her memory. They're holding her for no reason."

A couple of the inmates take up the chant, and the volume swells until it fills the entire hallway. "No chip! No chip! No chip!"

I can't take credit for this. I doubt it takes much to get this group going, since they're already furious with FuMA. Still, a smile spreads across my face, as I listen to total strangers repeating my words. I might not be so alone, after all.

A guard appears at the end of the hall and snaps an electric whip against the wall. Sparks shoot out the end, and even from my cell I hear the sizzle as the weapon cracks through the air.

"Silence!" he yells. Underneath the navy uniform, his shoulders are twice the size of mine. A nasty scar snakes up the side of his face. He could have easily gotten the blemish fixed. Which means he either deliberately left it alone—or he paid someone to make him look that menacing.

The chanting stops. Heavy black boots stomp down the hallway, and the guard halts in front of my cell. The gate slides open.

"You." The guard scowls, and his scar seems to fold in on itself. "You're the one who started this?"

I nod.

"Looks like you're going to get what you want. Come with me."

I swallow hard. This was a stupid plan. What's a few days of waiting—a few weeks, even—when I have my entire life in this place?

Scar Face prods me from my cell, and even though I'm in trouble, I hungrily soak up the change in scenery. I've been staring at the same gray blocks for so long, I can feel the photoreceptors in my eyes dying.

Detainment cells line both sides of the hallway, but they are staggered, to minimize visual contact among the inmates. Most of the girls stand right up against the bars, though, so I get a good look at them as I pass.

We could all be twins. Dirty hair, yellow jumpsuits. An ashen quality to our skin like we're missing some key nutrient. The only difference is that they each have a tattoo of an hourglass on their left wrist. And I don't.

I focus on their eyes. That's where all the personality lies. Blue eyes, brown eyes, green. Only the standard colors, since we don't have access to our eye tints. Blinking, narrowed, wide open and fearful.

Nobody says anything. Either they don't like me, or it has something to do with the electric whip guarding my back.

We stop at the entrance of the cell block. The door is thick, reinforced metal and looks nearly impenetrable. To the right is a glass-walled office filled with equipment. To the left is a closed-in room with actual walls. Maybe that's where the guards eat lunch or take naps when they're not cracking their whips.

Scar Face doesn't look like he's in the mood to answer questions. He presses a hand, palm-out, against a sensor on the door. Next, he inserts his index finger into a slot, where a pinprick of his blood is taken. His retinas are scanned, he enters a ten-digit code into a numerical keypad. Then, and only then, does the door open.

We are locked up tighter than a rocket ship sealed against the vacuum of space. I see no possibility of a successful escape.

He takes me into an elevator capsule, and we shoot into a different wing. I'm so distracted I barely feel my stomach drop. The instant we step onto the new floor, though, déjà vu hits me so hard I nearly fall.

I've been here before. Overly bright walls. Green linoleum floor with computer screens embedded every few feet in the tile.

Oh. Dear. Fate. It's the hallway from my future memory. Is my memory about to come true?

No. There's no shattered ceramic pot on the floor, no burning smell of antiseptic. Not the same hallway. Just a similar one.

Still, this could be where my memory will take place. My sister might soon be in a bed here. I have to find out. I need to know for sure.

We turn a corner. The handle of the whip digs into my back, and Scar Face's hand is draped loosely around my bicep. I glance over my shoulder. He's not even looking at me. The scar on his face twitches; his eyes glaze as if he is bored with escort duty.

I take a deep breath. It's now or never. I may never get this chance again.

At the next intersection, I break out of his grasp and take off down a side hallway.

"Hey! Stop right there!" Scar Face yells.

I run even faster. I don't have to get far. I just need to find a room with a doorway. I just need to see—

"I said, stop!" The electric whip crackles, and the smell of smoke fills the air.

I turn a corner. There! A doorway—

The whip wraps around my legs, and I pitch forward. Lightning zaps through my body for one blinding, mindless second. Every cell in my body blows up, and I'm left weak and cooked and panting.

Before I can catch my breath, the lightning flashes again. And again.

I guess Scar Face's not happy I ran.

But that's okay. My back arches when another bolt hits me. Pain like I've never known spreads through my entire body, burrowing into every nook and crevice. My skin feels like it's been ripped into ribbons. My veins feel like they've been chopped into confetti.

But Scar Face can whip me as much as he wants. Because before I went down, I found my answer. There is a placard next to the door where I collapsed—a golden rectangle with four snail scrolls decorating each corner.

The room number is different, but it doesn't matter. I know where my future self killed my sister: in a room numbered 522…

Somewhere in this very wing.

few minutes later, I am hunched in a chair in front of a simple card table. Sweat soaks through my jumpsuit, and my heart sits in my chest like a worn-out toy. My fingers continue to clench and spasm, still battling the ghosts of the electric whip.

Scar Face stands behind me, the handle of the whip jammed in my back, as if I'm in a condition to be a threat to anyone.

I twist around, even though my body screams, and give him my biggest smile. "I hope I didn't make you look bad. Wouldn't want anyone to think it was easy to get away from you, especially when you have that big, scary whip."

His lips press together, as if he would like to hurt me for such comments. But he can't because the Chairwoman is coming. "Face forward. Now."

"I'll be sure to warn you if I make another break for it. That's why you had to whip me so many times, huh? Because you were afraid you wouldn't be able to catch me if I crawled away."

In response, he shoves the handle deeper into my back.

The door opens and Chairwoman Dresden, head of the Future Memory Agency, strides into the room. Even though this is exactly what I wanted, I'm not sure why they sent the most important person in the agency to meet me. Aren't there plenty of cases like mine?

She looks like she did on the morning of my birthday. Silver hair cut closely to her head. Impeccable navy uniform. Her features as cold and beautiful as an ice sculpture.

She nods dismissively at the guard. "You can wait outside. I'll take it from here."

The pressure of the handle eases off my back, and he leaves the room.

She turns to me. "Lovely to see you again, October Twenty-eight," she says, as if she knows me. "I regret it's not under more pleasant circumstances."

I rack my mind for something biting to say, but my bravado seems to have fled with the guard.

"You've made my life difficult, October Twenty-eight. Very difficult." She taps her fingernails on the table. They're long and narrow, polished translucent silver so they resemble ice picks. One wrong word and she may stab one of those nails into my eye.

"You're not convinced," she says. "I see the incredulity written all over your face. But you have no idea what your little show of defiance may have cost us."

Standing, she stalks around the room in her five-inch heels. If her nails fail to do the trick, those heels can always double as a weapon. "I was ready to write you off. We have your administering guard's account of what happened in your memory. I was ready to let you languish away in Limbo for the rest of your life. Just another screw-up in the system. But your little stunt today changes things."

She stops in front of me, and I tuck my bare feet underneath my chair, away from her heels. "We've built our society around a system of future memories. This system is efficient, productive, and very, very prosperous. But it is also delicate. It depends entirely on the assumption that the memories come true. The slightest change in a person's life may cause ripples that spread throughout the rest of society—ripples which we cannot predict and for which we cannot prepare."

She places her palms on the desk. "You grasp, then, the dilemma we face when we encounter the future memory of a crime. While we have an interest in protecting society, we also have a very strong interest in making sure these memories cause as few ripples as possible."

I nod, unable to say a word.

She settles back in her chair, crossing her ankles to the side. "Most of the ripples are meaningless. They affect only a small circle of lives. But once in a while we get a future criminal whose personality is so aggressive, we can tell her ripples will be stronger than most. They may even have an overarching impact on society."

"I'm not aggressive," I burst out. "I haven't said a word since you came in here."

"You're playing meek. I like that. I appreciate intelligence as much as the next person. But it's no use, October Twenty-eight." She leans forward, her eyes glistening. "We scanned your brain when we first arrested you, and our computers have been busy analyzing the videos of your behavior. I saw the way you raised your hands and marched straight to our officers. The uproar you created in the detainment cells. But the clincher was how you risked—and received—multiple lashes of the electro-whip just to run down a single hallway. You weren't going to escape. You must have known that. But you still tried. That's the mark of a girl who will stop at nothing to win. Our computers have given us a definitive answer. You, my dear, qualify as aggressive."

No! I want to shout. You've got it all wrong. I wasn't trying to escape. I was looking for the placard. Trying to figure out where my sister will be killed. That's all.

But I don't know how to explain without revealing my memory.

"This is our compromise," the Chairwoman says when I remain silent. "While we have changed the course of the future by arresting you, we will endeavor to make pieces of your memory come true. Where's the black chip, October Twenty-eight?"

I lick my lips. I really don't think knowing the color of my shirt or getting my sister's hair style right will make a difference in anyone's life. "I must've dropped it in the woods, before the officers arrested me."

She arches her eyebrows. They're dyed silver, to match her hair. "We searched the grounds and didn't come up with anything."

"I don't have it." With any luck, it was smashed between the river boulders or washed downriver and lost forever. "Why don't I tell you what happened? I'll be happy to go over every detail until you're satisfied."

"That won't be necessary," she says, baiting me, waiting

for me to say the wrong thing. "We already have William's account. From you, we need a more precise picture of the future, so we must resort to…other methods of getting the information."

My mouth goes dry. "What other methods?"

She doesn't respond. She just raises her eyebrows as if to say, "What do you think?"

Torture. They're going to torture the information out of me.

My teeth knock against each other, so hard they might chip. As if the whippings weren't enough. I don't know if I can handle any more. Razor blades carving into my cheek. Drowning in a bucket of water. My fingers broken one by one.

I squeeze my eyes shut. I have to be brave. But I'm not brave. Not really. I'm not anything. I'm just a girl. Only a girl. Nothing but a girl.

No, that's not true. I'm a girl who will kill my sister in the future.

My teeth stop clicking, and I take a deep breath. That's right. I'm going to kill my sister. The worst is already going to happen. There's nothing they can do that will hurt me more. If anything, I deserve their torture.

I open my eyes. Chairwoman Dresden watches me the way one might look at a line of ants carrying away bits of food ten times their body weight—curious, but ultimately unconcerned if she squashes me beneath her platform stilts.

Without taking her eyes off me, she raises her hand and snaps. A moment later, the guard comes to the door.

"Please escort October Twenty-eight down the hall,"

she says. "Dr. Bellows is waiting to examine her."

I find my tongue again. FuMA already has the hour-glass insignia. So which agency has the snail scrolls? "Where are we?"

The Chairwoman smiles. "The science labs, of course."

A cold dread seeps into my stomach. I knew it. TechRA. I've spent the last six years protecting my sister from these people, doing everything I can to make sure they don't treat her brain like a science experiment.

I never worried about myself. But maybe I should've. Because I'm about to suffer the exact same fate I tried so hard to prevent for Jessa.

8

A hard, plastic chair sits in the middle of the room, reclined so far it is almost horizontal. Sort of like a dentist's chair, but worse, because a thousand different wires poke out from the armrests, winding around the nearby machines like coils of snakes. At the dentist's, only my teeth are at risk. Here, those little wires could slither right into the deepest regions of my brain.

A man, presumably Dr. Bellows, sits at a desk next to the chair, his hands a blur of motion as they move around a spherical keyboard. His hair and beard are black, like sticky asphalt before it hardens, and a small yellow stub is tucked behind his ear.

A pencil. Nobody uses pencils anymore. I probably wouldn't have even recognized it if my father hadn't done the very same thing.

The memory hits me right in the stomach.

I'm climbing on my father's lap. The smell of rubbing alcohol surrounds me, and his sandpaper beard brushes against my cheek. Quick like a hummingbird, I dart in and snatch the prize from behind my father's ear.

"What is it?" I turn the yellow cylinder over in my hands.

"A pencil. A tool our ancestors used for record keeping." My father wraps his large hand around mine and shows me how to scratch out the letters I see on my desk screen. "We're surrounded by the most advanced technology civilization has to offer. But the best inventions don't have to be complex." He spreads his palm over his chest. "They come from right here. The heart."

"Is that why you wear the pencil? So you don't forget?"

"No." My father's almond-shaped eyes flash. "I wear it so I remember."

I was too young, then, to understand what the difference might be. And by the time I was old enough to ask, he was long gone.

Bellows turns from his desk, waves my guard out of the room, and jerks his thumb at the wire-infested chair. "Sit."

I limp to the seat, a shiver running through me. Dr. Bellows might have the same profession as my absent father, but that doesn't mean I trust him. Quite the opposite, in fact.

He looks me over, clucking his tongue. "What did they do to you?"

"A few lashes of the electro-whip."

He sighs, as if majorly inconvenienced by my pain. "They know I need my subjects to be in top physical condition. The formula takes better that way. But never mind. We'll give it a try. If it doesn't work, we'll have another go in a couple of days. Good thing injuries from the electro-whip don't last. You'll be back to normal in a matter of hours."

"Give *what* a try?"

He fastens three thick harnesses around my body. "I understand the black chip recording your future memory was…misplaced?"

I nod.

"Well, your future memory isn't gone. It's stored in a part of your brain called the hippocampus." He taps the side of his head. "I'm going to root through your brain and induce the memory. Make you relive it, in order to give us a second chance to record it."

The breath gets stuck in my throat. "What do you mean?"

He blinks, as if he is a camera snapping consecutive images. "The memory will come to you again. Like the first time. Only this time, we'll make sure the black chip isn't lost."

No. *No.* In the future Jessa will be at the mercy of TechRA. The moment Bellows sees my real memory, he'll recognize the hallways and the placard. He'll know my sister will be a subject in these labs.

My memory will give him the evidence he needs to arrest Jessa now, in the present world.

I can't let that happen. My future self is already going to betray my sister. I refuse to do it in the present, as well.

"Will it hurt?" I ask, stalling.

"Only if you resist."

So resistance is possible. But how?

He squirts gel onto oval sensors the length of my thumb

and sticks them all over my head. The gel feels cold and sticky against my scalp.

He attaches the wires sprouting from the chair onto each sensor. "Open your mind, the way you did before. The memory will come to you." He reclines my chair and leaves the room.

I don't need to open my mind. I can call up the memory in an instant and it will play across my mind like a movie. I can freeze images and zoom in on shots. I can do everything at least as well as his recording device.

A light hiss fills my ears, and gas enters the room through nozzles positioned in the ceiling. The fumes disappear instantly, but I feel the chemicals in the air, pressing down on me.

I clamp my mouth closed. The gas is going to make my memory rise involuntarily to the surface. I can't let that happen.

The harnesses pin me against the chair. Think! I'm not going to be able to free myself. How can I keep the memory out? Bellows said to open my mind. Maybe I need to close it instead.

I can't hold my breath any longer. I take a sip of air — but as soon as I take one, I want more. The air makes me feel peaceful, relaxed. All of a sudden the chair doesn't feel quite so hard. The plastic is cool and inviting, the kind of surface on which you want to stretch out and take a nap.

No. Those are the fumes talking, not me. I need to close my mind. Close it. I think of a door, made of thick, solid wood. I turn and twist a dozen locks, slide a dead bolt across. I waterproof the door. Add insulation. Reinforce it with concrete. Layer on other metals—gold, silver, platinum, brass. And then I repeat the process.

A thousand tiny swords jab at the door, trying to puncture a hole through my skull. Each moment, by itself, is tolerable. But the swords never stop. They keep poking and prodding, slicing and biting, looking for the window where I let down my guard.

It hurts. And it's never-ending. That's what kills me, the incessant stabbing of the swords. I just need a second. One tiny second for the pain to stop, a moment to catch my breath and gather my strength…

I am walking down a hall. It has green linoleum floors, with computer screens embedded in the tile. The lighted walls shine so brightly I can make out a partial shoe print on the ground.

No! I bite my lip until the metallic taste of blood fills my mouth. The swords come back. They're sharper this time. They slice and slice at my self-control. But I can't give in. This is all I have left. The last thing I can do for my sister.

I scream inside my mind. I claw and yank and rip. I fight and elbow and jostle. But I do not let go.

Finally, finally, it stops. The swords withdraw, and I melt back against the recliner. I should be grateful. I should feel relief. But I'm so tired I can do neither.

Bellows walks into the room with a different guard. The scientist shakes his head. "I knew it. The formula isn't performing at peak efficiency because of your injuries."

My head lolls back and I stare at the ceiling. That wasn't peak efficiency? I'd hate to encounter those swords on a healthy day. I try to answer, but I can't open my mouth. All I can do is watch as water squirts out of the gas nozzles and rains all over us.

Well, "rain" in the sense of the raging summer storms that flood our rivers. Already, the water begins to accumulate on the floor.

The back of my reclined seat rises until I'm looking at Bellows. Water pools around his ankles and his beard drips like tangled moss. "Not to worry. The formula will break through to your memory, sooner or later."

We stare at each other. The water rises to his knees, his thin cotton shirt sticking to his chest in wet, unattractive patches. He doesn't even flinch.

The water laps at my legs, getting higher by the second, and I creak open my jaw. "Um…should we get out of here? We'll drown in a minute."

Bellows sighs and pinches the bridge of his nose. He pushes a button and the harnesses fall away from my body, leaving me free to go.

"Take her back to her cell," he says to the new guard. She's young and pretty and has a row of piercings along both eyebrows. "I'll talk to her later, once the gas has worn off."

"But sir?" She watches as I climb on top of the headrest and crouch there. "Will she be okay?"

"She'll be fine," Bellows says. "She's hallucinating, that's all. It's a side effect of the formula."

Hallucinating. This isn't real. Now that I think about it, the water doesn't feel wet. Or cold. In fact, I don't feel it at all. I look at Bellows and the guard. The flood has submerged their mouths, but they continue talking as if sound waves are not hindered by liquid.

I guess in my hallucination they're not, because I hear Bellow's next words, loud and clear.

"We'll give her a couple of days to recover, and then we'll try again. We'll keep trying until she gives up that memory. Until she inhales so much formula she forgets what's real and what's not."

The guard helps me off my perch, and together we swim to the exit.

9

dream. Or, at least, I think it's a dream. It's not a hallucination because I remember this actually happening. Except it's not a regular memory, hazy and indistinct. I live the moment, feeling every sensation, every texture, every detail, like I did in my future memory.

I wish it were real. Oh, how I wish I could go back to that time again.

So, yeah. I guess the best word for it is "dream."

lean my forehead against the cool glass sensor on my locker door. My eyes are all hot on the inside, but I'm not going to cry. That would be stupid. I mean, my mom could've let the baby miss her nap for one morning. It's not every day my pot roast is chosen for the school's Art Extravaganza. But it's fine. Whatever. The baby needs her sleep. The baby needs to stick to a routine. Anything for the baby.

The locker beeps at me. "Access Denied. Fingerprints Undetected." Sighing, I replace my forehead with my palm. A second later the locker swings open, and I see, among the jumble of measuring cups and skin tints, a single, orange leaf.

I suck in a breath. I don't know how he does it. These lockers are supposed to be vandal-proof, but I find a new leaf inside every single day.

As I do everyday, I pick up the leaf and twirl the stem with my fingers.

"I love your entry in the Extravaganza," a voice says behind me. "It tastes so different from the manufactured version."

I drop the leaf like I wasn't just caressing it and turn to face Logan. His hair is wet, as though he's tried to smooth it down, but a few strands stick up in the back. My heart stutters.

"Yeah," I say, trying to sound casual. "It's one of my family's favorite dinners."

What I won't admit to anyone, especially my mother, is that I made the pot roast because it's one of the few dishes Jessa can eat. The carrots and potatoes are soft enough to mash, and whenever I put some in her mouth, my sister claps her hands and reaches for more. In those moments it doesn't matter that my mother's forgotten about me since the baby was born. It's Jessa and me together against the rest of the world.

"So you made it for your mom?" Logan asks.

Maybe I did, but she couldn't even bother to come to school and taste it. A spurt of anger rushes through me. "No. I made it for my father."

"I thought he was gone."

Gone. That's one way to describe it. Eight years ago, my father left for work—and never came home. My mother has never explained where he went.

I slam my locker shut. "He's coming back."

Logan blinks. No doubt he's heard his own version of what happened to my father. "How do you know?"

It was only a distant hope before. Something I would cross my fingers and wish for when I heard my mother crying at night. But now, saying it to Logan, I know it's true. I feel it down to the very core of my being.

"My mother loves my father too much to have a baby with anyone else." And Jessa's baby pictures look just like mine. We are the products of a mixed heritage. We have my father's eyes, which taper at the corners. And my mother's seashell skin. "So he's been back," I say slowly, working it out in my head. "Maybe he had to leave again for work or something, but now that Jessa's here, he's going to come back and take care of us." I look at Logan, almost pleading, "Wouldn't you? If you had a little baby like Jessa, wouldn't you want to be with her?"

"If I had someone like you in my life, I would never leave to begin with," he says, his voice steady and sure.

Except he does.

A few short weeks later, his brother Mikey made a racquetball hover above the court, and Logan stopped being my friend. I kept the final leaf in my locker until it crumbled. I even left my locker door open a few times, to make it easy for him.

But a new leaf never showed up. And neither did my father.

When I wake my brain feels sluggish, like I have to push every thought through a sieve before it will register. It's been a long time since I felt that resentment toward my sister. Could this be why my future self kills her—because I'm harboring some jealousy toward Jessa that I won't even admit to myself?

No. I didn't feel jealous or resentful in my memory. I just felt . . . dread. I sit up and pull my knees to my chest. Jessa's the good one, the sweet one. She doesn't argue with my mom, doesn't forget her chores. I've never once seen Mom clutch her temples and moan because of Jessa. So what if Mom loves her more? I would love her more, too.

At least one thing's clear. My mind can manipulate more than my future memory. I can "live" other memories, too.

Testing the theory, I pull up the image of Logan's face, just as he tells me he will never leave me. I zoom in on the picture until all I can see is the sharp edge of one cheekbone. And yes, there on his cheek is a single, stray eyelash.

I let out a deep breath. So there's my answer. My brain can zoom like a recording device. It's not something weird about future memories. It's definitely me.

The ability started the day I received my memory. Could that process have something to do with these powers?

"Powers" feels like too strong a word. It's not like I can see the future or make things float. At most I'm a glorified digital camera. Does that really qualify as a psychic ability? If so, it's not like any psychic ability I've ever heard of.

I get to my feet and walk around the cell, swinging my arms back and forth. Now that I'm getting used to the idea, I think I'm okay with it. The worst thing about having a psychic ability is that TechRA will be after you. But they've already got me locked up. And the best thing? Well, maybe I can find a way to use it against them.

"Hatchie. Hey, hatchie."

I halt. Who's that? The voice seems to have come from right next to me, but there's no one else in my cell. No one outside the bars, either. I must be hearing things.

"Hey, hatch. When you're done with the calisthenics, why don't you come talk to me?"

Calisthenics? I realize my arms are still swinging. Hastily, I tuck them behind my back.

"Over here. In the corner. There's a loose brick."

I cross the room in the direction of the voice. Dropping to my knees, I run my hands along the wall. Dust covers my fingertips as they dip into the grout. At the very bottom, I feel empty space where a brick has been removed.

I stretch on the ground, aligning my face with the hole.

An eye looks back at me.

My pulse jumps. The eye is round, with long black lashes that stick straight out. Back at school, those lashes would've been the envy of all the girls. She could've crimped them, even attached tiny beads. But here in detainment, without the proper beauty tools, the lashes look overgrown, like weeds in an untended garden.

"How come I never noticed this hole before?" I ask.

"Because, hatchie," the voice says like I'm stupid, "I never took out the brick before. I didn't feel like listening to a sniveling wimp cry about missing her mama. But after you riled up the girls yesterday, I thought you might be able to amuse me."

That's the second person who's taken my actions to mean something they're not. I didn't yell out those things because I'm aggressive or interesting. I was just…impatient.

"Why do you call me hatchie?" I ask.

"Because you're like a baby bird about to step off a branch and plummet to your death. I call all the new girls that."

"Who are you?"

The eye blinks. "You can call me Sully."

"Sally?"

"No. Sully. Either because I'm sullen or because I'm the one who sullies everything up. Take your pick."

The voice is young, so she must've been a newbie herself not too long ago. But her tone is heavy, weighed with the kind of complexity you get only with experience.

"So Sully, when will they let me see my mother?" I don't want to see Jessa. Too dangerous. But maybe I can warn my mom. Let her know I saw Jessa as a lab subject in a future world, so she can take extra precautions to prevent it from happening.

The single eye rolls. "You don't get to see your family, hatchie. This ain't detainment, you know. No visitation rights in Limbo."

Huh? My skin's rubbed raw from the coarse jumpsuit, and I live in a cell with buckets of urine and feces that have been festering for days. Of course this is detainment.

"What are you talking about? What's Limbo?" As I ask the question, I realize I've heard the term before, from Chairwoman Dresden.

Sully's eye closes and I see lines etched into the eyelid, too precise to be veins. She must have a picture tattooed there. I move a little closer, but my head blocks the already dim light, so I ease back again.

The eye opens. "You're in Limbo because you haven't done anything wrong yet, so they can't convict you of anything. But they can't let you go, either, because you *will* commit a crime. So they keep you here until something changes."

"But what could possibly change?" I ask. "I can't commit the crime if they've got me locked up. Right?"

The eye blinks. "Maybe, hatchie. Maybe not."

"What does that mean?"

She doesn't respond. I wait an entire minute, but the eye just continues to look at me.

I try a different question. "Sully, have you ever seen them use a needle here? A syringe about the length of my palm, and, you know, cylindrical?"

An emotion I can't read passes through her eye. "Yes."

I suck in a breath. "When was it? What do you know about it?"

She considers me for a long moment. Blink, blink, blink. "What's in it for me?"

I'm not so much of a hatchie I don't know that information doesn't come for free. There's only one problem. I don't have much to bargain with.

"You want my glop?" I ask.

She snorts. "Please."

"I'm a good listener. I'll listen to you whenever you want."

"Even more pathetic. I didn't say I needed a friend,

hatch. And if I did, it wouldn't be you."

I want to bang my head against the wall. "What do you want from me?"

"That's the problem, isn't it?" She laughs. "You don't have anything I want." Humming a tune I don't recognize, she nudges the brick back into place.

"Wait—" I say, but it's too late. The conversation's over.

I run my fingers over the wall. The loose brick doesn't come out as far as the others. I push against it, but it doesn't budge. She must've braced something against it.

Smart girl, that Sully. The half-inch makes it impossible for me to grasp the brick, giving her absolute control over when to start a conversation.

Sighing, I retreat to the opposite wall. I have to find out about this needle, figure out how my future self gets ahold of it, if only to make sure my present self *doesn't*.

But whatever Sully knows remains out of my reach. That is, until I figure out how to give her something she wants.

10

lie flat on my back, staring at the ceiling, and try to remember everything I learned from the Meditation Core.

Inhale through my nose. Exhale from my mouth. Focus on a single, freeze-frame image from my future memory. Jessa's hair falls to her shoulders, tangled and unbraided.

To her shoulders. How long does it take for hair to grow three inches?

Long enough. So no need to panic. Not yet. I can figure out my memory. I can stop it from happening.

I inhale. Exhale. Try to get in some kind of zone. I probe my brain, stretching and distorting the memory. Walking through the scene again, I focus on one specific detail: the teddy bear with the red ribbon. I zoom in until all I can see is that bear—its fluffy, white fur; the gleaming, black eyes; the tattered, red ribbon. Then, I change it. I throw all of my mental power into one image: a crisp, blue ribbon. For just a moment, the color flickers from red to blue, but I don't have time to see which color wins out before I snap out of the vision.

Dear Fate. My limbs feel like spaghetti left too long in the Meal Assembler. I may pass out.

But the FuMA guards have other ideas. A horn blares through the cell block. I bolt upright, just in time to see my gate slide open.

Open. I move to the door and peek out. Are we free to go?

Wishful thinking. Two heavyset guards stand at the end of the corridor, metal rods clamped in their hands. The batons might look less menacing than a whip, but I've seen the news footage scrolling across our desk screens. Those rods contain so much energy they can send you flying five feet.

Footsteps shuffle on the concrete, and girls begin to emerge from their cells. As one of my fellow inmates lurches past, I grab her arm. She has pale eyes and translucent lashes. Not Sully. "What's going on?"

She shrugs, and her arm slides from my grasp. "The Outdoor Core. Half of us go out today, the other half go out next time, since fifteen minutes a week is all we need to maximize our potential."

My heart leaps. We're going outside. The sun! I fall in line behind the others, bouncing on my toes. The girl in front of me shakes her head. I smile in return. Fifteen minutes! Fifteen entire minutes to bask in a light I never thought I'd see again.

In the glass-walled intake office, the machines flash their lights. The door to the other room is shut like last time. One of the guards goes up to the entryway. He scans his body, punches in the numeric code, and then we are out.

He leads us to a small courtyard. It is surrounded on four sides by the buildings, but there's grass and blue sky and the slightest hint of wind. Brightly colored leaves fall from two large trees, and the sun sits high in the clouds.

It's even better than I imagined. The rays are warm on my neck, and the air smells like honeysuckle. I tilt my face up, absorbing every ounce of sunshine.

"You act like you've never been outside before," a voice says.

A girl stands before me. Friendly brown eyes. Dark fuzz on her scalp. If she had hair, it might be the same color as Marisa's, like chocolate swirled with butter as it cooks on the stove.

"It feels like it's been forever." I crouch down and pick up a leaf. But my hands don't stop after one. I pick and pick, until I have a small pile in my hands. Red, yellow, orange, brown—the colors remind me of Jessa.

A slight breeze blows through my hair and I shut my eyes. *The next leaf that falls will be yellow.* Opening my eyes, I zero in on the falling foliage—dark brown. I was dead wrong. I crack a small grin, feeling closer to home just for imitating Jessa's game.

"My grandmother used to make flowers by folding leaves and wrapping them together," the girl says. "Of course, this was when she was a little girl, and there were parks and trees on every corner. Is that what you're doing? Making roses out of fallen leaves?"

I look at the girl, my heart pounding. This might be the thing I'm looking for. Not sure if sullen girls have any use for imitation flowers, but it's worth a try.

"My sister does the same thing." I move to another patch of fallen leaves. "And yes, that's exactly what I'm doing."

She falls to her knees next to me and begins picking up leaves, too. A couple of girls racing up and down the courtyard vault over us. "My name's Beks, by the way. Are you new here? I don't think I've seen you before."

"I'm Callie. I have the cell next to Sully's." No need for her to know I'm the girl with no black chip.

"Lucky you. She's not exactly sweet, but she's got that loose brick in her wall. Some company's better than nothing, right?"

She gestures behind me. Most of the girls are clumped together in groups of twos and threes, trying to squeeze a week's worth of conversations into fifteen minutes. But a lone girl slouches against the wall, not looking at anyone. Her skin is stretched taut over a frame of bones, and horizontal marks decorate her arms from wrist to elbow.

"Is that Sully?" I ask.

"That's what she calls herself. The rest of us call her Calendar Girl."

"Why?"

Beks puts down the leaves and holds out her forearms. "She cuts herself every time we go outside, to keep track of time. It's pretty gruesome. Instead of doing it to ourselves, the rest of us use her as our calendar."

Even as I watch, a couple of girls approach Sully and count the marks on her arms. They don't speak to her, and she doesn't acknowledge them in any way.

I think suddenly of the tree that grows in the middle

of our school lobby. Students cover the bark with their initials and drawings—the only place in school where graffiti is tolerated. The only place it's even possible. Everything else is metal and plastic.

Living things, it seems, are easier to disfigure.

"How does she do it?" I whisper. "Does she have a knife?"

Beks wiggles her fingers. "You might think someone's smuggling in nail tints. But that's not tint on her fingernails. It's dried blood."

My stomach churns like I've eaten too much glop.

"When I got here, she only had five marks on her arms," Beks says. "And Gia over there arrived when she had twelve. You should go count her marks, so she can be your calendar, too."

"Um…that's okay." I turn back to the leaves. My fingers chafe from handling their crumbling surface, and my mouth is dry at the thought of a girl who cuts herself to keep track of time. "Beks, have you seen anyone use any needles here?"

Maybe I won't have to win Sully over after all. Maybe I'll be able to keep the imitation roses for myself.

She shakes her head. "You mean, as a weapon? I've never seen the guards with anything that subtle. Why do you ask?"

Disappointment blooms in my chest, and I scrape up some grass along with the leaves. "No reason."

We work in silence until the horn blares, signaling the end of the fifteen minutes. As I carefully put the leaves in my pocket, Beks holds out her pile.

"For me?" I ask, shocked.

"I don't have any use for them." She shrugs. "It was fun to feel close to my grandmother for a few minutes."

I take the leaves, and we fall in line behind the other girls. Before we go inside, I turn back to Beks, plucking a red leaf from my pocket.

I hand it to her. "To remind you of the sun," I say and hope it gives her a fraction of the comfort Logan's leaf gave me.

I fold a leaf in half and roll it into a tight cylinder. Taking another leaf, I wrap it around the cylinder. Fold and wrap, again and again, until the creases resemble the petals of a rose. I tie off the bottom with a sturdy stem, repeating until I have enough "roses" to form a bouquet.

Biting my lip, I survey my handiwork. Fallen leaves are fragile by nature. I lift the bouquet gently, praying it holds. The action opens a floodgate and questions rush in, one on top of the other. Did they call my mother yet? Does Jessa miss me? Who does Marisa joke with in class?

I shouldn't care. I'll probably never see them again. This is my life now. These walls. A tray of glop. A loose brick with an eye on the other side. The sooner I get used to that, the better.

"*Nooooooo!*"

My fingers close over the roses, and at the last second, I stop myself from crushing them. That noise. High-pitched. Keening. The wail of a soul being separated from its body.

I hear it again, louder this time, coming from the hallway. "You can't make me!"

I lurch to the front of my cell and press my face against the bars.

It's Beks, being propelled down the hall by a burly guard with whiskers. Her hands are caught behind her in a pair of electro-cuffs. He pushes her with the butt of his baton. She pitches forward, and he yanks her back up. The whole process starts all over again.

"I won't do it!" She curls into a fetal position on the ground. "I won't!"

The guard lifts her by the arm, and her body unfurls. Up and down the hallway, I see elbows poking out of the cells. I imagine the girls from the courtyard, all with their faces straining against the bars. All with their hands pressed against their chests.

The guard prods Beks with the baton. She flies forward, landing on her stomach in front of my cell.

She looks around wildly before locking onto my face. I can't be sure she recognizes me, but she reaches through the bars and grabs my ankles.

"You have to stop them," she says hoarsely. "You can't let them do this. To me. To any of us. You've got to stop them!"

I crouch down. I want to touch her face, but I can't reach it.

"Please." Beks's eyes reach right inside me and yank. "Help me."

Before I can respond, the guard wraps his arm around her stomach and lifts her up. He flings her over his shoulder and carries her down the rest of the hallway. He stops in front of the mysterious door at the end, the one that's always been shut until now.

"I'm sorry," he says gruffly. "But you have no choice."

He tosses her inside the room beyond. The next few moments are a blur. I hear a rush of footsteps. The screech of a table as it's being pushed to one side. A man yells, "No!"

And then, a gunshot sounds.

11

I rock back on my heels. What happened? Was Beks... shot? For what?

My stomach heaves. I want to crawl to the darkest corner of my cell, curl up into a ball, much like Beks did, and stay there until my ears stop ringing, until the image of her wild eyes fades from my mind. Until I forget everything that happened.

But I can't. I press myself against the bars, straining to see. The elbows begin to disappear. One by one, the other girls retreat into their cells, to nap or sleep or cry. To dig their fingernails into their arms until they break skin. To do whatever it is they do to make this mockery a life.

I don't. I stay by the door. Because she asked me to help her.

Me. Poor Beks. You got the wrong girl. What could I have done?

Hours pass...or maybe only minutes or even seconds. Time doesn't make sense anymore. What is future and what is past? Did I kill my sister or didn't I? Can I still save her? Like I didn't save Beks?

The door of the interrogation room finally opens. The burly guard with the whiskers walks out, and Beks follows him. Her hands and feet are bound with electro-cuffs. But before the pent up breath even leaves my lungs, another guard exits the room, carrying a black body bag. The corpse.

So somebody was shot after all. Just not Beks.

Burly Whiskers goes to the entry and does the whole routine. Handprint, blood sample, retina scan, numeric code. The entire entourage leaves. And they don't come back.

Where did they go? What did they do with Beks?

No matter how long I wait, the black bars imprinting lines onto my forehead and cheeks, I don't get any answers.

I remember Sully's words. *They keep you here until something changes.*

This must be the change she was talking about. The change that takes you out of Limbo and puts you some-where else.

Which can only mean one thing: Sully knows. Whatever it is that happened to Beks, Sully has the answer.

I'm waiting for her when she removes the brick. We stare at one another, blinking back surprise and the loose dust the movement of the brick stirred up.

"Tell. Me. Everything."

"About Beks or the needles?"

"Both," I say. "Beks first."

Sully's eye narrows. "So demanding, hatchie. Haven't you learned? You don't have the power here. I do."

If my fingers could fit, I'd reach right through the wall and shake her. "This isn't a game, Sully. Somebody is dead."

"You want something from me. I need something from you."

I push the bouquet of "roses" through the hole in the wall.

Her eye disappears as she examines the gift. A moment later, she's back. "What is this, a bunch of leaves? What do I want with some dead leaves?"

"They're not just leaves, Sully. This was my sister's favorite craft project. And when I felt cooped up at school, the boy I used to like gave me a red leaf."

Her eye rolls. "You are super boring to me, hatch. Who cares?"

I take a deep breath. "There's this line by Emily Brontë. It was in an old book of poems my mom gave me. She wrote, 'Every leaf speaks bliss to me/ Fluttering from the autumn tree.'" I wet my lips. "I hoped these leaves would make you feel that way, too. We may be stuck inside, away from the sun, but I hoped the leaves would remind you how it feels to be free. To be able to take whatever path we want and land anywhere we choose."

I wait, bracing myself against her laughter, anticipating her ridicule. The eye blinks at me. Blink, blink, blink. And then it crinkles a little at the corner. "You're all right, hatch."

The breath whooshes out. "So you'll tell me?"

She disappears, as if she might be putting the roses in a safe place, and comes back a moment later. "What do you know about Beks's story?"

"Nothing. She mentioned a grandmother," I say. "It sounded like they loved each other."

"Her parents were arrested when Beks was young. They were suspected of having psychic abilities. Beks lived with her grandmother until she got her future memory." Sully's voice softens with something I don't expect. Something that sounds almost like regret.

I swallow past the lump in my throat. The memory can't be good, not if Beks ended up in here. Not if Sully sounds like that. "What happened?"

"In the future, a robber breaks into their house. The grandmother gets in the way, and he puts a bullet through her chest. In a rage, Beks tackles the robber, wrestles the gun from his hands, and kills him."

The softness disappears from Sully's voice. "FuMA arrested Beks, and she's been in Limbo ever since, waiting to see if she would be deemed aggressive."

I freeze. The conversation with Chairwoman Dresden replays in my mind. *You, my dear, qualify as aggressive. Aggressive. Aggressive.*

"What do you mean?" I ask faintly.

"FuMA leaves most of us alone. But once in a while, they decide one of us is too aggressive. Our ripples are too strong to be left unchecked. That's why Beks was so hysterical. Because she knew her grandmother's dead."

"I don't understand." The pieces don't fit together, no matter how hard I jam them. "Why would her grandmother be dead? FuMA knew about the robber. Why didn't they stop the crime from happening?"

Sully laughs, harshly. "Where are we, hatchie?"

"You said we were in Limbo."

"That's right. But where are we housed? Are we in the PuSA facilities, with the rest of the criminals?"

"No," I whisper. "We're in the FuMA building." If we were truly criminals, even future criminals, we should've been shipped to the Public Safety Agency.

"Do you get it now?" The words are tired. Not regular tired, not even bone-tired. The kind of tired you can't cure, even with a lifetime of sleep. "It's not FuMA's goal to prevent crime. It's to facilitate the receipt and fulfillment of future memory. The fulfillment, hatchie. It's FuMA's goal to make sure our memories come true."

The truth crashes over me. *We will endeavor to make as many details come true as possible*, the Chairwoman said. I thought she meant the ancillary details. I thought she was talking about the color of my shirt.

No. I don't want to be right. I can't bear to be right. "So who was shot in the interrogation room? Are you saying it was…the robber?"

"He wasn't supposed to live, hatchie," she says, her voice as dull as the cinder blocks. "By arresting Beks, FuMA messed up the chain of events. When they decided she was aggressive, they had to fix her ripples. The only way they could do that was to bring the robber here and make Beks kill him. Just like in her memory."

I jerk back from the hole so I no longer have to look into Sully's eye. So I can stop listening to her.

She keeps talking, anyway. "Now that Beks has fulfilled her memory, now that they forced her to do it, they're moving her to PuSA. Because she's a real criminal now. Just like her memory predicted."

I turn away from the wall and bring my knees to my chest. I've made a terrible mistake. The worst miscalculation of my life.

Because the Chairwoman said I was aggressive. And when the scientists discover my real memory, FuMA will make sure it comes true.

They're going to make me kill my sister.

12

Sully's voice drifts over me. "You still there?"

Our transaction is finished. I gave her the roses; she explained what happened to Beks. So why is she still talking to me? "No, I'm not."

I keep my back to the wall. But she won't go away.

"I didn't even tell you about the needles," she says. "Don't you want to hear about the needles?"

Hot tears pound at my eyelids, but I refuse to let them out. Everything is working against me. FuMA. Fate itself. Why did I ever think I would be able to fight them?

"Listen, hatch. I know it's a lot to take in. I remember when I first found out. I was catatonic for a week."

I have to try. My sister's counting on me, and I can't fade away. I have to keep fighting. For her.

Mustering all my strength, I crawl back to the wall. "Tell me about the needles."

"Before you came here, a girl named Jules lived in your cell. She was as crazy as they come. She screamed insults from morning to night. Heckled the guards when they walked past her cell. Once, she even threw her bucket of urine in their faces. No one was surprised when they deemed her aggressive."

A smile tugs at my lips. I would've liked to see the urine dripping from Scar Face's cheek.

"A few weeks ago, they made her fulfill her memory." Sully pauses. "Or at least, I think they did. Her fulfillment wasn't like any I've ever seen. Usually we hear gunshots or bodies being thrown around. Hers was deadly quiet. She went into that room with a guard, and a scientist followed with a rack of syringes. One row with clear liquid, a second row of red. A few minutes later, they all walked out, seemingly unhurt. And that was it."

I frown. "What was her memory supposed to be?"

"Attempted murder. She attacks her dad, I think. But where was her dad in all this? And what happened to the attack?"

"Maybe her dad was the scientist," I say.

"Maybe. Or maybe they weren't fulfilling her memory at all. Maybe they were performing some other experiment we don't know about."

I'm not sure what to make of the story. Not sure if and how it relates to my own memory. My syringe had clear liquid in the barrel, not red. What does the red liquid mean? Are we even talking about the same substance?

Sully mumbles something I don't catch. I turn and look through the hole. Her eye isn't there. She's sitting a few feet from the wall, and I see her face for the first time.

Oh, I'd seen her face in the courtyard. But that was from twenty yards away, when her features were shadowed by the building. For the first time, I see her slashing cheekbones, the perfect heart-shaped mouth. The mouth that's currently trembling, although her eyes are as steady as ever.

I gape. How many times did I look into her expressionless eye and assume she had no feelings? That entire time, her mouth would have given her away, if only I had seen it.

"What did you say?" I ask.

She lifts her head and turns toward the hole, although I know she can't see me from that angle. "Now you know why I keep to myself. My brain scans show that I'm not aggressive. I should be safe here in Limbo, for the rest of my life. But I want to make sure."

"Slicing yourself is aggressive," I say. "It makes you stand out."

"The cutting is my back-up plan." She holds her arms out. She sliced herself up, all right. But not with neat, surgical strokes. The cuts are jagged and crooked, as if she ripped up her skin with a coat hanger. Or her fingernails.

"The girls think I cut myself to keep track of time. It's easier to let them think that. Be their human calendar. But the truth is, I can't bear to do it more than once a week."

"Why do it at all?" I ask.

"I kill a man in the future, hatchie. But before that, he rapes me." She presses her lips together. "I know how FuMA thinks. If they ever decide I'm aggressive, it won't be enough to turn me into a murderer. They need to make every detail come true, for fear that the ripples will mess up their precious system.

"But I'll show them." Her voice hardens. "Rape is one crime they can't force. So if I cut myself up, if I starve myself into a pile of skin and bones, then the lowlife will be so disgusted, he won't be able to rape me. Right?"

Rape is about power, not sex. And besides, they have pills for erectile dysfunction. They can fix Sully's arms with the zap of a laser. If FuMA has ways to dig into our brains and drag our memories to the surface, I doubt they'll let a little disfigurement stop them from reaching their goals.

But I don't say any of this out loud. Because hope, no matter how irrational, is a powerful thing. When the odds are against us, when the battle seems insurmountable, hope may be all that keeps us going.

I will not destroy Sully's hope. I will not shoot down the one thing that allows her to survive.

So I press my eye to the hole. "Right. He won't be able to rape you. You'll be safe here."

She turns away without responding, and after a moment, I do, too. Retreating into the corner of my cell, I allow a single tear to fall down my cheek. I can't let them have my memory now. I won't.

I slam my eyes shut and throw myself back into my future memory. This time, I drag my feet as I walk down the hall, dreading what I will find in room 522. I open the door and try to look at anything but my sister. My eyes fall on the teddy bear, specifically on its blue ribbon.

Yes! I did it! I changed the color!

But my elation doesn't last long. There's work to be done.

I take a breath, summoning my courage. But Limbo has put my reserves into a sieve, and I have to grasp at what little strength I have before it drains away. Finally, I turn and face Jessa. Poor, sweet Jessa with her tangled hair and big smile. With her toes poking up the sheet three feet before the end of the bed. With a mental push, I imagine those same toes clumping the fabric just a foot from the baseboard. When I look again, it's as if she's grown two feet taller.

Excitement stirs in my stomach. I can do this. I can change my memory.

Turning my attention to her face, I sculpt a new one. I disintegrate the baby fat left on her cheeks and push her jawline out. This work is the mental equivalent of running a marathon. Already, my mind feels blurry and fatigued, like I haven't slept for seventy-two hours. But I can't rest, not yet. I push forward.

Jessa's eyes grow rounder and spread slightly farther apart. On her chin springs a small mole. Her button nose lengthens, curving up at the end. And for the finishing touch, her perfect little grin twists, displaying two rows of crooked teeth.

The spot where my six-year-old sister lay now holds my cheating husband. That bastard. I'm going to kill him.

But first, I think I need a nap.

A few hours later, I wake to the nightmare-inducing vision of Scar Face. The scar isn't even the ugliest part about him. Mean, narrow eyes, thin, sneering lips. Now that's an image I'd like to alter. He hauls me to my feet and shoves me out of the cell. We take the same path to Dr. Bellows' lab as before.

At the first intersection, I lunge right. But the guard's

hand is a manacle around my arm, solid and unyielding. He yanks me forward, and I stumble. "Not going to work, girlie. I'm under strict instructions to take you to the labs uninjured."

"Oh, really? Does that mean you can't whip me for doing this?" I work up the saliva in my mouth and spit right in his face. The slobber plops onto his cheek and slowly, stickily drips down. It's even better than urine.

Scar Face wipes his cheek on my jumpsuit. "Of course, Bellows didn't say anything about after the procedure," he whispers lecherously in my ear. "I think you and I are due for a private, one-on-one session."

The words are ice cubes clattering down my spine. I know I should defuse the situation. I know I shouldn't do what I'm thinking. But I can't help myself. I grab his neck, pull him close, and bring my knee up as hard as I can. "Looking forward to it."

He doubles over, moaning in pain.

I gawk. I can't believe that worked. I must've learned something in my Self-Defense Core, after all.

Before he can recover, I run down the hallway, but I don't get far. A couple of employees spill out of the rooms and converge on me, seizing my arms. Scar Face must've pushed a button to call them.

I'll pay for this later. After the procedure, without the protection of Bellows' instructions, I'll be helpless against Scar Face's rage.

But it was worth it. Because I can spit in the guard's face. I can knee him in the groin, and he still has to deliver me to Bellows, safe and unharmed.

And that gives me deep, extreme pleasure.

Does that make me a bad person? Or maybe Chairwoman Dresden was right. Maybe I am aggressive after all.

The guard deposits me at the lab without another word. Before he leaves, he twists the flesh of my arm, a menacing promise of what's to come.

I thrust the incident from my mind. I can't think about Scar Face right now. I need to focus on this room. This fight. This memory.

Bellows is accompanied by a young woman. She sits at the table, a backpack hanging on her chair, her hands wrapped around the keyball. Medium build. Light eyes. Brown hair that curves around her ears and ends in a question mark above her shoulders.

"Looks like Chairwoman Dresden's taken a special interest in your case." Bellows fiddles with the pencil stub behind his ear. "She sent over her personal assistant to make sure we stay in line."

His tone is neutral, but a muscle ticks at the corner of his mouth. He's not happy to be supervised. And really not happy at me for causing it.

"Not at all." The assistant gets out of her seat and smiles. "Chairwoman Dresden was merely curious why the first treatment didn't work. Please, sit down."

Something flickers in my mind. William said he was dating the Chairwoman's assistant. Does that mean this woman is his girlfriend?

If she knows who I am, she gives no indication. She

helps me into the wired chair and fastens the harnesses over my body, her floral scent wafting over me. It's not perfume, but a pill she took to change the composition of her sweat.

"My name's MK," she says.

I know she's not my friend. Even if she's William's girlfriend, she is personal assistant to the Chairwoman herself, one step removed from the enemy. And yet, I can't help but warm up to her. She's the first ComA employee who's been kind to me since I've been arrested.

"I'm Callie," I say.

"Full name: Calla Ann Stone." Bellows slaps the sensors onto my head. "Birthday: October Twenty-eight. Status: in Limbo. Are we done with the niceties here? Some of us have work to do."

MK squeezes my shoulder and retreats to the desk screen.

Bellows jams wires into the sensors. "I've doubled the potency of the formula. You're at full health. If the memory's in there, we're dragging it out."

He nods at MK, and she flips a switch. My skin breaks out in goose bumps.

"Have you experienced anything strange since the previous treatment?" he asks.

Oh, sure. I've found out FuMA facilitates violent crime because of some twisted notion about preventing ripples in the future. Is that strange enough?

"No, sir," I say out loud.

"Are you sure? If you have any inherent psychic ability, these treatments have been known to enhance them."

I lick my lips. Does he know about my mind's machine-like abilities to manipulate memories? But that started before the last treatment, not after. He couldn't know.

I fall back on the answer I practiced with my mother. "I do not have a psychic ability. You can read my school record. Not a single report."

"Hmmm." He cups his chin with a hand. "Even with your genetic background?"

My heart stops. They know about Jessa? But how?

"I don't know what you're talking about."

"Your father," Bellows says.

My father? What?

It's doesn't matter. My heart starts beating again. I don't care what my father has to do with anything, so long as Jessa's safe.

"You thought I didn't know?" Bellows smirks. "Your name sounded familiar. It reminded me of a man I used to work with. He was so proud of his firstborn. He came to the labs and crowed about how he named her after the great Callahan."

He walks to his desk and lifts his hand. The keyball jumps to meet his fingertips. A moment later, my father's image appears in the air. It's the same one my mother has programmed into her locket, the one she wears when she's not wearing the cross.

"I did a little research," Bellows says. "Turns out this same man is your father."

I stare at the picture. My father's lips are relaxed, his expression stoic. I've seen this image a hundred times, but I've never seen the panic banked in his eyes before. Or is that my imagination?

"What do you know about my father? What does he

have to do with me having a psychic ability?"

Bellows studies me. Behind him, MK waits, her fingers poised above the keyball. "It's classified," the scientist finally says. "If your mother didn't tell you, I can't divulge it."

He nods at MK. She keys in a few commands, and they exit. The moment the door clicks shut, smoke pours into the room.

I'm not ready. My mind isn't a steel cage. Bellows' news has split it wide open. Stupid, stupid, stupid. He did this on purpose. The scientist wasn't ever going to tell me about my father. He probably made the whole thing up, just to rattle me.

My mind is open. As open as the patch of sky over the courtyard, as the ductwork that twists and turns out of this room. Open as the bottomless pit of a ready mind.

I am walking down a hallway. It has green linoleum floors, with computer screens embedded in the tile. The lighted walls shine so brightly....

No! I won't do it. I'm not giving them this piece of me.

...I can make out a partial shoeprint on the floor. The acrid smell of antiseptic stings my nose.

I grit my teeth. I clench my jaw. I cannot let the memory get to the door. I don't know if my changes stuck. I have no idea if I will murder my cheating husband or my baby sister. My fingers dig into my palm, ripping open my skin. I form the tightest fist I can. Tight because it is closed. Locked up. It will never open. Not for Bellows and not for anyone else.

This is my sister I'm trying to save. My sister.

Closed.

I don't know how long we fight, the fumes and I. Sweat drenches my entire body, gluing me to the chair. My heart thumps like it's in hyperdrive — too hard, too fast, too much for my fragile human body. I can't hear anything but the roaring in my ears. Can't see anything but the deep blackness behind my eyelids. Can't taste anything but the sharp, metallic flavor of blood.

CLOSED.

At some point, the machines go haywire. *Beep! Beep! Beep!*

MK rushes into the room, keying commands into the sphere and yanking the sensors from my head.

Bellows follows closely behind. "What are you doing? We almost had her."

"Her vital signs were off the charts." She pushes a button, and my harnesses fall away. "This memory is important, but we will not sacrifice her life in order to retrieve it. Is that clear?"

Nausea sets in and I fall to the ground. The room spins. Wires, computers, and both FuMA employees rush around me in a funnel of wind.

"You're right." How can Bellows talk when he's flying sideways? Why do his words come out clear instead of garbled? He is the tornado, and I am the eye. He will not stop moving, and I am eternally, consistently still. "She cannot die until she fulfills her memory. Her premature death will put the entire system in jeopardy."

He wavers in and out of my vision, and I clap a hand over my mouth. How can he stand it? I'm getting sick watching his motion.

"I'll tinker with the formula." His body elongates until

it stretches all around me. I whip my head back and forth as I try to lock in on his face. "Take her back to her cell and get her symptoms under control. By this time tomorrow, we'll have her memory."

It is a relief when MK slips her arm around my waist and takes me out of the wind.

13

MK half-carries, half-drags me back to Limbo. I try to help, but my legs don't work. I fall to the floor, pulling MK and her backpack down with me.

"You're going to be okay." She helps me to my feet. "I'm going to inject you with a quick-acting antidote. It's not standard issue, but Bellows signed off on it. He wants you back to full health as soon as possible."

We lurch past the glass-walled office. Burly Whiskers sits behind the desk. No sign of Scar Face. His shift must be over already. How long was I in the labs? All the walls in the cells are dimmed, so it must be nighttime.

We enter my cell, and MK lowers me to the ground, arranging my limbs as if they were precious silverware. I can almost believe she cares about me. Almost believe her primary concern is my well-being, not the success of the project.

Until she pulls the needle out of her backpack.

Hard, cylindrical. The length of my palm, with yellow

liquid swimming in the barrel.

I swallow hard. "What...what are you doing with that?"

"It's the antidote. Won't hurt a bit." She pushes up the sleeve of my jumpsuit, and I feel a sharp pinch in my arm.

An antidote. Maybe that's what I slammed into Jessa's chest. Maybe my future self was trying to save her, not kill her.

I wish. I could wish on a thousand falling stars, and it still wouldn't be true. I know because the heart rate monitor went flat. I saw it. She died.

"You see?" MK's cool fingers move to my pulse. "Your heart rate's slowing already."

She turns and begins to rearrange the items in her backpack. I close my eyes halfway. She's right. I do feel better.

MK may work for the wrong people, but that doesn't mean her intentions are evil. Judging by the items in her backpack, she's a regular girl, like me and Marisa. Water bottle, compact, teddy bear...

Wait a minute. Teddy bear. It has white fur and a red bow, round ears and a black nose. Just like the bear in my future memory.

I struggle to sit up. "MK, where did you get that bear?" The words squeak out, rushed and panicked.

"Shhh." She zips up the backpack with the bear inside and swings it over her shoulders. "It's a stuffed animal, Callie. It can't hurt you."

"No, you don't understand. I'm not hallucinating. The bear—"

She covers my mouth with her fingers. "You need to

rest. No more talking, okay? I'll be back in the morning to check on you."

"MK…"

But she's no longer listening. She and the bear leave my cell, and the gate slides shut behind her.

I lie back down, my heart pounding. I'm being ridiculous. This probably means nothing. It's coincidence that the bear's twin was on Jessa's windowsill.

Except I don't believe in coincidence anymore.

I close my eyes and try to sleep. I have a big day tomorrow. Bellows is going to tinker with the formula. Make it even stronger. I have to resist the fumes. I *have* to.

Once more, I probe my brain. Falling into step with my future self, I run down the hallway to room 522. Opening the door, I see a fluffy white bear with a bright blue ribbon. Relief floods over me, and I break into a grin. I step further into the room and turn toward the bed to kill my husband. I drink in his ski-jump nose, squared jawline, and crooked teeth. As ugly as he is, I've never seen anything more beautiful in my life. But just as I raise the syringe, something changes. Our gazes lock and I see her eyes. Jessa's eyes.

Just like that, the whole ruse disintegrates. Jessa's face becomes soft and round, the mole disappears from her chin, and her lanky legs grow stubby once more. I plunge the needle into Jessa's heart. The last thing I see before I fall into reality is Jessa's final grin, full of crooked, little teeth.

My stomach sinks. I've failed. My abilities aren't strong enough to maintain the alteration, at least not yet. My only option is to fight the fumes. I have to hold off the memory. But how long will I be able to keep this up? Can I keep resisting day in and day out?

I sit up, and the floor tilts in waves. I clutch my forehead. Bellows said the formula doesn't work as well when I'm injured. I need Scar Face. I need him to beat me up, to keep me safe from the formula.

I stagger to my feet, but before I can run to the bars, I hear a mechanical whirring. As if in slow motion, the gate slides open and a figure steps through the open space. His face is shadowed, but his shoulders fill the doorway.

My breath gets clogged in my throat. Wish granted. Scar Face is here.

I back away, my feet tripping over themselves. I want him to hurt me, but fear wraps its icy fingers around my heart. The hair stands on my neck, and my body is already flinching from the pain.

"Get it over with." The voice crawls out of my throat on all fours, beaten and resigned. I can do this. Whatever injury he inflicts will be worth it because it will keep me safe from Bellows's formula, keep FuMA from finding out about my sister.

He strides forward, and the gate closes. Something is not quite right. He doesn't look like Scar Face. He looks like—

He seizes my arm, and I gasp, because I can finally see his face, and it's not the guard, after all.

It's Logan Russell.

14

My knees go weak, and the room spins like it did back in the lab. I must be hallucinating again. Clearly, my old friend isn't in my cell wearing a guard's uniform. The real Logan Russell is probably home in bed, resting up for a swim meet or a calculus exam or a hot date.

But oh, he looks so good. Can't fault my hallucination for its attention to detail. Even in the shadows I can see his biceps bulge under the short-sleeved shirt, and the cottony material clings to his abs.

And then I see his expression.

It's the same look he used to give me in class sometimes. During a lull in the teacher's lecture, I'd feel the burn of his eyes on my skin. When I glanced up, he would avert his gaze quickly. Automatically. But not before I saw the yearning, as if he, too, scanned the skies every night, searching for a shooting star to wish our friendship back into existence.

Back then I was too shy to do anything about that look. But I don't need to be shy now. He's not even real.

I close the distance between us and spread my palms across his chest. His muscles are hard ridges under my hands, and his heart thrums against my fingertips. As soon as I touch him, the illusion Logan sucks in a breath and goes still, as if he's been waiting for this moment for a very long time.

Can't fault my imagination for its creativity, either.

"You feel amazing," I say. Apparently, even hallucinatory Callie isn't smooth.

My skin flushes, and my pulse is a too loud bass line in my ears. I should move away, but this is my hallucination, and I want closer. I want more.

I shuffle forward, and our toes caress through our sneakers. I trail my hand across his chest, over his shoulders, and then up, up, up until I touch his smooth, newly shaven cheeks. I rub my fingers back and forth, fascinated by the silky texture. He exhales, a puff of air that seems to contain all the frustration and yearning of the last five years.

I skip my hand to his lips. His soft, warm lips. The lips I so badly wanted to taste before I turned myself in to FuMA. The lips I'm daring myself to kiss now.

But even in my imagination, I'm not that brave.

He reaches up and covers my hand, his fingers locking around my palm like he never wants to let go. And then he moves my hand from his lips, slowly, reluctantly, as though it's the hardest thing he's ever done. "I can't believe I'm saying this, but we don't have much time."

Wait a minute. Back in the science lab, when I hallucinated the flood, I couldn't feel the raindrops. But I feel every bit of Logan, from his soft lips to the calloused pads on his palms. "You're real?"

"As real as you can get."

Oh. Dear. Fate. I snatch my hand away, my cheeks hot enough to set the air on fire. Was I really fondling his chest? Rubbing my fingers across his lips? What is wrong with me?

"What are you doing here?" I mumble to the floor.

"Rescuing you." He lifts his hand, as though he doesn't know what to do with it. The moment's gone. The hallucination is over. He tucks the hand behind his back, and I'm painfully aware the connection between us was all in my head.

"It's not what you thought," he says. "You aren't safe from your future here. The Underground told me FuMA doesn't care about crime. All they care about is making the memories come true."

"I found out the same thing a few days ago," I whisper.

He stops. "Am I in time? Did your memory come true?"

"They don't even know my real memory yet." The saliva lodges in my throat. What would he think if he knew the truth? Would he still want to save me?

He waves a magnetic wand in front of the gate, and it slides open. The wand looks the same as the ones the guards carry, FuMA-issued, not available anywhere else.

My eyes widen. It's finally hitting me that he's breaking me out of here. "Where did you get that?"

"I'll explain later. We need to get out before the sleeping draught I gave the guard wears off." He guides me forward. I trip on nothing, and he catches me.

"What's wrong?" He tightens his hand on my shoulder. "Did they hurt you?"

"It's the fumes." The disorientation comes back full force. I can't even tell where the door is. "They're trying to draw my future memory to the surface. The side effect is dizziness. And seeing things that aren't really there. That's why I groped you earlier." I should drop it. Pretend it never happened. But my mouth is no longer attached to my mind. "I thought you were a hallucination. I wasn't trying to come on to you. Or cop a feel. Or molest your lips." Oh Fates. *Be quiet, Callie. Just close your mouth.* "Sorry."

"I wouldn't mind if you came on to me." He clears his throat. I guess real-life Logan isn't so smooth either.

We stare at each other. Did he actually say he likes me? No way. He's not interested in me. We're not even friends.

And yet, we're standing inches apart, and his breath is coming in quick pants. If I lean forward a little bit…

"We'd better get out of here," he says.

Right. In the middle of a rescue mission here.

We shuffle forward, trying to blend our footsteps with the snores of the sleeping inmates. With any luck, no one is awake to hear the difference.

We take a total of ten steps when a voice sounds at my elbow. "Who's there?"

I jump, but it's just Sully, standing at the bars. She looks different. Her eyes look less hard against her bony face. The long, straight lashes that seem so intimidating in the light appear vulnerable when bathed in shadows.

"It's me." I wrack my muddled brain, trying to figure

out the fastest way to explain. "Sully, this is the boy who used to give me the leaves. He's breaking me out."

She reaches through the slot and places something in my hand. One of the leaves I gave her in exchange for information. It's dried and crumbling, but otherwise intact.

"Take me with you," she says.

I look at Logan, and he shrugs helplessly. "We can't. This wand is only programmed with the code for your cell. I have no idea where to find her code."

I didn't know this girl a few days ago, but now I wilt at the thought of leaving her behind. Just like the leaf dying in my hand. "I'm sorry, Sully. If I can find a way to come back for you, I will. But in the meantime, you're safe here. You're not aggressive."

She presses her lips together, and a fissure opens in my heart. A few seconds later, though, not a trace of sorrow remains. "Go, hatchie. Fly this coop for both of us."

She backs away from the bars. I tuck the leaf into the pocket of my jumpsuit, my limbs solid with regret, and trail after Logan. I feel like a carbonated bottle, filled to bursting. A single flick is all it will take to make me pop.

But then we reach the end of the hallway, and the entry stands before us, as imposing as ever. Inside the glass-walled room, Burly Whiskers slumps over his desk, bear-like snores shaking his shoulders.

The pressure leaks away. I can't feel badly about Sully. I don't have time.

I turn to Logan. This is where he needs to work his magic. "Let me guess. You've got the numbered code and have found a way to bypass the fingerprint, retina, and blood scans."

"Afraid not. They change those codes on a daily basis, and to get those scans, we'd have to move three hundred pounds of unconscious guard." He grimaces. "Not happening."

"What then?"

In response, he opens the door across from the guard's station, the mysterious one that was always closed. The room where they made Beks shoot and kill a man.

We walk inside, and it's just a room. Four walls and a simple interrogation table. I don't know what I expected. Blood stains on the floor, the stink of a rotting corpse. Something to reflect the nightmares that took place here. Apparently evil can be washed out with disinfectant and a bottle of air freshener. Nothing remains but a cold, sterile canvas.

Logan crosses the floor and taps twice on the back wall. A panel slides away, revealing a locked glass cabinet chock-full of equipment. Everything we could possibly need to break out of jail. Tasers. Firearms. Cutters.

I swallow hard. This is his plan? Knees to the groin notwithstanding, I'm not much of a fighter. "Um, Logan? You should know my combat skills are a bit...marginal."

His brow furrows in concentration. "How'd you do in the Self-Defense track?"

"I took the basic core and then opted out. Too busy learning how to cook manually." I cringe. My former dream seems frivolous compared to the practical life skills I could've been learning. "But if your Meal Assembler ever breaks down, I'm your girl."

He smiles as though I'm a live comedian, and I want to kick myself. I'm your girl? What possessed me to say that?

"We're not battling our way out," he says. "This place is like a fortress. We wouldn't get two feet."

I scan the weapons in the locked case, stopping on an electronic pulser with more buttons than I have fingers. "Then why are we here?"

"It's not what's in the cabinet, but what's under it."

The cabinet hangs a foot above the floor. Underneath, I see the same concrete blocks that make up the walls of my cell.

Logan gets on his hands and knees and backs into the space. He inches backward until his body disappears into the concrete. One moment, he's there. The next, he's gone. Talk about being swallowed whole.

"Logan?" I blink. "I think I'm hallucinating again. I just saw you disappear."

His head pops out of the wall, as though he's a taxidermic animal. "You're not hallucinating. The wall's not really there. It's a holographic projection."

I crouch down. The concrete looks so real, as solid as any wall.

His head disappears again. "Come on, Callie. There's an air shaft back here that will lead us to freedom. What are you waiting for?"

Nothing. There's nothing for me here but a mad scientist who wants to experiment on my brain and a messed-up agency who will make me kill my sister.

I take a deep breath and back out the same way Logan did, straight through the concrete.

15

expect my feet to bump into solid rock, but they move past the floor and dangle in midair.

"Slowly." Logan's voice comes from underneath me. "There's a ladder. Swing your legs toward the wall and get your feet on a rung. I'll catch you if you fall, I promise."

Great. How far is the ground below us?

I scrabble for, and then find, the ladder. I ease myself down, one rung at a time, until my entire body is in the shaft.

I look down. I can't see a thing. This shaft could go on forever. If I slip, I'll hurtle through the air—but probably not forever.

My heart pounds. I can't breathe. I can't move. My heartbeat thunders in my ears, drowning out the ventilation fan, drowning out sensible thought.

Drowning. Everything.

"Callie?" Logan says. "You good?"

Sweat drips past my eyebrows, down my neck. I almost

can't find my voice in all that liquid. "I...can't...see... anything."

"I'm right here, Callie. You're doing great." His voice takes my jumbled nerves and irons them smooth.

He knows. Maybe I've told him the story of the woman jumping off the cliff. Or maybe he noticed when I refused to climb to the top of the rope during the Fitness Core. Somehow, he knows I'm scared of heights.

But more importantly, he remembers. I remember that his favorite candy is watermelon glass and that he's always been terribly afraid of spiders. But I never expected him to remember a thing about me. He's the one who forgot about our friendship, after all.

The thought warms my belly, and I manage to take a normal breath.

Below me, a light flicks on, and a thin beam cuts through the darkness. I see the hole I've come through and the room beyond. A small, black device, shaped like a spider, perches at the edge of the hole. This must be what created the hologram. The good news is that we're both facing our fears tonight. The bad news is he seems to be doing better than me.

"You can do this." He wraps his hand around my ankle, and his calloused palms pierce through my fear. "You went to prison to keep your future from coming true. You're not going to let a little phobia stop you from breaking out."

You can do this. You can do this. You can do this. I take a deep breath and then another. Quickly, before I free fall into oblivion, I take my foot from the safety of one rung and jam it up onto the next one.

"That's it. One foot after the other. As easy as popping a pie into the Meal Assembler. That is, if you even use the Meal Assembler."

I try to laugh proudly. Manual pies only for me. I will not think about how high I am. I'll pretend the ground is five feet below me. Surely, I can handle five feet.

My palms are wet, my grip slippery. Rust or paint or dirt flakes off the rungs under my hands. In my mind, I see the bits falling, falling into the darkness below. With each rung I get higher, and the distance I have to fall gets farther. It is against my every instinct to keep scaling this building with him.

"Talk to me." My voice shakes and echoes off the walls. I have to think about something else. I can't keep imagining my imminent death. "Who put the hole and hologram here?"

There's no way Logan did it himself. The guy may have hidden depths, but come on. This job is the work of professionals.

His shoes squeak against the ladder. "The Underground."

He mentioned them before. "You mean the secret community that set up that haven in the wilderness? The one made up of all those psychics?" We climb a few rungs. "How did they get this technology?"

"Most psychics have an aptitude for the sciences. That's always been true. Newton, Einstein, Darwin—all those guys were psychics, although Callahan was the first one who admitted it. How do you think they made all those leaps of intuition?"

We settle into an easy climbing rhythm. Logan touches

my ankle every few rungs, and each contact gives me another shot of strength.

"The Underground's got a group of scientists inventing technologies we don't share with ComA." He brushes my ankle again, and this time his fingers seem to linger. "The holographic projection is one of them."

The ladder dead-ends at a mesh silver screen. I try to swallow, but the saliva's dried in my mouth. How long have we been climbing? How many yards do I have to fall?

"I'm at the top." The words scrape out of my throat.

"You see the screen above you? Give it a good punch."

Oh, sure. A good punch. I'll slip right off these rungs as I wind up for the throw.

"I'm right beneath you, Callie. I'm not going to let you fall."

He believes in me. He thinks I can do this.

I adjust my grip on the ladder and jam my fist upward with all my might. The screen blows right off.

A rush of night air greets me. We climb out of the shaft and find ourselves on the roof of the building. I could kiss the solid surface beneath me.

A zillion stars sparkle in the black sky, and the wind carries a scent of trees and soil. The full moon hangs like a perfect white orb, shadowed with craters. It provides almost as much light as the sun on a cloudy day.

A lump forms in my throat. The freedom is almost unbearable. "I've never seen anything so beautiful," I whisper.

"This is where we part ways." His voice is so heavy it pulls me back from the stars.

I realize how bare the roof is. No other ladders. No doorways. Not even a nearby building to which we can cross.

"What do you mean? How am I going to get down? And where are you going?"

He guides me to the edge of the roof and I look down into white rapids crashing over enormous boulders. The river. Again.

"No." I back away, horrified. "I can't do it. I can't jump off this roof."

"You climbed up that ladder like it was nothing. You can do this, too."

My heart sprints as though chased by an enemy, and the roaring is back in my ears. But he's right. I did climb the ladder. Which means I'll do this, too. For Jessa, I'll do anything.

I take a deep breath, and it coughs and stutters out of me. "Okay. Where do I jump?"

He points to an area right below a rocky incline, where the river widens drastically. "Right there, where the current is weakest. There are no boulders for at least a hundred yards, so you can't miss. When you get across the river, head south. Stick close to the water and look for some boulders piled in a pyramid. There will be a boat hidden underneath the brush. The Underground leaves it there for people like you. Inside, you'll find a backpack with a laminated map that will lead you to Harmony."

He gestures over his shoulder. "I'll go back down the shaft and hide until morning. I'm sorry I can't go with you. Underground orders." His voice is thin and patchy with guilt. "The cliff doesn't end for miles, and by the time we find flat land for me to cross back into the suburbs, the FuMA guards will be patrolling the city limits."

"That's okay. You've already done enough."

I look at the water below, and the panic flutters in my chest again. Someone's done his homework. This part of the river seems downright calm compared to the ferocious currents I'm used to seeing. If I'm going to jump, this is the place to do it. There's only one problem. I can't believe I didn't think of it before.

"Logan," I say. "I can't swim."

He gawks at me, a swimmer first, and then a rescuer. "How is that possible?"

"I don't know. My mom never liked the water, so I never learned how."

He wrinkles his forehead, thinking hard. I want to tell him it's over. He went to all this trouble to break me out, never realizing I was such a pathetic escapee. Scared of heights. Unable to swim. My knees buckle and I want to collapse onto the hard cement. I've failed him. Failed Jessa. Failed myself.

But then, he grabs my hand. "All right. Let's do it."

"Do what?"

"I'm going with you."

What? *What?* "Don't be ridiculous. You just said—"

"Look, Callie. Five years ago, I stood by and did nothing when they took my brother away. I'm not about to let it happen again."

It is generous, so generous that hot tears stab my eyes. "I'm not your sister. I'm just a girl you haven't spoken to for five years."

He touches my cheek, briefly. "You've never been just

a girl to me, Calla Lily."

An alarm sounds. Dimly at first, and then louder and louder. "That's for you," he says. "The guard must've woken up and discovered you missing. They'll start combing through the building. They'll be on the roof before we know it. There's no time." He grips my clammy hand. "We jump on three."

I take a deep breath and face the open sky. There's no time to be scared. No time to worry I'm flinging myself into open space. No time to let my phobia out of its cage.

"One."

I'm so sorry, Jessa. I never meant to hurt you. I never dreamed it would come to this.

"Two."

If I die, then you'll live. That's all that's important now.

"Three."

You see, Mom? I told you I'd keep her safe.

A valley of nothingness looms before me. I jump.

16

hit the water. It's cold. Ice cold. Bubbles fizzle all over my body, and I plunge so deep I might tunnel a path all the way through the Earth. But my feet don't hit ground. Instead, the water buoys me up and flips me around. White foam engulfs me, and beyond that is darkness.

Up. Which way is up?

The moon will show me the way. I arch my neck, wildly searching for a ray of light. Nothing. I can't see more than six inches in front of me. I claw forward and kick my feet. If my pathetic maneuvering changes my position, I don't notice.

I need a breath. My lungs begin to burn. I imagine them expanding like overfilled balloons, stretching bigger and bigger until *pop*!

I'm going to die here. After all Logan's done for me, I'm going to drown, tucked into the river's watery sheets like a long forgotten doll.

Suddenly a vise clamps onto my feet and jerks. My

body sails through the water, twisting and turning as it fights the current's pull. And then, air. Sweet, beautiful air. I take a deep breath. And then another. But the vise isn't finished. It claps across my chest and pins my arms to my sides.

I thrash against the hold, grappling, kicking, squirming. Anything to get free.

"Calm down!" Logan yells in my ear. "You'll drown us both!"

He repeats this twice before the words sink in. I let my limbs go limp, although I'm still sputtering for breath.

"You okay?" he says.

"Yeah," I gasp.

Something sharp jabs me in the middle of my back. His hip bone. He's on his side, balancing me against his body. And then we're moving, slicing through the waves, as he swims with one arm and two legs.

The glass and steel building is already a craggy rock in the distance, and if my pursuers stand on the roof, watching us, they're nothing but a blur of dots. I think I hear the faint echo of the alarm, but all around us is water. Nothing but water.

Logan Russell is dragging me to shore. Saving my life, in every sense of the word.

That's my last coherent thought before I pass out.

When I wake, I'm in a boat, shaded from the sun by a blanket rigged up by a couple of sticks. A backpack lies under my head, and Logan is in front of me, pulling the oars with powerful, rhythmic strokes.

His shirt is off. For more than a moment, I stare. His muscles glisten under a sheen of sweat and sunblock. A thick white cream is smeared across his nose, obstructing my perfect view of his face. A sudden urge to wipe the stuff away washes over me. I'm reminded of the times I used to sneak into his swim practices. He always had time to help a teammate with his stroke, always left the best swim lane for someone else, even if he was the first one in the pool. That's Logan—generous to a fault. That's why it killed me when he stopped talking to me. It was so uncharacteristic.

He glances up now, and I drop my eyes. My stomach darts around like a hummingbird, and I'm intensely aware that each pull of the oar brings his knuckles inches from my knees. It's almost painful the way the heat threatens to dance across my body before fading away as he pulls the oar back into himself.

Oh, we've touched. In the last twenty-four hours, I've touched him more than any other boy in my life. But those circumstances were extenuating. Now that we're not breaking out of detainment, now that I'm no longer under the influence of Dr. Bellows' fumes, we're back to the girl and boy we used to be—the ones who barely spoke, much less came within an arm's length of each other.

"How long did I sleep?" I ask in order to fill the silence.

"A few hours. I didn't want to wake you. You looked like you needed your rest."

His words are neutral, but his gaze is too direct. In the harsh sunlight, he must see the stamp Limbo leaves on all its inmates. The pale, ashen skin. Bruises like thumbprints under my eyes. Hair that hasn't been washed in days.

So. Not. Attractive.

Flushing, I study the scenery as it whizzes by. The raging current has turned into the placid waters of a lazy river. Gone is the imposing cliff, with the metallic spirals and jagged towers rising above it, architectural feats dreamed up by Eden City's most enterprising minds. We've even passed the suburbs surrounding the city, with their residential homes and athletic fields.

Instead, I see color. Brilliant reds, sunset oranges, emerald greens. Every color reflected in Jessa's falling leaves, and then some. Dense forests line both sides of the shore. There's not a manmade structure in sight.

I look back at Logan. His stroke is strong, but fading. Exhaustion edges his features. He's probably been rowing the entire time I was asleep.

Every stroke takes him farther from civilization. Every length of the boat is more distance from where he's supposed to be. Where he belongs.

"What are you doing?"

"I'm taking you to Harmony," he says. "It's fifty miles upriver, and they're expecting us."

The community on the edge of civilization. A chance to leave my future—and my family—behind like a bad dream.

I swallow hard. I may have to abandon the people I love best, but he doesn't.

"No." I grab the oar and stick it in the water, trying to turn the boat around. Unfortunately, I only succeed in making us rock and buck in the current. "You can't go to some community in the woods. In the future you're a professional swimmer. You have to get back to Eden City and live out your memory."

"It's too late. By now the patrols will be stationed at every bullet train into the city."

My eyes get so big I feel wrinkles in my forehead. "So you'll walk." I point the oar toward the flat, forested shore. "Cross the river here, hitch a ride to the suburbs, and then make your way back to the city on foot."

My attempts to turn the boat are only making my arms ache. Giving up, I pull the oar back in, and the boat drifts gently down the river.

"Maybe I've changed my mind," he says, his voice thick with an emotion I can't identify. "I've been hearing about Harmony my whole life. Maybe I want to check it out for myself."

"It's not your future."

He reaches for the oar. "My memory doesn't take away my free will, Callie. I still get to make my own decisions. And right now, my decision is to go to Harmony. With you. I'll make sure you're settled, and then I'll go back to Eden City."

"But why?" I shouldn't ask. I should leave well enough alone. But the words roll out of me like they've been pressed against the door, waiting for five long years to be let out. "You don't even like me. You stopped talking to me ages ago."

He stiffens, and I know I've crossed a line. We never agreed not to talk about the past—but from the moment I saw him in my cell, our interaction has had the quality of a dream. Or a hallucination. My statement plunks us squarely back into real life.

"I kinda stopped talking to everybody," he says.

"Yes, but you *ignored* me. It was like I didn't exist. No 'hello,' no 'excuse me.' Not even 'get out of my way.'"

He sighs. Okay, so I'm a terrible person. The guy dragged me across the river. He left civilization so he could deliver me safely to Harmony. And here I am, badgering him about something that happened when we were kids. "Forget it. It was a long time ago."

"No, I want to answer. I'm just trying to figure out the best way to do it." He swallows once, twice, and then dips the oar in the river. But his stroke is no longer sure and steady. His motion is jerky, uneven. Almost as though he were nervous. Of what? Me?

"Do you remember the day they took Mikey away?" he asks, staring at the waves in the water.

"Like it was yesterday."

Mikey was four years ahead of us, and I didn't really know him, but he looked just like Logan, except with longer hair. I was sitting in the T-minus five classroom when we heard sirens, followed by the clatter of footsteps. We crowded around the door, craning our necks to see into the hallway. And then we saw him, Mikey Russell, flanked by two TechRA officials, his tanned arms wrenched behind his back in a pair of electro-cuffs.

"So you remember what you said to me?"

I shake my head. The image of Mikey being led away is imprinted in my mind, but everything else is a chaotic blur. "I'm sorry?"

"You turned to me and you grabbed my arm, just as Mikey was passing in front of our classroom. 'Do some-thing,' you said." His hand clenches, and the oar vibrates.

"And I stood there like an idiot, while they took my brother away from me. I stood there and watched like the rest of you, even though my life was never going to be the same again."

"Oh, Logan." My heart squeezes. "You were twelve years old. What could you have done?"

"Something." He looks up, and I see the little boy again. The one who cared so much and tried so hard to do the right thing. The generous thing. The one who shut down that day, and I never knew why. "I could've talked to the officials and convinced them it was some magic trick we pulled. Or maybe get the other kids to agree it was all a big joke, that they didn't actually see what they'd said they saw."

"I don't think any of that would've worked," I whisper.

"Maybe I should've been brave enough to look into his face as they dragged him away. Tell him I loved him so he wouldn't feel so alone. But I didn't. And that's why I couldn't talk to you. I couldn't even look at you without hearing those words. *Do something*." He inches forward on his knees, and the world fades away. There are no oars digging into the water, no sun's rays warming my shoulders, no leaves fluttering in the wind. There's just Logan and me and these words between us. "I didn't mean to hurt you. I just couldn't bear to see the blame in your eyes."

"I never blamed you. Not for a second."

For a moment, we don't speak. The air around us is stuffed with so many thoughts, so many emotions. Any second now, it will burst and the excess will rain on us like a hailstorm.

"Maybe I blamed myself." His voice is low, so low, as

if these words have never been spoken before, and he's scared to speak them now. "And I took it out on you. I'm sorry."

You sure did. But the old anger fails to rise. My chest is too blocked up. There's no room for anything but this ache that's splitting me in two.

"That's what you meant on the roof," I say. "You jumped with me to try and make up for the past."

His lips curve, the ghost of a grin that died five years ago. "I want him to be proud of me."

Your poor parents. First, they lose Mikey, and now you.

I don't say it out loud, though. If I do, he might get upset, and then I'll start crying. Once I go down that path, I'll think of my mom and Jessa, and then where will I be? A blubbering fool, no good for anything.

Instead, I smile so big it makes my cheeks hurt. "How much longer before we break for the night?"

17

The sun is low in the sky when Logan suggests we stop. We pull the boat onto the shore and walk until we find a clearing not too littered with rocks. Moss-covered roots jut out of the ground, and all manner of plants—fan-shaped, spiky, broad—crowd under the soaring trees. It smells like the earth here, of worms and raindrops, so unlike the steel and pavement of the city.

I step behind a tree and change out of the yellow jumpsuit into a clean black shirt and pants, identical to the uniform I used to wear at school during the Fitness Core. It's remarkable what a change of clothes can do to a person. I almost feel refreshed. When I come back, Logan is sitting on the ground, arranging the contents of the backpack into piles.

I fold the jumpsuit and set it next to the backpack, even though I'd rather burn it. I sneak a look at Logan, only to find him watching me, and we both look away. The old awkwardness looms between us. I chew my lips and try to figure out what to do with my hands. I clasp them behind my back, but that looks stupid. Cross my arms over my waist. Too defensive.

Come on, Callie. Get it together. He's just a boy.

No, never, a voice inside me whispers. *Like you've never been just a girl to him.*

The warmth begins in my stomach and creeps out to my skin. I give up on my hands and crouch down to study the piles of supplies. Anything to avoid the weight of his gaze.

Tins. Lots of metal tins, labeled on the side. Rope. A compass. Extra clothes. A map.

And then... What on earth? Packs of underwear, in varying sizes, and the largest pair of sneakers I've ever seen. I don't get it. I'm not a wilderness expert or anything, but why do we need so much underwear? Size fourteen sneakers probably fit two people in Eden City.

Logan tosses me a metal tin. I look on the side and read "basil." I grab a few of the others, and each tin is some sort of seasoning. Thyme. Rosemary. Mint.

I rock backward. It took weeks for me to grow these herbs on my windowsill. I had to scrounge and beg and bribe to get the seeds from my Manual Cooking instructors. And here they are, every herb I can imagine, packaged neatly into little tins. Ready to be used.

"I knew you'd be happy about the spices," he says, grinning like a little boy handing out his first Christmas present. His smiles are like a candle to my heart, heating it up slowly but steadily.

And I couldn't ask for a better present. I'd take curry and turmeric over a diamond bracelet any spacetime. "I'm thrilled." There are enough tins to supply the graduate studies program for a year. "But why are all these herbs here?"

"The backpacks are a handy way to bring stuff to Harmony," he says, comfortable now that we're talking information and facts. If only our whole relationship could be comprised of data streams. "They don't have any modern technology, and it's not easy to get back to civilization when they're running low on supplies. So one way for them to get stuff is for people like us to bring them."

I run my finger along the tins. "So they don't have digital communication? How does the Underground know what to pack?"

"Oh, um." Both the grin and the comfort disappear, like a flame doused with water. "I'm not sure. They must have their ways. Or maybe they're guessing. I don't know."

Guessing about size fourteen shoes? I don't think so. I watch him stack the tins into a pyramid. He's hiding something. But what?

"You said they were expecting us." I say slowly. "How do they know about us, if we can't communicate with them?"

"Did I say that?" His face is bright red now. "I must've misspoken. I don't have any actual connection with Harmony. I only know what my parents told me."

He clearly doesn't want to talk about it. I should drop the subject. But if I hadn't asked why he stopped talking to me, he never would've confessed. I would still believe he gave me the silent treatment because he didn't like me.

"What aren't you telling me?" I ask.

"Nothing! The situation is complicated, that's all." He stands and edges away from me. With each step, he becomes less the guy on the boat and more the boy who ignored me for five years. "I can't discuss this right now. Try to keep an open mind."

I watch him leave. Try to keep an open mind. About what? Our friendship?

I'm willing to be open about that. I'd forget about our five years of silence. I'd forgive him for all his secrets.

If only he would trust me like he used to.

An hour later, I sling the stainless steel canteen over my shoulder and head for the river to fill it. Rolling up my pants, I wade in until the water splashes around my knees. The sun has dipped below the horizon, and streaks of purple chase after the orange glow, against a backdrop of wispy clouds.

I take a deep breath and hold it. I like the sun even when it isn't here.

Logan gave me this, and I couldn't be more grateful. So maybe he's right. Maybe I should keep an open mind.

The breeze rushes over my skin, making the hair at the back of my neck tingle. I unscrew the cap and dip the canteen in the water.

An open mind. I roll the concept around my tongue, my brain. What does it mean? How does it work? Your future spread out before you. Open. An infinite number of possibilities. Open. Paths branching out in every direction. Open.

A rush of something flows through me. I feel it everywhere—in the cuts on my legs, the ache in my lower back, my hands holding the canteen in the water.

What on earth? I've already gotten my memory from the future. There's only supposed to be one. Right? So why am I feeling this rush? Why do I feel like I'm about to receive another memory? Another *memory*. OPEN.

I am curled in my mother's lap, hugging a stuffed dog. The dog's fur is purple, and she has a green ring around one of her wide, sad eyes. She smells like a mixture of peanut butter and stale crackers, but when I dig my chin into her body, she envelops me with a softness that is only slightly matted.

My body feels strange. Out of sync. Like I've put on the wrong skin. "Why did she have to leave?" I ask. "Where did she go?"

I don't know who "she" is. I don't know why I'm sad. All I know is there's a gulf inside me so large it may never be filled.

My mother strokes my hair. It curls around my ear and stops under my chin. I must be young, so young, to have hair this short. "I don't know, baby."

Why doesn't she know? My mother always knows. Even if she has to make them up, she always has the answers.

"She promised," I say. "She promised she would stay all night. She promised she would stay forever, but she left me. She's gone."

"Sometimes, people can't keep their promises."

"But I miss her." I catch the ear of my stuffed dog between my teeth. When I spit it out, the ear flops over, faded and wet. "I need her."

"I do too, baby. I do, too."

jerk. The canteen plops into the water, and I lunge after it. What *was* that? I must've been dreaming. But it's not fading, the way dreams do. I can hear my mother's voice, feel her arms around me. I can smell Princess's soft fur, that lingering scent of a mid-afternoon snack.

Wait a minute—Princess? *Princess?*

Princess isn't my stuffed dog. She's Jessa's.

My mind spins, and I wobble onto the shore. If the dog belongs to my sister, then so must the vision. But how can that be? How did her memory get into my mind?

I trip over a rock and sprawl across the dirt. The canteen crashes to the ground. Water gushes out, seeping around my fingers. She promised she would stay all night, my sister said. She promised she would stay forever, but she left me. She's gone.

"Callie?" Logan materializes in front of me. "How you doing with that water?"

I look down and realize I've got a vice-like grip on handfuls of pebbles. I open my fists, and the rocks fall away, leaving tiny cuts all over my palms. Tears threaten to well over, and not from the little gashes. No matter how hard I try to be strong, I can't keep the words from spilling out.

"The last thing I said to my sister was a lie. She asked

me to stay the night with her and I said I would, even though I had no intention of doing it." Can my heart break any further? Really, can it? "Why did I have to lie to her? Why?"

He reaches out his hands like he might want to help me up and then puts them in his pockets again. "You're a great sister, Callie. Anyone can see that."

I rub my face on the polyester fabric of my sleeve. We'll see how good it really is at wicking away moisture. "Was our entire relationship fake? Was my love for her nothing but a lie?"

"Of course not. She means the world to you. Anyone can see that."

I lower my sleeve and look right at him. "Logan, I killed her. In my future memory, Jessa was in a hospital bed in TechRA, and I stabbed a needle into her heart. I murdered my baby sister. How can I love her? And if I don't love her, how can I love anyone?"

I wait for the horror to cross his face, the automatic recoil when my words register. I've pictured his expression a million times. The one that says I'm evil. The one that shows his disgust. The one that tells me more clearly than any words what a horrible person I am.

But the expression doesn't come.

Instead, he grazes his fingertips against my arm. It is the slightest touch and yet it burns all the way through me, searing my feet into the pebbled ground. "That's a terrible burden to bear."

I look at his hand, at the long, artisan fingers that could've easily given him a career as a concert pianist. "You don't think I'm a monster?"

"The only monster here is your future memory. It robs you of your peace and makes you doubt who you are. I know who you are, Callie, and you are full of love."

My knees turn as squishy as the river mud under my feet. "Thank you," I whisper.

"For what?"

"For not judging me."

"How can you judge someone's future actions without understanding the circumstances?" he asks.

How, indeed. But I don't say this out loud. I can't. Because I don't know if he's as sincere as he sounds. Maybe he's gifted at knowing exactly what to say and when. Maybe his words have no more meaning than the laughter that bubbled out of him five years ago.

Or maybe, just maybe, he's still the same boy I remember.

We don't talk much during dinner. Logan builds a brace to dangle his canteen over the fire—thank the Fates for his Ancient Methods elective—and I cook the rice in the makeshift pot.

My hands shake as I measure out the grains. Bring the water to boil. Stir the canteen.

After my mom and my sister, cooking is what feels the most like home to me. And I missed it while I was in detainment. I feel a bit of my old self returning as I drain the water and transfer the rice to broad green leaves. I'm not much use out here in the wilderness, but at least I can prepare a meal.

We settle underneath a big tree after we eat. The

pine needles scratch my face, and the chill in the air bites through my clothes. Logan lets me have the fleece, taking the parka for himself. We spread the lightweight space blanket over us.

I pull my corner of the Mylar over me and turn my back to him. The stars glitter in the sky like gems against a jeweler's black cloth. Jessa must be looking at these same stars now. I imagine a line being drawn between me and the brightest star, and then another line connecting the star to my sister. *You see, Jessa. I never left you. We're linked together through these imaginary threads.*

My breath comes faster. Is it possible? I clearly have some sort of special ability, or I wouldn't have been able to manipulate my memory. That would explain everything. Why we've always been so close. How her memory got into my head. Maybe I can even talk to her now.

Jessa! JESSA! Can you hear me?

I fling the thoughts out into the universe, send them spiraling down those invisible lines connecting us to the stars. I wait, teeth gnawing lip, for a response. Some sort of sign. I'd settle for that vague rushing sensation again. But there's nothing. Just the rustle of Logan shifting on the pine needles.

I roll onto my back. I guess my psychic abilities don't extend that far. And I'm pretty positive that's what this is — an enhancement of my ability to manipulate memories, maybe from the fumes Bellows gave me.

Too bad I'm not back at the labs. TechRA would be interested in this development. But why? Why are the scientists so interested in psychic abilities?

Sully's voice echoes in my mind: *Where are we housed,*

hatchie?

I suck in a breath. Of course. All along, I thought that TechRA and FuMA just happened to share the same building. I didn't think there was any link between the two agencies. But what if that's not it at all?

Maybe the two agencies share the same building because they're intrinsically related. Maybe the scientists are studying psychics to *find out* about future memory.

The more I think about it, the more convinced I'm right. This is why the fumes have the side effect of enhancing psychic ability. This is why my particular abilities seem to revolve around some sort of memory manipulation.

Whatever reason the scientists want Jessa, it has to do with future memory.

The Mylar blanket crackles, and Logan's ankle brushes against my calf. We spring apart.

"Callie?" he says.

I swallow. "Yes?"

I can only make out the outline of his form in the darkness, but my mind's eye remembers every detail of his face. The dimples in his cheeks. Eyelashes so long I worry they might tangle. Straight white teeth in a devastating grin.

The silence balloons between us, taking on the significance that precedes a major declaration. My heart raps against my chest. If only he would trust me. If only he would reveal whatever secrets he's hiding about Harmony. I would tell him everything in return. My new psychic abilities. The conclusion I just drew.

But he doesn't. An agonizing minute passes, and then he says, "Get some rest. We get to Harmony tomorrow."

18

In the morning, my back is pressed against Logan's chest. His arm is draped over my hip. We're curled up like mice in a nest.

I should move away. Now that I'm awake and aware of where our bodies drifted unconsciously, I should put distance between us. But I don't.

I can't.

His warm breath tickles the sensitive nape of my neck, right next to my ear. Part of me wants to squirm. The other, more in-control part stays exactly, perfectly still so I don't wake him. So I can enjoy this exquisite torture for as long as possible. His chest rises and falls against my shoulder blades, steady and even, nothing like the heart that's ricocheting inside me. And his arm—it holds me close, traps me possessively, like I belong to him and him alone.

This is nothing like my daydreams. My hand's gone numb beneath me, and pine needles jab my cheek. And yet it is better, more delicious than anything I've ever imagined. I could lie here the rest of the day and pretend. Pretend he's not keeping secrets. Pretend he's not leaving me in a few days. Pretend he's zero gravity falling for me the way I am for him.

"Good morning," Logan says.

I jump, and my heart nearly slides out of my throat. Oh Fates. Has he been awake this entire time? Does he know I'm awake?

I start to pull away, and his hand tightens on my hip, just briefly, before letting go.

"Hi." I flip over to face him, scooting to the edge of the Mylar blanket.

We look at each other. Other than the brief interlude after I got Jessa's memory, we've been talking in nothing words, substituting pregnant pauses for actual communication. I turn before the silence gets too dense and head to the river, to clean up as best as I can. When I return, Logan's sitting on a boulder, shaving off the knobs from a branch, so he can use it as a walking stick. When he finishes, he offers me the knife. "You want to make one, too?"

"No, thanks." I pick up the canteen and gulp the water. I used knives in the eating area all the time, but I haven't touched one since I got my future memory. Maybe I'm being silly, but after feeling my arm slicing through the air, jabbing the needle into my sister's heart, I don't trust myself with sharp objects.

"Go on." He wraps my hand around the bone handle.

The knife feels heavy. Foreign, but at the same time familiar. I hold it up to the sunlight. The blade is thin and flat, ending in a clipped point. The bottom half is serrated.

It looks innocuous enough, a general-purpose blade used for ordinary camping chores. But it could be used for something else. The sharp teeth could pierce through human skin as easily as it cuts into an animal's body.

Trembling, I slide the knife back into the sheath. "I really don't think this is a good idea."

"Why not?"

"You said so yourself. My future memory makes me doubt myself." I walk back and forth in front of the boulder. "Truth is, I have no idea who I am. Chairwoman Dresden said I was aggressive, and I never would've called myself that a few weeks ago. I never would've kneed Scar Face in the groin, either. Or jumped off a cliff. There's no telling what I'll do next." I take a deep breath. "I'm dangerous."

"Oh yeah?" He grins. "You look real dangerous, shaking like a leaf at the sight of a little knife."

"This isn't funny. What if I flip out while I'm holding this knife?"

His eyes crinkle at the corners. He's still not taking me seriously. I've got to make him understand. I have to make him see he's not safe with me.

Lunging, I thrust the sheathed knife toward Logan's throat. Just to see if I can do it. Just to see if the killer instinct lives inside me.

In one smooth motion, he deflects the knife. "You may not know who you are. But I do."

All of a sudden, his mouth is hovering above mine. A dozen live wires zip along my skin, stealing my breath and electrifying my nerves. My heart beats so loudly it drowns out the drone of the insects, the twitter of the birds. A few more inches and our lips will touch. One tiny sway and we'll be kissing.

"Who am I?" I whisper.

"Calla Ann Stone. A girl who seeks out the sun like a flower soaking up its rays. A girl who loves her family with everything in her heart. A girl who is so brave she'll do anything to save her sister." He moves closer. And closer still. "You're doing everything I should've done for Mikey but didn't. I'll always respect that."

I swallow, but there's no moisture left in my mouth. I'm not at all sure he's right. I don't know this girl he's describing. I don't know if I can be her. But I'd like to be.

My eyes flutter close, and I lift my chin. The warmth of his breath mingles with mine...

And then something presses into the side of my neck. My eyes fly open, and I realize I'm no longer holding the knife. Logan has it, and he's holding the sheath right at *my* throat.

"I don't think you need to worry about me." He taps my collarbone with the point and then moves the knife away.

Dear Fate, I actually rose onto my tiptoes. Heat floods my face and I back away. "Is that what you were doing? Proving a point?"

He grins and those dimples beg me to touch them. "Well, that and the fact that I used to stay up nights wondering what you smelled like. Now I know. Apples and honey."

"You are such a liar. I haven't had a shower in days!"

"Why did you think I put a leaf in your locker every day? You didn't think I was a budding horticulturalist, did you?"

I stare at him and then burst out laughing. It's a chortle that comes from the pit of my belly, one that jerks my entire body. I remember tickling Jessa, but for the first time, the thought of my sister doesn't make me sad.

Maybe it's those wacky endorphins from all the laughing. Maybe it's because being around Logan makes me giddy. Maybe it's because he's confirmed, more clearly than any words, that I'm not a cold-blooded killer.

Whatever it is, I'll take it. When your entire world has been destroyed, when you're on the run from FuMA and your future, when the biggest threat to your sister is yourself, you take whatever you can get.

"This is it," Logan says a few hours later, consulting the map in his hands.

We're standing in the middle of the forest, after hiking several miles inland. Next to me a network of exposed tree roots rises as high as my knees. Pinecones mingle with dirt and pebbles on the ground, and thick white trunks spear into the sky.

"This is *what*?" I ask.

"Harmony, of course. Listen."

I wrinkle my forehead. Now that he mentions it, I can hear indistinct shouts echoing from the woods and the repetitive dull thud of one object striking another.

But there are no shelters. No smoke. And certainly no people.

"Where's the noise coming from?" I ask.

He points to my right. I squint. There's something

clinging to the bark of a tree, something that almost blends right in with the wood. I move forward a few steps and gasp. It's a spider-like device, like the one in the airshaft.

"Are you saying this is one big hologram?" I wave my hands in the air.

"There are at least a hundred holographic spiders around the circumference of Harmony," he says. "All projecting holographic images so the community goes undetected by the outside world." He looks again at the map and gestures at the moss-covered boulder in front of us. "According to this, all we have to do is walk twenty feet forward and we'll see Harmony as it really is."

He holds out his hand. "Are you ready?"

I hesitate. Not because I don't want to touch him, but because I do. I want to take his hand and hold it forever. I want to go back to being the Logan-and-Callie team we used to be—except different. Because five years ago, I never noticed the way his upper lip rested on his lower one, soft but assured. My breath didn't quicken when he was near, and my stomach didn't flip-flop whenever he touched me.

Our friendship has entered unfamiliar terrain. Terrain I've never crossed with anyone, terrain I shouldn't cross with him. As much as I like him, I know Logan isn't mine. Soon enough, he'll go home. He'll leave me again.

And yet, it's just a hand. A single touch. We held hands when we jumped off the roof. My body was plastered against his when he pulled me across the river, and this morning we snuggled together in our sleep.

Maybe it's okay to take his hand, just this once.

"We're in this together," he says. "Whatever happens,

I want you to remember that."

With shaking nerves and a trembling heart, I put my hand in his. Our fingers weave together, my seashell-colored ones crossing his tanned ones like the braids in a loaf of bread.

"I'm ready," I say. And we walk into the woods.

19

We walk into a large clearing, and I feel like I've stepped into another world. Rows of dome-shaped huts flank three sides of a square. An actual log cabin dominates the center, and in front, I see several long tables constructed from saplings, and a fire pit made from stones.

And then I spot a man thirty feet away, working on the carcass of a deer. Everything else fades. The deer hangs from its hind legs on the branch of a tree, what's left of its belly facing us. The torso has been split wide open, and I can count each of the gleaming, bloody ribs.

I bring a hand to my mouth. I read about this in my Manual Cooking classes. This is where meat comes from. But it's so red. So raw and slick.

The man grasps the animal and makes an incision from the groin up the inside of the leg. The knife cuts through the fur like it's tissue paper. Yes, fur—sleek, brown fur, which has somehow stayed clean despite the butchering.

The bile rises in my throat. I'm glad my instructors aren't here to see me.

The man slides his knife under the skin, cutting *what* I don't even want to think about, and then slowly, meticulously, he peels the skin back. It comes off in one piece, revealing a dark red-blue hunk of fresh meat. My stomach rolls.

I lurch forward and trip over a string stretched across the ground. *Squawk! Squawk! Squawk!* A bevy of black birds bursts into the sky, tearing off in different directions. I grab my ears and reel backward, my heart racing. What did I do?

The man turns, shifting his knife from one hand to the other. He's huge. As in, the-largest-man-I've-ever-seen huge. Probably two of me could fit within his shoulders, and he towers over Logan by at least half a foot.

"We're fugitives from the Underground," Logan calls out. "Uh, we seek Harmony, a haven for any who desire a new start in life."

That must've been some secret passphrase. Please, oh please, get it right.

The man stares, and then he sets his knife on a rock. The breath whooshes out of me.

"Don't mind the birds. They're our alarm system, so we don't have intruders sneaking up. I'm Zed." Walking toward us, the man looks at his palms. "I'd offer to shake, but I don't think you want to be touching these right now."

Up close, the man looks younger than I thought. Mid-twenties, I'm guessing, and handsome, despite his size. I clear my throat, trying not to shy away from his hands. "I'm Callie." I nod toward the backpack on Logan's shoulders. "I think we've got something for you. Size fourteen sneakers?"

"I think I love you." Zed lifts an enormous foot. He's wearing oversize socks made from buckskin, slit down the middle and laced together with long thin strips of the same material. "I've been lining these suckers with grass, but they're not much for insulation."

"Did you make those?" I ask.

"Nah. My friend Angela did. You'll meet her soon enough. She's the heart of Harmony." He turns to Logan. "I'm sorry, I didn't catch your name…"

And then he does a double take. "Mother of Fate. You're Logan Russell, aren't you?"

"Guilty," Logan says.

Apparently forgetting what he's been touching, Zed grabs Logan's hand and pumps it. "Took you long enough, man! I've been hearing stories about you for years."

What? Logan said he didn't have a connection with Harmony. He said he only knew what his parents told him. I knew he wasn't telling the whole truth, but I didn't think he was an actual celebrity around here.

So much for being in this together.

"What stories?" I ask, but my one true "ally" shrugs as if he doesn't know. Oh, he knows, all right. He just doesn't want to tell me.

"Come with me." Zed claps a hand on each of our shoulders. I wince. Now the deer parts are all over me. Unconcerned, he guides us down the dirt path.

We walk along the row of huts that line one side of the square. Each shelter is neatly shingled with a thin wooden material that looks like bark. A couple of girls cross the open space in the middle, right in front of the log cabin and the fire pit, carrying armfuls of wood. One wears a mesh shirt similar to mine. The other girl has on a buckskin tunic, cinched at the waist to give it shape. They look at us curiously but don't say anything other than "hello."

"So." Zed turns and gives me a huge grin. "What brings you to Harmony?"

Exactly how am I supposed to answer this question? "To see the sights?"

He laughs. "Oh, you're funny. But seriously, why are you here? Are you running from TechRA or your future?"

"None of your business," I stammer.

Zed squeezes my shoulder. "Oh, sorry. I've been living in Harmony too long. Didn't mean to pry."

I blink. "This is considered small talk in Harmony?"

"Well, yeah. It's the one thing we have in common, so we do our best not to judge each other."

"If that's true," I say, "I suppose you won't mind me asking: why are *you* here?"

"I said we try not to judge each other. I didn't say it always works."

Something crosses his face, a pain so deep, so raw, so *familiar* it makes my heart throb. A moment later, the look is gone. He drops his hands from our shoulders and walks a few steps ahead.

"But I asked you first, so it's only fair I answer." He turns and wets his lips. "In the future, I beat a woman to a bloody pulp."

I shudder. I've heard of bad memories. I mean, I lived in a cell block filled with would-be criminals. But I've never heard such a stark, unapologetic description. No excuses, no justifications. Just the facts.

"That's why I'm here," he says. "Not because I have to be. Ten years ago, FuMA still didn't know how to view or record the memories. So nobody else knew about my crime. But I didn't fit in anywhere. This was the only place that could forgive me." He pauses. "The only place where I could try to forgive myself."

"Have you?" I whisper. "Forgiven yourself, I mean?"

He shakes his head. "Working on it."

We reach the last hut in the row, and he clears his throat. "Here we are."

As far as I can tell, the hut looks like every other one we've seen—ten feet across, bark shingles, a large piece of hide for the door. But next to me, Logan's entire body stiffens, and his fingers dig into my elbow. He's been so quiet I'd almost forgotten he was still here.

Zed lifts the rawhide. "After you."

Logan swallows hard. He didn't act this anxious when we were jumping off the roof. "Can you...can you go first?" he whispers to me, his voice heavy with guilt. I don't know where the emotion comes from, but I'm in no position to turn him down.

He's never asked me for anything before. He risked his freedom when he broke me out of detainment. He gave me the warmer jacket, the bigger piece of dried fruit. But not once has he asked me to do something for him.

He's asking now. Even if I'm walking into a lair of hungry lions, I'll do it. I'll go first.

But please, let the lions be sleeping.

Taking a deep breath, I go inside. It's dim, and there's a bed made from five or six poles lashed together. A stone pit lies a few feet inside the door, and the sun shines through the hole in the roof. A figure stands up and comes forward. He walks into the sun, and his features catch the light.

Mother of Fate. I would recognize him anywhere.

He's taller now, broader through the shoulders. A man, not a boy. But the features of Mikey Russell are unmistakable.

Logan's brother.

20

Mikey doesn't even see me. He only has eyes for the boy who stepped into the shelter behind me. They stare at each other, and then Mikey's face crumples. He crosses the room in two strides and wraps his arms around his brother.

"Look at you. Just look at you," Mikey says.

I can't look anywhere else. Tears stream down both their faces. They stand at practically the same height, give or take an inch, the family resemblance as striking as ever. Same discerning eyes, same straight nose, same blond hair. Mikey, however, wears his hair long, pulled back with a piece of rawhide, and sports a straggly beard.

"I thought I'd never see you again," Mikey says.

Logan swipes at his face. "Same."

They break apart. Mikey slaps his brother on the back, punches his shoulder, rubs his head. It's as if he can't stop touching Logan, can't stop reassuring himself his brother's real and not the result of a hazy, mid-afternoon nap.

Logan gestures in my direction. "You remember Callie?"

Mikey looks me over. I want to shrink into one of the saplings that form the internal structure of the hut. "Is this the girl you couldn't stop talking about five years ago?"

"Yeah."

Mikey gives me a nod. "You grew up nice." Since my hair's a mess and my skin is streaked with dried mud, I know he's just being polite. Or maybe this is the look they go for in the wilderness, I don't know.

"I had no idea you escaped. I thought TechRA carted you away and you never came back." Even as I say the words, I realize how foolish they are. If the Underground went to all this trouble to break me out, of course they would've rescued one of their own members' sons.

"I was the very first breakout," he says. "And only because my dad had this idea for a secret community and insisted I be the one to lead it. We don't rescue someone often, as you can imagine. It's a huge risk to our members inside the agency. A huge risk to the entire Underground." He slants a look at Logan. "My brother must have put up a really strong case to the board, to get you out."

Logan flushes and darts a glance at me. "I explained about my future memory. They listened."

His memory. The one that made him talk to me that day in the park. The one that he warned me was unexpected. It must've concerned me, if it caused the board members to authorize my rescue.

Curiosity thrums through my body. What could the memory be? But Logan has clamped his mouth shut. If he didn't tell me in private, he's not about to tell me here, in front of his brother.

"I'm glad you're free," Mikey says to me and then turns to his brother. "But that doesn't explain what you're doing here."

"The board said if I wanted Callie out, I had to do it myself." Logan's words are slow and even, as if he's practiced this answer for days. "They would provide me with the resources, but I had to take the risk myself."

"Yes, I'm well aware of the policy." Mikey's voice rises. "But the policy doesn't explain why my little brother was concerning himself with Underground business in the first place. Why he would risk his swimming career before it even began."

"They were going to make her fulfill her memory, Mikey. She went to detainment to stop her future, but if her memory was going to happen anyway, how could I leave her cooped up like that? She can't even stand to be away from the windows at school." His breath comes in big, anxious pants. At that moment, he sounds more like the nervous T-minus five boy I knew than the brave guy who rescued me. "I wasn't intending on coming with her, I swear. But she doesn't know how to swim. So I jumped in the river with her."

Mikey puffs out a breath. "Ah, romance. Isn't it grand? It screws with your mind and makes you do stupid things like throw your future away. So, tell me." His face tightens, and he gestures between Logan and me. "When did this begin?"

This? I dart a look at Logan, not sure what "this" is. Should I tell Mikey we held hands as we walked into Harmony? That's something, right?

Across the hut, Logan's face wavers in and out of the shadows. But he doesn't respond.

"Um," I say. "We kinda just started talking again."

"Explain," Mikey barks.

"We used to be friends five years ago," I say, still looking at Logan, still wanting him to take the lead. "And then we stopped. He started speaking to me again the day before I got my memory."

Mikey wraps his hand around a stool made from a tripod of sticks. There's a platform in the middle, but he's certainly not offering me a seat. "You haven't talked for five years?"

"That's right."

"I don't believe this." His grip tightens and I can see the white of his knuckles even through the dimness of the hut. "I wouldn't have approved, but I could understand, at least, if you put your life on hold for the love of your life. But this girl's a stranger! You have no connection with her other than a childhood friendship a lifetime ago. For this you risked everything? Logan, you're not a kid anymore. You have a responsibility to everyone here. We rely on you. You can't go running off on a whim with some girl."

Logan finally speaks up. "Maybe Callie's only part of it. Maybe the other part is because I wanted to see you again. Did you ever think of that?"

This stops Mikey. Because it's not an excuse. It's not something Logan is saying to defuse the situation. The pain in his voice is too raw for that.

I ache to comfort the boy in him, the one who lost his brother at too young an age. I want to smooth away the long-standing cracks in his heart, but I can't. Logan has never let me into that part of his life. And besides, I wouldn't know what to say. I don't understand what Mikey is talking about. Logan's only seventeen. How could a teenager from Eden City put the entire community of Harmony at risk? It doesn't make sense.

Mikey places a hand on his brother's shoulder. With a single touch, he offers solace where I cannot. A pang runs through me, but I can't bring myself to be jealous. Not when Logan has finally gotten what he's clearly wanted for so long—to be with his brother again.

"I'm happy you're here," Mikey says. "More happy than you will ever know. But that doesn't change the facts. This girl is nothing to you. Your life wouldn't have changed one iota if you left her to FuMA. But us? We can't make it without you, Logan. What were you thinking? How could you do this?"

Logan's got to confess now. He's got to explain the guilt he felt when they took Mikey away. How his sacrifice for me was a way to make up for his inaction all those years ago. But he doesn't. He just bites his lip, taking the criticism, as his fingers trace a pattern on his leg.

"You weren't thinking. That's the long and short of it. No brother of mine would deliberately make such a stupid decision."

I remember, all of a sudden, something Logan said about his brother. *I want him to be proud of me.* And I can't stand it anymore, can't stand to watch anyone tearing him down, most of all the brother he so wants to impress.

"He didn't do it for me, okay?" I say. "Yes, I was there, and yes, I needed his help, but it wasn't *for* me. Logan jumped into the river because of who he is—because he's brave and honorable and selfless. The most selfless person I've ever known. Maybe it makes no difference to you what happens to me. But I'll never forget what your brother gave up to save me."

"What he gave up?" Mikey's lips twist into a smile. "His life, sure. He's welcome to throw that away if he pleases. But the future of Harmony? The stability of our very community? I really don't think that's his to sacrifice."

"What are you talking about?"

Mikey glances at Logan. "You didn't tell her?"

"Of course not." He won't look at his brother. Won't look at me. He studies the woven mat like he's counting the number of fronds. "I don't go around blabbing our secrets to strangers."

Okay, I get that he's frustrated with his brother. But he offered me his hand. He said we were in this together. Hearing him call me a stranger slams me right in the chest.

"So she has no idea what she's caused?" Mikey asks, his voice so hard it feels like it's reaching across the hut and slapping me.

"Don't be so dramatic. It's not that big a deal."

"It's a big deal, all right. We can improvise a lot of things in the wild, but there's a whole lot more we need from civilization. We depend on those backpacks, Logan. We need to be able to communicate with the Underground."

"I understand," Logan says. "But you'll figure something out, Mikey. You always do."

I'm listening as hard as I can, but I still don't follow.

Mikey slumps on the mat. It's as if the conversation's drained him, and he doesn't have the energy left to be angry. "Callie, do you know why FuMA took me?"

"Yeah," I say. "You made a racquetball hover above the court."

"I suppose everybody knows that. What people don't know is I'm not the only Russell brother with psychic abilities. Logan's more discreet about it, that's all."

I blink, and then his words register. Logan has psychic abilities? To do what? Hide information? I shift my gaze to Logan and wet my lips, almost afraid to ask. "What… what can you do?"

The brothers look at each other. Something passes between them, but it's too subtle for me to catch. The air feels like it's about to burst with pent up energy, and Mikey laughs a little, shaking his head. I think he's going to ignore my question, but then he turns to me.

"The telekinesis is a preliminary ability, the one that manifests in childhood. It's a neat trick, sure, but it has no real power. I can't levitate anything heavier than a ball." He takes a breath. "Our true ability is, we Russell brothers can communicate mind-to-mind. Or rather, I can talk directly into Logan's mind. For the most part, he can't reciprocate, other than a brief thought here and there, but his reception of my words is crystal clear."

His glare pins me to the wall. I feel as helpless as a moth mounted on display. "For years now, Logan's been our contact in Eden City. He's our means of communication with the Underground. He's the one who sends us the backpacks with the supplies we need to survive. Of course, now he's here, instead of there. Because of you." He bites off each word. "I'd say our lifeline has been cut off, wouldn't you?"

21

run outside. After the dim lighting in the dome hut, the late afternoon sun blinds me, but that's okay. I'm blinded, anyway.

I stumble down the dirt path. I didn't know. I swear I didn't know. I tried to stop him, truly I did, but everything was moving so fast. He wanted to jump. Why did he want to jump?

Excuses. I collapse against a tree, the bark rough against my forearms, my breath coming in pants. If I want to call them what they are: lies. The truth is, I wanted Logan to come with me. I could've made him turn back at any point in our journey, but I didn't. I didn't care what he was giving up, because I didn't want to be alone. If he had gone home, the entire community wouldn't be in jeopardy. If I wasn't so curse-the-Fates helpless, he would be where he belongs.

The future was right about me. If I needed proof that I'm toxic to the people around me—well, here it is. Logan's life is a shadow of what it could be, and the very future of Harmony is in jeopardy. All because of me.

"Callie." A gentle hand drops onto my shoulder. "Are you okay?"

I turn and bury my face in Logan's chest. The hard contours of his muscles press against my cheeks. I should be furious with him, but this is my fault, too. Why couldn't I get myself here? Why wasn't I strong enough?

"I'm sorry," I whisper. "I'm so sorry."

"Don't apologize." He winds his arm around my back. "You've done nothing wrong. I'm the one who should be saying I'm sorry, for not telling you everything sooner."

I pull back and look into his face. We're standing in the shade of one of the dome huts, and the breeze carries on it the scent of fresh pines. I breathe it in, realizing that I've never been this far from civilization. So far that I can't even smell the city.

"Why are you so nice to me?" I ask.

He sighs. "You look at me like that and it makes me want to keep pretending I'm the hero you make me out to be. When I'm no hero, really. Far from it."

I lean my head against the tree. In my book, he's only made one decision that's been less than heroic. "Couldn't you have told me one thing? I understand I'm a stranger to you. I understand we've only been talking again for a short time. But I told you my memory. Wasn't there one secret you could've shared?"

"I was scared," he says.

"Of what?"

"It's a long story." He fidgets with the hem of his shirt, as if he's deciding whether or not to confide in me. "When

I stopped talking to you five years ago, it was because seeing you made me remember what I didn't do. But everyone else? I avoided them because I saw the way they looked at Mikey, like he was a freak. And I didn't want them to look at me that same way."

I take his hand. I know how he feels. I've seen Jessa on the playground during the Outdoor Core, standing by herself, pretending not to notice the other girls as they shrieked and giggled and played tag. Her classmates may not have known why she was different, but she clearly was.

All that lost time. While Logan was hiding his abilities from the world, I was hiding Jessa's. We could've trusted each other. We could've suffered alongside one another, comforted by the knowledge that someone else understood.

"You should've told me," I say. "I wouldn't have judged you."

"I know. And I wanted to tell you. Especially that day in the park, when I saw Jessa calling out the color of the leaves. But I'd just gotten my future memory, and it changed everything."

I wait, my breath caged in my lungs. My hopes hemmed in my chest.

"My memory wasn't what I expected." The words drip from his mouth like molasses from a tree—slow, sticky, and worth every second. "Like I told you, I saw myself as a gold-star swimmer. I was warming up for the final heat of the national meet, and I was a shoo-in for the win. But that was only part of it. Every detail leaped out at me. The wet concrete under my bare feet. The smell of chlorine saturating the air. A scar down the center of my palm."

He holds up his hand, and we both stare at the smooth, still-unblemished skin. "And then I looked out at the audience, at this girl, and I had this overwhelming feeling of belonging, of being totally accepted for who I am."

He kicks his foot rhythmically at the base of the tree. The bark chips away, leaving a smooth, naked patch of wood. "I was so mad when I got the memory. I didn't even understand what it meant, so how on earth was it supposed to guide my decisions in life? And then I saw you at the park." He stops kicking. "And I thought, maybe the memory was telling me to trust this feeling, to go after it. Maybe it was saying: this is the feeling that makes life worth living."

"I don't understand," I whisper. "What does that have to do with me?"

"The girl in my memory was you." He shifts until his shoulders block my view of the huts, with the smoke curling out of their roofs. Until his eyes loom above me, as green as forest grass plump from soil and rain. Until his face becomes my entire world. "You make me feel like I belong. You've always made me feel that way. And that's why I didn't tell you about the backpacks. Because I was afraid it would change the way you felt, and I wanted to hold on to that feeling for just a little while longer."

22

don't think I can speak. My heart feels too large for my chest, like I'm a Russian nesting doll put together in the wrong order. I lift my hand and place it against his cheek. A few days ago, he was clean-shaven. Now, the newly grown bristles prickle my fingertips, and a shiver climbs my spine. It winds down my arms and blows a cool breeze at the nape of my neck.

He leans closer. "Does it? Change the way you feel, I mean?"

"Only for the better."

His lips touch mine, as light as a moth dancing on the breeze. I'm lost. In school, we learned about the butterfly effect, that something as insignificant as the flapping of insect wings could cause a hurricane on the other side of the world. Well, that's me. There's a storm inside me, swirling violently, threatening to sweep me away. For once I would be happy to drown.

The kiss deepens. Heat spreads from the contact of

our lips all over my body, enveloping me in the warmth that is Logan. I wrap my hands around his neck, and he backs me up until my shoulders hit the bark of the tree. His mouth moves across my lips, my tongue, my teeth. And then, his hands touch my face.

I die. That one brush of his fingers against my cheek, at once tender and aching, slays me. I didn't know a kiss could be so exquisite. I didn't know a boy could mean so much. I didn't know I could be this happy ever again.

I move my hands to his face, touching his cheeks the way he's touching mine, and it's like we're holding the very essence of each other between our fingers. No secrets between us. No misunderstandings or hurt feelings or fears of the future. Just his mouth and my lips; his ribs, my chest; his thighs, my hips. I don't think of our five-year distance. I don't think of the separation yet to come, when he goes back to Eden City. All I can feel is our convergence. The togetherness of our bodies and souls. In that moment, Logan and I are one.

An eternity later, he pulls back and smiles. We are so close, I can sense the contours of his lips, feel the rush of air as it leaves his mouth and enters mine.

"Well," I say when I can finally talk again, "if that's the reaction I get from an overdue confession…any other secrets you want to share?"

He laughs and pecks me on the lips. "I'm clean out at the moment."

Hand in hand, Logan and I walk down the path toward Mikey's hut. As we approach, Mikey lifts the flap of rawhide and steps outside. I thought the brothers looked like twins before, but in the stark sunlight, I see differences I missed earlier. While Logan has a nice golden tan, Mikey's skin resembles the dark brown bark of pine trees. What's more, his veins pop and protrude against crazy cords of muscle—the kind of build that must come from living in the wilderness.

He scowls at our linked fingers. "You lovebirds kiss and make up?"

Flushing, I drop Logan's hand. Clearly Mikey doesn't approve of our relationship. And why should he? Logan may be here for the moment, but he belongs in civilization. What we have can only be temporary.

What we have can only be temporary.

The words frost my spine. Oh Fates. How could I forget? Logan's future is back in Eden City, where he is a gold-star swimmer with a room full of medals. Where he's needed to communicate telepathically with Mikey and stock the backpacks with essential supplies.

The ice settles in my lungs, stacking up until I can hardly breathe. Holding Logan's hand feels so good. Kissing him feels so right. When we're together, I don't feel like a monster. I feel like the girl he sees, the one who can be strong when she needs to be. But none of that matters. I don't get to keep him.

I wait for Logan to respond to his brother, to explain that it's not important what Mikey thinks he sees. It will all be over in a few short days, anyhow.

But he doesn't say a word. That's when I get it. I have my weaknesses, and he has his. Logan can save me from FuMA. He can drag me across a river. But the one thing he can't do is protect me from his brother's wrath.

That's okay. In this one area of our lives, I can stand up for both of us.

I face Mikey and lift my chin. "I'm sorry I took away your source of communication with the Underground. If I had known, I might've made a different decision. But it's done. I can't go back and change either of our choices, and resenting me isn't going to make that any less true."

The wind sweeps over my hair, and the harsh sun burns my forearms. Mikey studies me, and then he gives a curt nod. "Fine."

I understand I'm not forgiven. He's merely putting his resentment on the back burner. The problem with the back burner is that the pot continues to simmer, and sooner or later, its contents overflow…or burn to a crisp.

I turn to Logan, desperate to change the subject. "Is this ability rare? Can Mikey communicate with someone else in Eden City?"

"It doesn't work that way," Mikey says. "I can't send a message to just anyone. There has to be a genetic connection, and the closer the DNA match, the better." He runs his fingers over his beard. "My link with Logan is the strongest, but I can also communicate with our mother. Nothing like the whole sentences I can speak into Logan's head, but I can usually convey a concrete image, if I focus long enough."

My chest loosens. "That's great. You'll still be able to send messages."

"No, it's not great," he snaps. "Tedious at best, ineffective at worst. It's not an answer, just a stopgap measure. It will do for a few days, but it's not a long-term solution."

He glares at me like it's my fault. Clearly, the issue's not resolved, not by a long shot. It's just shoved to that nasty back burner again.

23

Mikey leads us into the woods west of the village. After half a mile, we come upon a large field with rows and rows of plants. Several people are scattered across the plot, digging in the dirt, pulling weeds, and piling up root vegetables. I see lumpy brown potatoes. Fat, papery onions. And carrots! The orange skin is dulled by dirt, but the leafy tops are green and lush.

I suck in a breath. I've read about how they grew food in the pre-Boom days, but I never thought I'd actually see it. We had a small garden in the Manual Cooking classroom, but most vegetables these days are produced in hydroponic greenhouses, in elevated rows to save room and increase efficiency.

Mikey steps forward, cupping his hands around his mouth. "Hey, Angela! Got a minute? I want to introduce you to your new roommate."

A woman stands up and hoists a basket of carrots onto her hip. A rag covers a thousand tiny braids in her hair, and dirt streaks her pants from the knees down. As she walks toward us, her brilliant eyes shine. That smile could power Eden City.

She reaches our group and trails her hand down Mikey's arm, with an ease that only comes from a long relationship. Their hands link, and matching bracelets woven from the fronds of a plant flash in the light.

I slip my own wrist—with its conspicuously absent hourglass tattoo—behind my back, as Angela draws Logan into a hug. "You must be Mikey's brother. Welcome to Harmony. Although I've got to say, I'm sorry to see you. I was pulling for at least one Russell brother to live peacefully in civilization." She gives Mikey a loving look then winks at Logan. "And, between you and me, I was pretty glad it was you."

"Well, I'm happy to be here." Logan gestures to me. "This is Callie."

Angela directs her blinding smile at me. "Welcome. I'm done with the carrots here. Why don't we let the boys get reacquainted, and you can help me prepare dinner? You're not afraid to get your hands dirty, are you?"

"Oh, no," I say, my fingers itching to grab a carrot from the basket. "I live for this stuff. I can't believe you get to cook manually every day."

Angela laughs. "Most of the community sees it as a hardship, not a luxury. If I burn the stew, they have to eat it anyway."

"But that's the beauty of it!" I give in and snatch up the orange root. Bringing it to my nose, I inhale deeply. This is how vegetables should all smell—as if they came straight from the earth, because they did. "Who cares if your food tastes good, or if it tastes the exact same every time? It's the variety that brings the flavor to life."

"Callie here was in training to be a chef of the pre-Boom era," Logan says. "She was at the top of her class."

I lower the carrot. "How would you know?"

"I sampled your dishes every year at the Extravaganza," he says softly. "And you're right. I like food better when it's not subtle. I heard some people say your guacamole had too much cilantro. But I thought it was sublime."

Our eyes meet and hold. I shouldn't be doing this. Shouldn't be feeling this tingle in my spine. Shouldn't store his words in my memory so I can take them out later. He might be the most perfect boy in the world, but he doesn't belong with me. He belongs in Eden City, where he is needed to keep Harmony alive. Deep down, I know this. I force the tingling sensation away, smothering it with my guilt.

Mikey clears his throat. "We'd better get going, Logan. I've got a lot to show you before dinner."

I say good-bye to the boys and turn to find Angela watching me.

"What was that all about?" she asks.

I put the carrot back in the basket. "What do you mean?"

She adjusts the basket on her hip and walks into the woods. I trail after her.

"This may be none of my business," she says. "I know I've just met the two of you, but I've been hearing stories about Logan for years. I love him because Mikey loves him, and I don't want to see him hurt. So what's going on between you two?"

I rub my chest, but it does little to soothe my aching heart. How do I sum up our history in a few words? But when it comes right down to it, it's not all that complicated. "We used to be friends, and then we weren't. And now we are again, and maybe we could be something more…but he'll have to go home soon. It could never work in the long run."

I pull my shoulders back with new resolve. Forget the long run. It's not going to work now. Which means I have to fight our attraction. Logan won't keep us apart, but for his sake, I must.

She turns left at a tree that looks identical to every other one. "Half of us are here to escape our futures, Callie. We can't dwell on what might happen tomorrow, so we focus on the day-to-day. That's all we have."

I skirt around boulders and hop over roots, thinking about her words. My entire childhood has been a countdown to the day I receive my future memory. I spent so much time anticipating tomorrow—making plans, imagining scenarios, worrying endlessly—I'm not sure I know how to live in the present. I wouldn't even know where to begin.

We step around a tree, and all of a sudden the village is there, with its rows of huts lining three sides of a square. I push thoughts of Logan from my mind. Plenty of time to feel sorry for myself later. Now, I've got a whole way of life to learn.

Angela heads for the log cabin and dumps the carrots on one of the long tables in front. "We call this the village square," she says. "It's the center of life in Harmony, where we eat, cook, hang out. The general store is inside the cabin, and we all sleep there in the winter."

She moves to two wooden basins standing side-by-side in front of the log cabin and takes the lid off the first one. "We're out of drinking water. I'll have to make some more."

She scoops some water out of the second barrel with a large aluminum can and takes it over to a tripod of sticks. It looks kinda like Mikey's tripod chair, but instead of a seat, three levels of porous material are tied to the sticks. Angela pours the water into the first level, and it drips through the three tiers into a basin below.

I peer at the porous material in each tier. Grass, sand, and charcoal. "Unbelievable."

"Haven't you heard stories about this stuff?" she asks. "Mikey says all the Underground kids these days talk about coming to Harmony. Logan's been practicing building fires for years."

So that's how he learned how to do it. It wasn't his Ancient Methods elective, after all.

"No, I never heard of the Underground before, even though my sister has psychic abilities."

"That's weird," she says. "The Underground's got a way of reaching the right people. Your parents must really have their heads stuck in the concrete."

Stuck in the concrete is right. We've always kept to ourselves, and my mom's always taught me never to talk about our family. I thought the big secret was Jessa's psychic ability.

But there's a whole group of people with the same abilities. And they've banded together to help one another. Mom should've wanted to be part of this group. It would've been easier to protect Jessa with the resources of the Underground.

Unless Jessa's ability isn't the secret, after all. Unless my mom's hiding something else entirely.

I frown as Angela sweeps up the basin of freshly filtered water and pours it into the cauldron. "I need to warn my mother about my future memory. A few months from now, my sister is going to be arrested by TechRA. When her hair reaches her shoulders. I know Logan's your usual source of communication, and he's here now. But do you think Mikey could pass a message through his mom?"

"Sure. I'll talk to him," she says. Just like that. No questions, no conditions. I should ask Mikey myself, but no doubt he'll be more receptive if the request comes from Angela. "Your mom's Phoebe Stone, right?"

My mouth drops. "How did you know?"

Her hand stills on the cauldron. "Isn't your mom an Underground member?"

"I don't think so."

"Oh. I must've heard her name somewhere else, then."

I furrow my brow. Is it possible my mom is a member and she just never told me?

No way. We used to tell each other everything. We had to. It had been our family against the world. Three sides of a triangle. My mom would never keep such a big secret from me. Right?

I stand and scoop another can of water to pour into the tripod. I have no idea what to think anymore.

I've felt so alone ever since I received my future memory. But maybe it's always been that way. Maybe I just never realized it until now.

24

Perfectly diced pieces of carrot and potato swim with chunks of venison in a thick brown broth. I add another dash of oregano to the stew simmering over the fire, and a delicious aroma wafts into the air.

"That smells amazing." Angela lines up wooden bowls on the long table. The sun sits like a glowing egg on top of the trees. She assured me the dinner service would start when the sun was "right there" in the sky. But was she pointing at the tops of the trees, or a few inches above it?

"I think my job as Manual Cook might be in danger," she says. "One taste of your stew, and the people will kick me outside the holographic screens."

I drop my ladle into the cauldron and have to carefully fish it out. "I'm not after your job, I promise. I'm just trying to be helpful."

"I'm teasing." She hands me a clean rag so I can wipe the stew off the ladle. "Besides, I'd be happy to step aside for someone as talented as you. I only volunteered because nobody else did. If you want the position, say the word."

My dream job. I should be leaping at the chance to cook. But when I open my mouth, the acceptance slides down my throat. That's when I realize I still haven't left my old world behind. My body might be here, but my heart and mind are still with my mom and sister in Eden City.

Stalling, I ladle up a healthy serving of stew and hand Angela the bowl. "There's nothing I would like more. But I don't know if my stay here is…permanent."

She sets the bowl next to the others on the table. "Where would you go? Back to Eden City?"

"Of course not. I would never tempt Fate like that." I turn the thoughts over in my mind, trying to figure out what I mean. "TechRA's going to arrest my sister sometime in the next year. I don't know what, if anything, I can do from afar. But if there's somewhere I can go to figure out what they're up to—why they want my sister, why they're so interested in her psychic abilities—maybe it will give my mom a fighting chance to protect her."

"You don't have far to go," she says.

"What do you mean?"

"Think about it. Who established Harmony? The Underground. And who makes up the Underground? A bunch of psychics. I bet whatever information you're looking for is right here."

I put the ladle down. "Angela, you're brilliant."

She flashes me her one-thousand-watt grin. "So they tell me."

We fall into an easy rhythm. I ladle, and she wipes the side of the bowls and sets them on the table.

Over the next hour, I must meet all of Harmony's fifty inhabitants. There's a man whose gray beard reaches his waist. A redheaded girl with dreads that reminds me of Sully. A scrawny little kid named Ryder who's here without his parents. They seem nice enough, especially Ryder, who shoots me a shy smile after giving Angela a big hug. But I feel very much like the new girl. I'm glad I have a pot of stew to hide behind.

The Russell brothers show up as we're scraping the bottom of the cauldron. Mikey walks straight to Angela and whispers something to her. His arms slip around her waist, creating a barrier between the two of them and everyone else.

"What?" Her hand jerks, and stew sloshes over the bowl. "No."

He continues whispering, his hand coming up to stroke her hair.

"No. It can't be." Her shoulders shake, and she brings her knuckles to her mouth.

Mikey looks around, lost. It's the first time I've seen him not in control. "Callie, can you finish up the service? I need to get Angie out of here."

I barely have time to nod before he leads her away. My last glimpse of Angela is of the tears streaking down her cheeks.

I turn to Logan, my stomach flipping up and then down. It's been hours since I've seen him. Hours during which he could've rethought the kiss and decided it's not worth pursuing a relationship. Sure, I'd come to a similar conclusion, but on top of everything else, I'm not sure I can deal with a rejection from Logan right now. *I* want to be the voice of reason, not him. Maybe that's selfish; maybe I'm being childish. Guiltily, I scold myself for having these thoughts, but still they remain.

"What happened?" I ask, struggling to sound normal.

"No clue. We spent the afternoon fishing, and when we got back to the hut, Mikey found an envelope in the backpack we brought from Eden City." He rubs the crease on his forehead. "It had something to do with Angela."

He steps behind the table, next to me, as if it's the most natural thing in the world. As though it's a given he'd want to spend time with me.

My pulse speeds up. Maybe he hasn't reconsidered anything. Maybe, like me, the hours only made him miss me more. Maybe his mind is telling him one thing, and his body, his heart, his soul are telling him another. I can always wish.

I serve up the last of the stew. A few more people trickle by and grab bowls, but pretty soon, it's obvious no one else is coming.

"Have you eaten?" he asks, his breath tickling my shoulder.

"I sampled the stew so many times, I'm stuffed."

"Come on, then. I want to show you something."

He takes a bowl of stew for himself and leads me through the village. We walk a quarter-mile into the woods and slip behind a wall of trees.

My breath catches. Green tufts of grass poke through the brightly colored leaves littering the ground, and butterflies flit among the purple wildflowers. The trees shield us from the wind and noise. Maybe from the entire outside world.

"How'd you find this place?" I ask.

"Mikey showed it to me. He likes to come here when he needs to think."

We sit on a log nestled against a tree, and he digs into his stew. We don't talk as he eats, but this silence feels different than the one we've been used to for five years. It's not filled with unspoken words and hurt feelings. It's not like the whining of the dentist's drill a moment before it descends. It's just…nice.

Logan scoops up a piece of carrot and picks up the bowl to drink the broth. "This is delicious."

Simple words. I've heard them dozens of times this evening. But coming from Logan, the compliment makes me giddy. "Thank you."

"I feel bad being the only one eating." He fishes out a hunk of venison and holds it up. "Here, have some."

"I don't want to take your food."

He brings the meat to my mouth, as if to feed me. "Go ahead. I'll enjoy my dinner more if I have company."

Hesitantly, I lean forward and take the meat from his hand. As soon as my lips brush his fingers, a spark shoots through me, a lone firework that sizzles every nerve in my body. The flavor of the venison is hearty and rich. I should know; I seasoned it myself. And yet, it's nothing compared to the taste of Logan's skin. Soft but firm. Warm. Slightly salty and all-the-way irresistible.

The sun's fallen behind the trees, and I sneak a look at Logan in the dimming light. He's not mine to keep, but Angela said to focus on the day-to-day. That means enjoying the view in front of me, even if it's temporary.

"What?" he says, and I realize I'm staring.

Flushing, I drop my gaze. "Nothing. I, uh, wanted to tell you about this weird…thing… that happened to me. I think it's some kind of psychic ability, but I'm not sure if it's my power or Jessa's."

He turns to face me, pulling an ankle over his knee. "Go on."

"I had this vision. Or maybe it was a dream, I'm not sure. But it felt like a future memory, except I was seeing it through my sister's eyes."

I tell him about sitting on my mother's lap, feeling sad, and speculate whether this vision has anything to do with TechRA arresting Jessa in the future.

When I finish, his brows furrow. "I've got an idea. It's a long shot, but if it works, it might give us some answers."

"What is it?"

"I want you to open your mind, like we were taught in the Meditation Core."

I frown. "Why? What are you going to do?"

"*I'm* not going to do anything. I just want to see what happens."

All of a sudden, I feel the stiff breeze cutting through my thin clothes. An experiment. A logical one, since the last vision came from unintentionally opening my mind. But what if I repeat the experience? What if I *don't*?

Only one way to find out.

Open. What is open? The hole at the top of Mikey's hut. The carcass of the deer, split open at the ribs. The hollowed-out center of the log we're sitting on. Open, open, open.

I look for it, I wait for it—and yes! There it is. That rush of something filling my fingernails and teeth, my eyelashes and toes.

My memory. Jessa's memory. Whoever's memory. OPEN.

I'm straddling a metal plank inside an open pod. My hands grip the handles on either side of me. I fly into the air and fall back down again. Up in the air, and down again.

A seesaw. I'm on the playing field during the Outdoor Core, but whose class?

I have that out-of-body sensation again, but I look through the spokes of the sphere, hoping to see Marisa's trademark smirk in the pod opposite of me. Instead, I glimpse the precisely cut bangs of January One, Olivia Dresden. Daughter of Chairwoman Dresden and Jessa's classmate.

"I'm thinking of a number between one and ten." Olivia flies into the air. "What is it?"

Pressing my lips together, I grip the handles and brace my feet against the spokes.

"Come on," Olivia whines. "I know you know the answer. You can tell me. I promise I won't say anything."

I shake my head. "Sorry. I don't know."

Up. Down. Up. Down. All of a sudden, I crash to the ground so hard my teeth hurt.

"Fine." Olivia's twin braids bounce on her shoulders as she swings the hatch open and jumps out. "I didn't want to be your friend anyway."

gasp, and the memory shatters. I'm back in Harmony, sitting next to Logan on a log.

"I did it!" I say. "I got into another one of my sister's memories." Briefly, I describe the scene I saw.

"I knew it!" he exclaims. "You're a Receiver, just like me."

"A what?"

"A Receiver." He stands and begins pacing, his shoes scattering pine needles as if they're grasshoppers jumping to safety. "It's what they call my type of ability. I can't do much other than receive messages. If there's no Sender around, you would think I was like anybody else."

My mind whirls. "So you're saying the ability is both mine and Jessa's?"

"That's what it looks like. Senders and Receivers typically occur in pairs, like me and Mikey. In your pair, the Sender is your little sister, but she seems to be sending whole memories, instead of words, into your mind."

I look at the patches of bare dirt Logan's left in his wake. "I don't understand. How could I have missed this?"

"Jessa's six. That's the right age for the primary ability to manifest." He wrinkles his forehead. "She already has some sort of precognition, right? That's how she knew the color of the leaves before they fell?"

I nod. "She's been able to see a couple of minutes into the future since she could talk."

"I'm thinking the precognition is a preliminary ability, like Mikey's telekinesis. Jessa must have come into her real powers recently. She may not even realize she's sending you memories." He walks back to me. "When you received the future memory on your seventeenth birthday, it must have triggered something in your brain. Showed you, in a way, how your powers worked."

"That's when I started being able to manipulate memories." I tell him how my mind was able to replay my memory like a recording device, even change aspects of the memory itself. With disappointment, I note that I have yet to make the changes permanent. "And then Bellows gave me the fumes, and he said it would enhance any inherent psychic ability I had."

"The fumes, in turn, probably triggered something in Jessa. Helped her come into her primary ability."

"But how? I sniffed the fumes, not her."

"If the two of you are a true Sender-Receiver pair, there's a deep psychic connection between you. That's why the pairs manifest most often in siblings, and even more strongly in twins."

That's why meditation has always come so easily to me. It's like a muscle I'd never flexed, but as soon as I did, it became second nature. That's how I was able to open my mind by accident. Why I was able to close it successfully against the fumes. It's all tied up in my abilities as a Receiver.

I leap to my feet, vibrating with excitement. I haven't left Jessa behind, after all. Sure, I can't talk to her, but I can access her memories, and that's almost as good. I'll be able to see her anytime I want. Be with her. Watch her grow up.

Laughter bubbles out of me and I spin around, my arms outstretched. I slip and slide on the pine needles, but I don't care. A magical mirror. That's what this is. A mirror into my sister's life.

I can't wait a moment longer. Now that I know she's here, within reach, I have to see her, if only for a few minutes. Logan will understand.

I stop spinning and try to slow my galloping heart. I can't calm my mind if I'm about to burst out of my skin.

Let's see. Open. Think open. The inside of Jessa's toy cradle. Her mouth in an "o" when I gave her the purple stuffed dog. My sister opening a door and welcoming me home. Open, open, open.

I wait for the rush of sensation, I close my eyes and focus and yes! There it is! The memory. OPEN.

'm straddling a metal plank inside an open pod. My hands grip the handles on either side of me. I fly into the air and fall back down again. Up in the air, and down again.

frown, falling out of the memory. "I don't understand. I got the same memory again."

"I expected as much," Logan says. "Remember, this is a passive ability. You don't get to decide when you receive a new message. If it works anything like mine, Jessa has to send the memory before you can open your mind to it."

"But that's crazy. How would we ever connect?"

"You don't have to be doing it at the same time." He lowers himself onto the log, and I sit down next to him. "Think of it this way. When she sends you a message, it's stored somewhere, in another dimension maybe, waiting for you to retrieve it. Until she sends a new one, when you open your mind, you'll retrieve the same one over and over again."

He reaches up and catches my earlobe between his fingers. "You have really nice ears. Anyone ever tell you that?"

The air gets stuck in my chest, until I feel like my lungs might burst, along with my heart. If Logan keeps touching me, I'll have no organs left. *Breathe, Callie.* It's just a touch, a slight sensation I might not even notice in a crowd. But we're not in a throng. We're in a magical clearing at the edge of the world. And now that I've felt his touch, I never want to be without it again.

But never is a long time. And no matter what Angela says about focusing on the present, I have to remember today will disappear like sand falling through an hourglass. Before I can grasp more than a few grains, it will be gone.

Just like Logan will depart, leaving me with nothing but a handful of memories.

He releases my ear. The sun has ducked behind the trees. Dusk falls in purple shadows around us, and invisible insects flit around my arms.

"What does this mean?" he asks. "Does it help you figure out why TechRA wants Jessa?"

I shake my head. "Not really. If anything, it opens up more possibilities. They could be studying her precognition or her abilities as a Sender."

"Don't worry. You'll figure it out."

He puts his arm around me and tucks my head onto his shoulder, nestling it under his chin. Our bodies touch in a line, and it's like he's thrown a warm down blanket over us and lit a crackling fire for good measure. We're in the middle of nowhere, with no electricity or running water. He's leaving in a few days, and yet I feel safe. He makes me feel safe.

I snuggle closer to him. I don't want to think about the future. I'd rather open my mind to see if Jessa's sent any new memories. It may be a few days too late, but I'm going to make good on my promise to my sister. I'm going to stay with her, all night long.

25

It's the first thing I hear when I get to Angela's hut—the gut-wrenching moan of a heart being split.

I don't think twice. Flinging aside the rawhide door, I rush inside. Darkness surrounds me, and I drop to my knees and crawl toward the noise. By the time I reach Angela, my eyes have adjusted enough to make out her balled-up figure.

As I've done for my sister all of her life, I take Angela into my arms. She turns to me, buries her face in my shoulder, and cries even harder.

"It'll be all right," I murmur into her hair. "There now. Everything will be okay."

But will it? Maybe it's because I can't see more than a foot in front of me. Maybe it's because I'm kneeling in a shelter that will never see electricity. Maybe I don't believe in happily ever after anymore.

Whatever the reason, my words fall flat in the air, revealed as the platitudes they are.

"My mother's dead," Angela whispers. "She passed away from a vicious strain of the flu. The ceremonial burning is in two days."

I pat her back helplessly. "I'm so sorry, Angela."

"I never got to say good-bye. A month ago, she sent a message through the Underground, begging me to come back to Eden City. I refused, and now it's too late." She bursts into fresh tears.

"Oh, Angela. Surely she understood you couldn't go back. Isn't FuMA looking for you?"

"No," she sobs. "No one's after me. My memory's not criminal. It was entirely my decision to come here. And I'll never go back, even for a visit."

"How come?"

She pulls back. I can't see her face in the dark, but the dampness of her tears makes my shirt stick to my shoulders. "You know as well as I do. Those of us running from our memories live in perpetual fear of tomorrow."

No wonder my words fell flat. What are empty reassurances in a world where you can see concrete images of the future?

"Do you want to talk about it?" I ask.

She sighs, and the breath of air flutters against my skin. Her hands grope for mine, and it's a jolt when her icy fingers wrap around my arm.

"I'm going to have a baby girl," she says in a low voice. "In the future, I have the prettiest girl you've ever seen. Hair as soft as spider silk, eyes the color of the sky at midnight. And when she coos at you, you feel as if you would go to the ends of the earth to keep her safe."

My nails sink into my calves. Oh, Fates. Please, don't

let anything happen to that little girl.

For a long moment, all I hear is the thundering of my heart, and then Angela speaks again. "In my memory, we were picnicking on a cliff by the river. One of the ComA-sanctioned ones, with the black metal railing along the edge. I turned away for one second, I swear. Just one little second to mop up the juice she spilled on my shirt. When I looked up, my baby's all the way over by the railing. I didn't even know she could crawl that fast. I started running toward her, yelling her name. She looked at me once, those beautiful black eyes searing into mine, and then she slipped under the railing. And crawled right off the cliff."

My heart skitters. Angela's eyes swim in my memory, so clear I can see thousands of tiny fractures in their depths. I blink, and all of a sudden, overlaid over the image, are the round, innocent eyes of her unborn child.

"Oh, Angela," I choke out.

"And that's why I couldn't go home to my mother. As much as I love my family, my number one priority is to make sure my memory doesn't happen. There are some things you can live with. And some things you can't." Her voice is stronger now, as if her convictions have cleared her conscience. "As unbearable as it's been to live with this memory, I know I won't survive a future where it actually comes true."

"But surely you could return for a short visit?" I ask. "Maybe you can go to the ceremonial burning. See your family. Say your good-byes."

"No." Her hair swishes against my face, as if she's shaking her head forcefully. "The pull of Fate is strong.

I've seen it happen again and again. As soon as you step within her reach, Fate will find a way to make you live your future. The only answer is to run as far as you can, and never look back."

I want to argue with her. But I can't. Because I saw Fate at work, in front of my very eyes. I thought going to detainment would be safe, but Fate found a way to twist the situation. If Logan hadn't rescued me, sooner or later Fate would have won.

"You can't straddle both worlds, Callie. You need to make a decision. Is the prevention of your memory paramount, or isn't it?" Her hand finds mine and grips it. "And if the answer is yes, you must never return to civilization again."

Later that night, I toss and turn on the woven mat on Angela's floor. She's layered moss, grass, and leaves underneath and given me a buckskin blanket. It's by far the most comfortable bed I've had since I was arrested, but the moon casts weird shadows through the hole in the roof. Plus, I can't quite forget that I'm lying underneath the skin of a dead animal.

I sit and pull my knees to my chest. After crying a few more minutes, Angela pulled herself together and gave me a stick to chew on. She showed me how to put a little soap on the end of the fibers, so I could brush my teeth before going to bed.

Squinting across the hut now, I can make out a heap on the floor. As I watch, the lump shifts, and I hear a sniffle and a low-pitched moan.

"Angela?" I say. "How are you doing?"

The shadows seem to shiver, but there's no response. She's either asleep or doesn't want to talk.

Lying back down, I pull the buckskin over me. Is Angela right? Of course, I have no plans to return to civilization. My number one priority is to make sure my memory doesn't come true. Even if Jessa is arrested, TechRA only wants to study her, whereas my future self might kill her. Clearly some life is better than no life at all.

But I can't watch from a distance, helpless in the knowledge that I deserted her. A piece of my soul will die if I stay here, safely tucked in Harmony, as TechRA bundles my sister off to their labs. I have to find some answers that will help her. But what if those answers lead me within Fate's grasp?

I don't know. The only thing I'm sure of is this: I miss my sister, and I want to see her. I open my mind, for the fifth time in the last hour, and Jessa flies up and down in the seesaw pod. Again.

Sighing, I turn over on the woven mat. There are only so many times I can look at Olivia's blunt-cut bangs and listen to her jeers. I'll try again tomorrow.

My mind drifts to open fields unfurling under an expansive sky. Sweet green grass that tickles the toes. Air so fresh you want to open your lungs and take a breath.

My body relaxes as fatigue takes over. My limbs sink into the ground, and my last conscious thought is: Open.

I am sitting at a wooden desk. My fingers scamper around the keyball of my desk screen. The zipper of my silver jumpsuit digs into my chest, and my hair curves under my ears, tickling my chin. All around me I hear the tap-tap-tapping of fingers against keys.

School. I'm at school, and I'm taking a test. My finger slips, and my nail gets stuck in the crevice of the keyball. Quickly, before the teacher notices, I yank it back out.

The door lights up. A woman in a FuMA uniform walks into the room. She has bright silver hair cut closely to her head, and plump Olivia Dresden calls out, "Mommy!"

Chairwoman Dresden. Head of FuMA. Who else?

The Chairwoman gives her daughter a curt nod before addressing the teacher. "I'm sorry to interrupt, but I need to pull one of your students out for a screening."

Mistress Farnsworth, the teacher, purses her lips. Her hair curls out riotously over her head. "What kind of screening?"

"I'm afraid that's confidential," Chairwoman Dresden says.

"Well, I'm afraid this isn't convenient. As you can see, my students are taking an arithmetic exam."

The two women regard each other. The Chairwoman turns her head and considers the twenty sets of eyes watching her. "Mistress Farnsworth," she says. "May I speak with you outside?"

The teacher nods. "Class, please return to your exams. I'll be back in a few minutes to download your answers."

They step outside and close the door. The tapping begins again, but I unplug my desk screen from the outlet and check the battery level. Half full. Tossing my portable charger to the back of my desk, I take the screen to the front of the room and plug it into the turbo-charger.

Low but distinct voices drift from the other side of the door.

"It's the only way," Chairwoman Dresden says. "We've received new information that the Key lies in a child with psychic abilities. How else will we find him or her without systematically screening every child in school?"

"Where's the reasonable suspicion?" Mistress Farnsworth asks. "Don't you need eye-witness reports?"

"Set aside the EdA guidelines for a moment. Nothing is more important than finding the Key. You know that."

Mistress Farnsworth clucks her tongue. "Exactly where does your information come from? How do we even know if we can trust it?"

The Chairwoman pauses. "I probably shouldn't be telling you this, but we've found a precognitive. A real one. Not these children who play at fortune telling. Their abilities to see into the immediate future are useless. The whole world knows what they know within seconds. This one's different. She can see years into the future. Decades. She doesn't see everything. She only sees snippets, but she's proven herself, and what she's telling us is the First Incident is rapidly approaching."

Mistress Farnsworth is silent. I check my battery level. Three-quarters full.

"Universal screening in schools is unorthodox," the Chairwoman continues. "But do you see now why we have to do it?"

Mistress Farnsworth sighs. "If people hear about this, you'll have a revolt on your hands. You know that, don't you?"

"*So keep it quiet. We'll do one student at a time, starting with the oldest. Space them out over a few weeks. If the parents ask any questions, tell them it's for academic placement.*"

"*I don't like this.*"

"*You don't have to. I have a ComA decree. Who's the oldest child in the class?*"

"*That would be January One. Your daughter,*" *the teacher says.*

Chairwoman Dresden pauses for a heartbeat. "*She's already been tested. Who's next?*"

Without waiting for an answer, I scurry back to my seat. My battery has reached full power, and I have no other excuse for being by the door. I plug in my desk screen and tap out as many sums as I can before Mistress Farnsworth comes back into the room.

26

wake, my heart pounding. Jessa's the youngest in her class. Her birthday is December Thirtieth. If there's going to be systematic testing, she'll be the last one.

Her hair, in my future memory, fell to her shoulders. In the memory I just received, it curved under her ears, tickling her chin.

I have time. I have time. I have time.

But no matter how often I remind myself, my stomach churns, spinning around the stew I ate last night.

I blink at the arched saplings holding up the roof. Angela's still asleep across the hut, the buckskin pushed aside and her arm flung over her eyes. If I had any doubt that the two agencies were intrinsically linked, here's the proof. Why else would Chairwoman Dresden, the head of FuMA, be talking to Jessa's teacher about TechRA business?

I pad over to the door and slip outside. The breeze cools the sweat on my body, and the rawhide flaps behind me. Dawn approaches. The sky looks like someone is shining a flashlight behind a navy blanket. Light creeps around the edges and infuses the entire swath with a backlit glow.

The village square is empty. A few birds twitter, but even they don't break into song, as if it's too early still for that level of cheer.

A person appears on the other side of the square. As he gets closer, I see that it's Logan, carrying a wooden pail. He stops in front of me and sets the bucket on the ground. Steam rises from the water inside and dissipates into the air.

"Hot water," he says. "Straight from the fire."

I draw in a breath. Vats of water warm in the sun during the day, so that the people of Harmony can rinse off with lukewarm water on a rotating basis. Logan and I were added to the end of the schedule, but our turn won't come for days.

"For me?" I've washed in the river, but not like this. Not with hot water that will sluice over my skin, making me feel truly clean for the first time since I was arrested.

He nods. "Couldn't sleep, so I had time to kill."

A lot of time, apparently. Angela explained that hot water is a personal luxury, so the kindling used to build the fire shouldn't be taken from the communal pile. To bring me this bucket, Logan had to gather his own kindling, build a fire, boil the water, and then lug it across the village.

"Logan, I'm…speechless. Thank you."

He winks and begins to walk away. "I'll leave before the water cools."

But I don't want him to leave yet. I want him here, with me, for a few more minutes. "Wait," I call, without thinking.

He turns back around. "Yes?"

I like you so much, I want to say. *I may even be in love you. Maybe I always was, from the time you gave me a red leaf to remind me of the sun. Whatever happens, I want you to know that.*

I can hear the words in my head. I can see myself saying them, imagine his intake of breath and the light in his eyes as he says, *Yes, yes. I feel the same way.*

But what if he doesn't? What if he brought me hot water because he really was bored?

"I got another memory last night," I say instead. "While I was sleeping."

Pushing aside my unspoken confession, I tell him about the classroom and Chairman Dresden's plan to screen every child. "Have you ever heard of 'the Key' or 'the First Incident'?"

He shakes his head. "No, but they sound familiar. You should ask around. I'm sure someone here knows something about them."

We both look at the bucket of water. Already the wisps of steam seem to be thinning.

"I should get to my shower," I say reluctantly. "After all your hard work."

"Enjoy every last drop," he says. "I'll come find you later."

I watch him round the log cabin, and then I pick up the pail. It's heavier than I thought, and my hand slips on the rope handle. Water sloshes over the edge. I grit my teeth and take a firmer hold.

As I walk past the hut, Angela comes outside, stretching her arms overhead. "Well. What do we have here?"

"Logan brought me hot water."

"He doesn't waste any time, does he?"

I flush. "Maybe he just thinks I could use a proper washing."

She dips her hand into the pail. "That's how Mikey courted me, you know. Brought me a bucket of hot water every day until he wore me down and I accepted his plant bracelet."

"How long did it take?"

She laughs. "Three days, maybe? The Russell charm is hard to resist."

I couldn't agree more, but it's not the kind of thing I want to admit. So instead, I say good-bye and hurry behind the hut to the "shower" area, which is a patch of dirt cordoned by woven mats hanging from tree branches. Inside, a wooden crate holds a cake of lye soap and some old T-shirts to use as washrags.

I strip off my clothes. The second the hot water drips onto my skin, I moan. Angela's right. Hot water's way better than a recited poem. More romantic than an invitation to view a memory chip. Frowning, I squeeze the T-shirt at the base of my neck, so water runs in rivulets down my back. I suppose Logan is courting me. But why? He's not thinking about the long-term. Four or five days from now, he'll be back in Eden City and I'll be here, in exile, for the rest of my life. There's no future between us. There will never be a future between us. No matter how much I want it, as long as he is needed at home, we will never be together.

I scrub the soap over my stomach, my arms, my legs. I'm temporary. I'm temporary. I'm temporary.

If I say it enough, maybe I'll get it through my head.

Even if my heart refuses to listen.

I hang strips of venison over three long sticks resting on an A-shaped frame. Now that the deer has been cut into manageable pieces, now that it looks like meat and not the animal, my stomach no longer rolls.

"Looking good." Zed arranges rocks around the low, smoky fire. The rock ring will get hot and cause the heat to rise, drying out the venison instead of cooking it. "You're a natural at this."

"This was one of our first lessons in our Manual Cooking class. After boiling water and frying an egg."

"So making deer jerky is okay. But not the part where you skin the animal?"

I wrinkle my nose. "You saw my face, huh? My stomach was even worse. If I really want to be a Manual Chef, I should probably stop being so squeamish."

I say the words without thinking. Of course I'm not going to be a Manual Chef, not with the memory I got. Even if I somehow got around my fugitive status, no program in their right mind would admit me. The profession is too competitive to take a chance on anyone without a proven future.

Somehow, in all the turmoil of what my future memory is, I forgot to mourn what it isn't—a vision of myself as a successful chef. I'll never cook for the rich of Eden

City—or any other city. I'll never have my own eating establishment for those who can afford to shun the Meal Assembler.

And yet the people of Harmony weren't concerned about my resume. All they cared about was how my stew tasted. In the end, that's what's important—not some award. Not the elite's idea of success. All I've ever wanted is to cook for people who will appreciate my food.

So maybe the dream hasn't died, after all.

"Skinning animals takes some getting used to. If you want, I could show you," Zed says. "I'll start you out with something small, like fish, and then work you up to squirrels and deer. We'll get you un-squeamish in no time."

I smile. "I would like that."

He finishes with the rocks and begins to erect a wooden shield around the fire, to protect it from the wind. I never thought I'd say this, but for a future woman-batterer, he seems like a nice guy. And as Harmony's assignment coordinator, he probably hears a lot of things.

"You've been in Harmony a while, right?" I ask.

"Almost since the beginning. Angela and I came here only a few months after Mikey."

I take a breath. All morning, the memory of Chair-woman Dresden has been running through my mind. "Have you ever heard anyone talking about 'the Key'? Or 'the First Incident'?"

"I'm not sure about a First Incident." He waves his hand to shoo the flies away. "But I think the Key refers to the person who figured out how to send memories back in time."

I frown. "No. The Key I'm talking about is something

that happens in the future, not the past."

"I don't know, then. But you know someone who would? Laurel. She's our resident poet, and she does all the record keeping for the community. There probably isn't any psychic lore she hasn't heard. After duties, you can find her at the convenience store in the log cabin."

"Thanks, Zed. I appreciate it."

The venison begins to shrink as it dries out, and he helps me move the strips closer together on the stick. It's hard to believe that a future version of this man beats up any woman. Maybe as hard as it is to believe my own future memory.

"Can I ask you a question?" I lick my lips. "Who was she?"

He freezes, his hands clenching the dark strips of protein. He clearly has no doubt which "she" I'm referring to. The woman whom his future self batters.

He puts down the venison. "I don't know." His voice scrapes out of his throat like flesh against broken glass. "I cared about her a great deal. I know that much. When I walked into the room, she wasn't wearing any clothes, so I assume she was my girlfriend. But I didn't see her face."

I almost jostle the venison strips myself. That's the devastating thing about future memory. You get a snippet of your future, so multi-dimensional and vivid, it feels like real life. But there's no context. No reason or explanation. You're left only with a fact, something you can neither defend nor justify.

As horrible as Beks's and Sully's future memories are, at least they had a reason. The robber killed Beks's grandmother; the man raped Sully. Zed and I have nothing.

"How do you live with it?" I whisper.

He sucks in the air, smoke and all. "I do everything in my power to avoid Fate. I came out here. I don't let myself get involved with women. This is probably the longest conversation I've had with a girl, other than Angela. And with each day that passes, I breathe a little easier because that's one more day where my memory hasn't come true."

He looks up, and my pulse leaps in recognition. On his face is an expression that is not quite faith. Faith itself is too scary, too unattainable. Optimism is reserved for the good people, the ones who go through their lives without harming anyone. But Zed's expression is something approaching faith, something that might eventually become faith if circumstances allowed it.

"Sometimes I see a pretty girl and I'm tempted, like anyone else," he says. "But there's a voice inside me and it stops me from doing anything stupid. It reminds me I have no business having a girlfriend. No business tempting Fate, not when I came all this way to escape it. What if I slip up? What if my control falters, even for a second, and I do the unthinkable?" His voice drops to a whisper. "What if I hurt someone I care about?"

I shiver, even though my skin is warm from the smoke rising off the fire. I don't have an answer, because the same voice springs to life inside me. And it says, in no uncertain terms: *Jessa is safe now.* By running away from civilization, I've finally gotten my guarantee. So long as I stay in Harmony, my memory cannot come true.

Clearly I would be a fool to return to Eden City. For any reason.

27

"It's going to smell like dirty feet," Logan says after duties later that day. We're standing in front of the log cabin. The sky rumbles, and dark clouds pile up as though they're assembling their forces for the upcoming onslaught.

"Why's that?" I ask, squinting at the sky. Good thing we're about to go inside.

"Mikey told me everybody crowds together and bunks inside once the weather turns cold. He said last winter he woke up with somebody's dirty sock in his mouth."

"Ew."

Bracing myself, I push the door open and walk inside. But I don't smell feet, dirty or otherwise. Instead, the scent of sawdust greets me. Small round tables hold hand-carved chess pieces, and parchment paper hangs on the walls. A girl and a boy sit behind a long counter covered with baskets. Deer jerky, dried fruit, soap, paper, socks, underwear, dried herb packets, even a few books.

Anything I could possibly want in the wilderness.

"Come on in, Callie, Logan." The girl waves us over. Her dark bangs and ponytail look familiar. I must've met her the previous night. "I'm Laurel and this is Brayden. Was there something you wanted to buy?"

"I don't have any credits," I say.

"Oh, we don't use credits out here." She indicates a paper with handwritten letters scrawled across it. "Or at least, not the credits you're used to. We're each allotted fifty points a month, and you can redeem those points for anything you see here."

I run my hands over a basket. Even the deer jerky? Zed and I pulled it off the drying rack a few hours ago.

"Even that, I'm afraid," Brayden says. Red hair falls over his forehead, and his freckles stand out like stars in the night sky. "It's the only fair way of dividing things up."

My hands still. "Do you have a psychic ability?"

His mouth twists to the side. "Oh, sorry. I hate it when I do that."

"You can read minds?"

"Only if you're having a specific thought. I can't dig into your memories or read your emotions or anything like that." A flush creeps up his neck, making his freckles disappear.

"What am I thinking now?" Logan asks.

"You want to know what we're talking about." The redness fades, like water seeping into the ground. "I was explaining to Callie the way we do things here. Take Laurel. She has to buy the paper like everyone else, even though one of her duties is making paper and walnut ink."

I pick up the parchment paper. The edges are frayed,

and the page looks like it's been crumbled into a ball and then smoothed out again. But it's paper. "You made this? It must've taken forever."

"I have a vested interest. I'm a poet, see." Laurel points to the sheets hanging on the walls. "Those are the poems I've 'published.' If I didn't step up to make the paper, I'm not sure anyone would."

I peer at the even letters covering the page. They look almost like the words on my desk screen. No wonder they elected her as record-keeper. "I'm not actually here to buy anything," I say. "Zed said you might be able to answer some of my questions."

"He did?" Her face lights up like a flint striking steel. "Did he say anything else about me?"

"Laurel here would do anything to get a plant bracelet from Zed," Brayden says. "I could've told you that even if I didn't read minds."

She tosses a dried herb packet at him. "Hush. I think Zed's sweet, that's all. If he has any points left over at the end of the month, he always buys me paper, so I can write more poems."

"He likes you. Anytime you're around, he's thinking how nice your…um, eyes are."

Her smile is equal parts embarrassment and pleasure. "I think he just likes my poetry."

I shuffle my feet, not sure how to respond. I'm sure Zed finds Laurel attractive, but given what he confided in me, their relationship doesn't have much of a future.

Logan clears his throat. "We're trying to figure out what the terms 'the Key' and 'the First Incident' mean. Have you heard of either?"

She exchanges a glance with Brayden. "There's a legend about a Key that helped Callahan unlock the secrets of future memory."

I frown. "That's not right. Tanner Callahan received the first future memory. He didn't invent it. I should know. I'm named after him."

"I'm just telling you what the legend says." She drums her fingers on the table. "The Key held the final piece of the puzzle. Without the Key, the legend goes, future memory never would have been discovered."

It's the same story, more or less, that Zed told me. But I don't care what happened in the past. I'm interested in the future.

I fight the sinking feeling in my stomach. What are the chances I'll figure out the Chairwoman's code words, when I'm not even in the same world as her? Murmuring my thanks, I turn to go.

"Wait," Laurel calls. "As long as you're here, would you mind filling out my log book? I'm keeping a record of Harmony's inhabitants." She reaches under the table and pulls out a bundle of parchment papers, bound together by strings of rawhide. "Here, take a feather and a pot of walnut ink."

We take the supplies to a round table and settle onto creaky, three-legged stools.

"You seem disappointed," Logan whispers, as he moves the chess pieces to one side. Our knees brush under the table. As with any time we touch, the air crackles with electricity.

But that could just be the storm outside. My heart keeps time with the raindrops splattering the roof—

furious and ferocious, an onslaught that may never stop. Will I always feel this way when he touches me? Or will my turbulent feelings someday smooth into something calm and serene?

I peek at him, at his eyes and his mouth, at the dimples in his cheek. Quickly, before I can get lost in the sight of him, I look across the room at Laurel and Brayden. "Not disappointed. I was hoping she'd have more information than just a recounting of our history."

"Keep asking questions. Sooner or later, you'll find something useful."

I pull my stool closer, so we can both see the book. My arm bumps into his—and my heart lurches and dances and sighs. He opens the cover, and I struggle to get ahold of myself.

I stare at the handwritten letters marching across the parchment. The page is divided into columns. I read the categories across the top:

NAME. DATE ARRIVED. DATE LEFT.

I turn the page. More columns:

NAME. PRELIMINARY ABILITY. PRIMARY ABILITY.

The next page concerns future memory:

NAME. MEMORY. DATE MEMORY RECEIVED. DATE MEMORY FULFILLED. DATE MEMORY SENT.

My hand pauses over the page. Every other column has lines and lines of text underneath. The space underneath the column DATE MEMORY SENT is completely empty.

"Why are all these spaces blank?" I ask Logan.

He shrugs. "They changed their futures by coming here. Maybe their futures changed so much that no memory is ever sent."

"But then, they never would've received the memory in the first place. Right?"

He shakes his head slowly. He doesn't know. I don't, either.

I look back at the book. "Not everyone here is escaping a bad future. Look here." I point to the column under DATE MEMORY FULFILLED. "Some of these memories have come true, probably the ones belonging to the psychics. Shouldn't at least one of them have a date recorded for the date the memory was sent?" I sit back on the stool. "Unless not a single person in Harmony has yet sent a memory to themselves."

"How do you even send a memory to your past self? I never learned how. Did you?"

"FuMA always said they would instruct us when the time came," I say. "But when is that? Do they herd all of us into the FuMA building on our sixtieth birthdays? I didn't see any groups of old people while I was there, did you?"

He shakes his head.

I wrinkle my forehead, thinking hard. "Laurel is the second person who linked the Key to the discovery of future memory. Past tense. I dismissed the connection because the Chairwoman was talking about searching for the Key in the future. But what if they're talking about the same thing?" I wet my lips. "What if FuMA's been lying to us all along?"

He frowns. "Lying about what?"

"What if future memory hasn't been invented yet?" I whisper.

"Of course future memory has been invented. You

and I are living proof of that."

"No," I say, my excitement growing. "We're living proof that future memory can be *received* in the present. Not sent. Don't you see? That's why all the spaces under the column are blank. That's why FuMA has never explained to us how to send a memory. Because they haven't figured out how yet."

I stop. I look back at the page, with the column of blank spaces. And it all clicks into place. "That's it. That's why the two agencies are working so closely together. FuMA needs the scientists to figure out how to send memories back to the past."

28

Mud squishes between my fingers, and a worm slithers around my wrist, leaving behind a wet, slimy trail.

Instead of screaming, I grit my teeth and dump the bait in the stream, where I've built a funnel-shaped trap by jamming branches side-by-side. The idea is that a fish will be lured by the worm and swim inside the funnel. At the first splash of water, I'll block the opening with a flat rock, trapping my prey inside.

As an introduction to slaughtering animals, it's not bad. Zed brought me here early this morning, with a knife, a bucket of worms, and a whole lot of instructions. Now that I've built three traps, all I have to do is wait.

I mop my head with a bandana and settle on the muddy bank. The water ripples and a bird swoops across the sky, its wings stretched out to ride the wind. The smell of smoke cuts through the air, and I'm comforted by the fact that Zed is somewhere close by.

If only my younger self could see me now. I remember

how excited I was to take my first Manual Cooking class. Back then I never would've dreamed that one day I'd be catching fish in a stream rather than taking it straight out of the freezer.

Wait a minute. Maybe she can.

I sit straight up. Psychic powers are related to future memory. So maybe I can send a memory to my younger self. True, I don't remember ever receiving a memory in my youth, but maybe I just suppressed it.

Taking a deep breath, I snap a mental shot of the scene before me and picture my twelve-year-old self. Chubby cheeks. Wavy hair caught in pigtails. Nut brown skin from too much sun.

"Send," I whisper. "Send."

Nothing. Not a twinge, not a tingle.

I open my eyes, frowning. That didn't work too well.

"How many times do I have to tell you?" a voice says above me. "You're a Receiver, not a Sender. It's not a reciprocal power."

My head snaps up. "You scared me, Logan! Why are you sneaking up on me?"

"I stepped on and cracked about a dozen twigs." He plops on the ground next to me. "Maybe you didn't hear me."

Maybe I should pay closer attention. I dart a glance at the fish traps. Sure enough, the worms are missing, although no fish are trapped inside the funnels. Sighing, I grab a few more crawlers from the bucket and replenish the bait. "I was trying to send a memory to my younger self. Nobody knows how future memory works, so I hoped the Sender/Receiver distinction wouldn't apply."

"Any luck?"

"Nope."

I wade back to shore. Water drips down the rolled-up cuffs of my pants. I try to wipe the sweat from my forehead and end up smearing dirt on my face.

He grins. "Maybe I should try sending an image to my younger self. Of you, just like that. Water soaking your knees, mud on your cheeks. I think he'd get a kick out of it."

"Don't do that." I laugh. "I don't want to scare him off."

"I doubt anything could scare him away from you."

After all these years, I thought I knew all of Logan's looks. But I've never seen this one. His lips are soft, his gaze heated. He sees the charred, blackened edges of my soul, and he likes me anyway. In his eyes, I am more. Smarter, prettier, braver, kinder. I want to be more. I want to be a girl worthy of his attention.

But this is selfish of me, and I know it. If I truly care for Logan, I should want to be the type of girl he can never fall for. Soon, he'll leave, and the best thing for him will be to forget me and move on. Yet, I want to make him proud. For Logan, I want to be perfect.

And when he looks at me like that, I am.

I take a shaky breath. "What are you doing here, anyway?"

He brings my hand to his lips and places a searing kiss on my palm. "I thought it was time you learned how to swim."

The water laps at my ears. It rises in a line all around my body, a sensation somewhere between tickling and vibrating. And then it engulfs me altogether as I sink into the stream…for the tenth time.

"You're not concentrating," Logan says.

I push the wet hair out of my eyes. The sun reflects off the water droplets in his hair, and he looks like a pre-Boom image of a god. The stream is chilly, but the afternoon rays beat down on my face and shoulders, keeping me from being cold.

I wrap my arms around my waist anyway. "It's a little hard to focus."

"Are you worried about Jessa?"

"Yeah." I skim my hands along the stream, scooping up water in my palms and letting it run through my fingers. "I know she's safe for now, 'cause her hair's too short. But sooner or later, they're going to test her. And then they'll find out about her psychic abilities and take her away."

"Was Mikey able to get a message to your mom through the Underground?"

"He's trying." I stare at my hands, distorted through the water. "He's not sure how clear the communication with your mom is."

I recline in the water again, and Logan supports my neck and back. If there weren't so much going on in my head, this would be nice. The water sways me, and his eyes flicker down the length of my body before returning to my face.

I lift my hand to touch him…and sink into the water once again. When I surface, he leans his forehead against mine. "You've got to focus, Callie."

His lips are right there, inches from mine, so I kiss him. As our lips spar, I push out all the images cluttering my brain. A woman in a FuMA uniform, with bright silver hair. Beks's wild eyes as she grabs on to my ankle. My arm slicing through the air and stabbing a needle into my sister's heart.

I kiss Logan until these images fade. I kiss him until white noise roars in my ears and my mind is frenzied static. I kiss him until I forget everything but the feel of his bare chest and arms slick against me.

But it's not enough. I jump up and wrap my legs around his waist. He staggers backward, and we sink into the stream, still kissing. My hair swirls around us, mixing with the ribbons of algae, and we're still kissing. The water creeps up our necks toward our chins, and we still… continue…to…kiss.

He breaks the contact with a gasp, his hot breath panting over me. "Maybe we'd better stop before we get carried away."

I wrap my fingers around his neck. "I like getting carried away with you."

"So do I." He gives me a peck on the nose. I know, somewhere in the back of my mind, that his eyes are green, yet at this moment, I'd swear they're made from the same murky blackness as the water. "But I get the feeling we're not talking about the exact same thing."

Aren't we? Because part of me is very sure I'm ready to take the next step. If I only have a short time left with Logan, I want to make the most of every moment. But the other part of me isn't sure, isn't ready.

I take a couple of steps away, to give both my emotions

and my body some space. The water laps against my ribs, cool and refreshing against my burning skin. With the amount of heat we generated, I'm surprised the stream didn't boil.

Lying back on the water, I kick my feet, trying to remember everything he taught me. Amazingly, I don't sink.

Something buoys me up, and I'm floating. Weightless. Skimming the top of the world.

"You're doing it." The words sound muffled through the water, and I smile. And then my heavy limbs take over and I sink.

"Twelve seconds," he says. "You were floating for twelve whole seconds."

I wipe the drops off my face. "Is that good?"

"Good enough for your first lesson."

We go back to shore. When we sit down, Logan's eyes have turned green once again. I show him the net I've been weaving out of plant stalks, as I waited for the fish to get caught in my traps.

He runs his fingers over the bumps where the fronds cross one another. "How come you don't know how to swim? You said your mom doesn't like the water. But couldn't your dad have taught you?"

I take a swig from my canteen, although the lump in my throat has nothing to do with thirst. "My dad hasn't been around since I was four."

"I knew he left, but I thought you said he came back. After Jessa was born."

"Nope." I drink more water. "I remember his last day so clearly. I was standing on the sanitation machine in my nightgown in order to hug him good-bye. He turned to my mom and said 'They're going to shave my head. I'll have to get a wig when I come back so Boo-Boo doesn't get scared.' That's what he called me. Boo-Boo."

The words come automatically. I've said them a hundred times before, as bedtime stories to my sister. This memory and a handful of others. Building a sand turtle by the dunes. Riding high on my father's shoulders. Shrieking as he carried me upside down by my feet. Stories repeated over and over, so Jessa could have a glimpse of him. So I wouldn't forget.

"Did he buy the wig?"

"No. That was the last time I ever saw him."

Surprise, then confusion, then understanding flit across his face in rapid succession, like one of those cartoon flip-books I used to make as a little girl. "So Jessa is your half sister?"

"She's my sister. There's nothing halfway about it." Taking a deep breath, I pick up a plant stalk and begin to weave another row onto the net. "But to answer your question, back then, I would've sworn we had the same dad. My mom wasn't involved with anyone else when she got pregnant. And when Jessa was born, she looked just like my baby pictures. Just like my dad. What were the chances my mom had gotten pregnant with someone else with those eyes? I waited and waited, because I knew one day he would come back to us."

I pick up another plant stalk, but my fingers don't work anymore. They feel too big, too clumsy. "Except he never did. And when I pressed my mom, she confirmed Jessa has a different dad. So technically, you're right. She is my half sister."

"I'm sorry, Callie. That must've been hard."

It's still hard. Time dulls all pain, but it can't erase the hurt. Not completely.

"You're right, you know," he says. "She does look like you. When I saw her in the park that day, I thought I was seeing you as we were entering the T-minus eleven class."

My lips crack their plaster mold. "My mom has photos where she swears she can't tell which of us it is."

"That's weird, isn't it? How you look so much alike."

The rest of his sentence remains unspoken. That's weird you look so much alike, when you have different fathers. Different blood. Different genes.

"It doesn't matter. I wouldn't care if Jessa had a different *mother*, too. I wouldn't love her any less."

"Of course not. Love isn't something you can give halfway." He takes the plant stalk from my hands and begins to twist it around his fingers. "I'm learning that now more than ever."

My sentiments exactly. I tried to give Logan only part of my love. I tried to hold back, knowing that he would leave me soon. But no matter how often my brain declared his impending absence, my heart affixed itself to him. And there's not a piece of logic in the world that can change that.

I tear my gaze from the ground and look back at Logan. He holds up the stalk. He's wound it into a perfect circle, the circumference of my wrist.

A hammer pounds against my chest. My mouth is desert-dry, despite all this water, and the rushing in my ears is back, and he isn't even touching me.

"I've decided I'm not going back to Eden City," he says. "Mikey will have to find another way to communicate with the Underground."

I suck in a breath. I never hoped for this. It may have been the secret wish of my selfish heart, but I never let myself dream of this moment. "But your future as a gold-star swimmer—"

"Can wait. Now that I've found you again, I'm not leaving. Not without giving us a shot." He picks up my hand and gently, so gently, slips the circlet over my wrist. "Don't forget, my future memory is two-fold. Half of it is the swimming. The other half is you. I want that part of my memory to come true. I want you in my life." His voice drops, and it seems to reach inside me and pick up the pieces that fell apart when my dad left. It puts those fragments back together, cementing them with his certainty. With his belief. "What do you say, Callie? Will you let me stay without arguing? Will you be my girlfriend?"

I look at my hand. The twisted green plant hangs around my wrist. I don't know how long it can keep its shape. But as long as it holds, can I really deny its chance to last? I've spent the past few days trying my hardest to quell the feelings I have for Logan. Would it be so bad to just let go?

All sense and reason is telling me not to accept. I know that Logan is needed in Eden City. There may even come a time when I need something that only he can send. But, at this moment, the only thing I need from Logan is himself.

I've been in love with him half my life. I know this now. For once I'm going to be selfish. I'm going to grasp my chance at a new life.

"Yes," I say. With that one word I wish, I shiver, I pray that I've sealed my Fate. And, desperately, I hope that I haven't sealed anyone else's.

29

The air smells of rosemary and grilled fish. Conversation and bits of food are flung around, as if the people of Harmony can't decide whether to talk or eat. I'm wedged on a bench between Logan and Brayden, trying to keep the hysterical laughter inside.

I had some sparkling wine once. A neighbor sent a bottle to our house after Jessa was born. Mom popped the cork, and white bubbles spilled out the neck.

"Here, quick." Mom pushed the bottle at me. "We can't waste a single drop."

I licked the side of the bottle and the bubbles exploded on my tongue. Even after I swallowed, I could still feel the fizz climbing my throat.

Well, that's how I feel now. Every time Logan speaks to me, brushes my shoulder, or even looks at me, my insides fizz a little more and bubble a little higher. Long forgotten are my guilt and caution. Now I'm brimming with heady elation. By the time I finish my dinner, I can't sit still any longer. I jump to my feet and excuse myself, leaving Logan talking to Brayden about his swim meets.

I wander over to the long table in front of the log cabin, where Angela is stuffing a fish with cubed vegetables.

"Dinner was delicious, Angela." Sliding in next to her, I pick up a fish and slice through its stomach with a knife. "I think I may have caught a few of these suckers myself."

"Did you? Well, hurry up and finish your hunting rotation. I miss having you in meal prep." She lays her fish on a tray and holds her hand out for mine. "You are going to be around at the end of your rotation?"

I hand her the fish. Its eyes stare at me, dead and lifelike at the same time. I rub the underside of my bracelet, twisting it around my wrist. I made Logan a matching one, too. These bracelets symbolize so much more than our relationship. They offer me another chance at life.

I flash back on a scene from this afternoon—cleaning the haul with the other fisherman on the shore. The air is ripe with fish guts. The bloated bellies of the fish flash in the waning light. And Logan, a few scales clinging to his cheek, wields a thin metal blade like a scalpel.

I could be happy here. No, scratch that. I *am* happy here.

"I'm not going anywhere," I say to Angela.

The smile beams out of her. "Welcome home, Callie."

We work in silence for a few minutes, and her smile leaks away. Her misery presses down on me. I can see the grief in the tightness of her lips, in the fish she's handling a little too roughly.

"Angela?" I ask. "How are you holding up?"

Her hands pause. "Still sad about my mum's passing.

And Mikey and I have been fighting."

"Over what?"

"The usual. Relationship stuff." She turns the fish over. "But don't worry. We'll work it out. We always do."

We prep the rest of the fish, and when Angela takes them over to the fire pit to grill, I walk back to Logan.

He's sitting with his brother now, his head bent as he listens to Mikey. I'd recognize his swimmer's physique anywhere. The broad shoulders that taper to a *V*, the muscular thighs and long legs. As if sensing my approach, he looks up and reaches out his hand to me. Our fingers intertwine and I forget how to breathe. When he looks at me, I don't need a memory to tell me where I belong. I could make a home here. With Logan by my side, I could carve a place for myself in Harmony.

At that moment, a scream rips through the air. Startled, Logan and I look at each other, and then all three of us jump to our feet and run to the fire pit, where Angela is cradling a little boy in her arms. He has long, scrawny limbs, smooth nutmeg skin…and a deep, bloody gash on one thigh.

It's Ryder, the little boy who had given me the shy smile, whose psychic parents were locked up by FuMA. The boy who came to Harmony rather than live in a city that might someday incarcerate him, too.

"It hurts, Angela," he cries, thrashing his arms and legs as though he can battle the pain away. "Make it stop. Please make it stop."

"*Shh*. You're going to be okay," she says, already dressing the wound. She rolls up a tube of antiseptic, squeezing out every last bit of ointment. "Mikey, didn't you say you sent a runner to get a new shipment of supplies? Could you—"

"On it." Mikey leaves even before she finishes her sentence. It's like they know each other so well he can anticipate her needs.

"A new shipment already?" I murmur to Logan, as Angela whispers in Ryder's ear. The little boy continues to moan, and a sheen of sweat shines on his forehead, but as she speaks to him he stops moving and lies still.

"We usually wait for the next fugitive to bring the backpacks," Logan says. "But Mikey wanted to test his telepathy with my mom, so he sent someone to fetch the pack from the meeting point, where we picked up our boat. The runner just got back today."

Mikey reappears with a navy backpack identical to the one we brought. Hurriedly he unzips it, and a dozen white tubes tumble out.

He picks one up. The logo of a smile gleams up at me.

"What. Is. This?" Without warning, he closes his hand over the tube and crushes it.

I gasp. If the tube had a life, it would be dead.

Logan picks up a tube, too. "It looks like toothpaste."

Mikey slams the tube on the ground; he'd squeezed it so hard the tube split, and white paste oozes out.

"It's okay, Mikey." Angela places a large piece of gauze over Ryder's leg. "We had enough ointment. Ryder will be fine."

"It's not okay," Mikey growls. "Do you know how many scratches you can get here in the woods? A knife slips, like Ryder's did today. A branch scrapes your leg. You nick your finger on a bone." He yanks up his sleeve, revealing a nasty red scratch on his forearm. "I did this just yesterday. Any of these cuts can become infected. If they go untreated, these little infections can turn life threatening."

He looks wildly around the fire pit, skimming over each face in the crowd, until his eyes land on me. "It turns out our stopgap measure has a leak," he says, as if he's addressing me alone. "I asked my mother to send us tubes of antibiotic ointment." His lips press together in a long, thin line. "This is what she sent."

My heart plummets. He was testing his communication with his mom. A simple message, a single concrete object — and it still didn't transmit properly.

"You two," Mikey snaps to Logan and me. "Come with me. Now."

He dips a cattail torch in the flame of the fire pit and leads us to his hut. Still holding hands, Logan and I trail after him. My stomach sloshes around uneasily. I don't know what he's going to say, but it won't be good. It can't be good. I've never seen Mikey so angry, not even on the first day we arrived.

Once we arrive at his hut, Mikey drops the torch into a built-in holder. The flame flickers, making our shadows dance on the wall.

Two buckskins are laid out on the dirt. This must be where they've been sleeping, as opposed to the soft piles of moss that serve as my bed at Angela's. I feel a pang as I remember the bed Logan made me out of pine needles during our trip to Harmony. He must've done that just for my comfort.

I look up to catch Mikey studying me. "You don't like

me," I say.

He opens his mouth as if he would like to agree, but then snaps it shut again. "That's not true. But your relationship with my brother will not work. I can't allow it to continue."

"What do you mean you can't allow . . .?" But the words die in my mouth, strangled by what I think—what I know—he's going to say.

Logan shifts behind me. His breath wafts against my hair, but the heat does nothing for the goose bumps that have popped up along my arms.

I lick my lips and try again. "Why won't our relationship work?"

Mikey looks between us. His shadow looms behind him, hulking and grotesque. A single bird screeches outside the hut, and I'm suddenly aware of the stillness in the air.

"Logan's not staying in Harmony. The day after tomorrow, I'm sending him back to Eden City."

30

The world tilts, and for one crazy moment, I think I might slide right off the edge. Then I hear Logan's voice, low and controlled, and it anchors my feet to the ground.

"What are you talking about?"

"You knew your time here was limited," Mikey says. "Harmony needs you in Eden City. We need you to communicate with the Underground. With the coldest months of the year coming, many will get sick, with illnesses for which we haven't prepared. Without you, they'll die."

"Shouldn't it be my decision?" Logan steps around me so that he's face-to-face with his brother. "What if I can find another method to deliver the messages? I...I don't know how, but we'll figure something out. What if I'd rather stay here with Callie? With...you?"

His voice falters on the last word, and my heart squeezes, squeezes, squeezes.

Mikey lays his hands on Logan's shoulders. Something

passes between them, some invisible force I can't sense in any physical way. But I know it's there. My mind recognizes it and carves its shape into my perception.

He's speaking into Logan's mind, words too personal for an outsider to hear.

I love you, my brother. I will not forget our days together. The bond between us is strong and true, and no one can take that away, no matter where you are.

Or maybe Mikey's not saying that at all. Maybe he's saying: stop your crying, little boy. You will do as I say. You will not disappoint me ever again.

Whatever passes between them, it seems to work. Logan takes a step back; he drops his head, as though he's considering Mikey's words.

My stomach plummets to the ground. No. I won't let my future be decided like this. I won't stand here observing like a passenger with no access to the controls as my life hurtles down a path I didn't choose.

Not again.

"You're not giving your mother a chance." My voice echoes in the hut, shattering the silence that's smothering me. "Her powers might improve with practice. She was able to figure out you wanted a white tube—it was just the *wrong* white tube. She'll get better with time. You just have to let her try."

Mikey tilts his head. "Why are you arguing with me? Even if we had a different option, which we don't, Logan doesn't belong here. You know it, and I know it. He's got a brilliant future back in civilization. He's going to be the best swimmer they've ever seen."

Mikey's not saying anything I haven't felt. And I know

I'm being selfish. I know I should accept the situation. I know I should let him go.

But my heart refuses. I've finally opened myself to him, after all this time. We're finally together, the way we're supposed to be. He can't be ripped away from me again. He just can't. "There has to be another answer. Another avenue of communicating with the Underground. We just have to find it. It doesn't have to be him."

Mikey arches an eyebrow, not saying a word. He doesn't have to. Until I come up with an alternative solution, these words are meaningless.

I reach for the only argument I have left. "If FuMA finds out Logan broke me out of detainment, they'll arrest him."

Mikey's pupils widen. In them, I see the soul-splitting scream that will tear through us both should such a thing happen. If they know he managed an escape before, FuMA will throw Logan in a cell where there'll be no hope of breaking him out. He'll spend the rest of his days rotting in an above-ground grave.

"He'll be fine." Mikey wipes a hand across his brow. "My parents will swear on their lives he's been sick at home. We have doctors in the Underground who will have no problem coming up with fake documents."

"You'll risk his life on that assumption?" I'm trying to guilt him, and I feel bad about it, but I can't give Logan up. Not now. Not after I finally let my feelings out.

"Yes." Mikey sets his jaw, the hard edges of bone visible through the taut stretch of his skin. "Your future memory has already destroyed one life. Don't destroy the rest of Harmony, too."

I sway, flinging my arms out to hold onto something,

anything. I close my hands around a sapling, gasping. Because with those words, he steals my breath, melts my muscles, upends my world. With a single sentence, Mikey wins.

In my future memory, I will kill my sister. I cannot—I will not—be responsible for the destruction of Harmony, too. Mikey knows this. He knows that with this argument, I'll have to let Logan go.

Slowly but surely, I wall myself back up. I begin the long process of blocking away the feelings I had foolishly allowed to run free. It might take minutes or maybe even years, but I can't allow myself to have feelings for Logan.

If he's leaving, I need to be prepared.

"I could stay," Logan says uncertainly. "I don't have to listen to my brother."

We're back at the clearing, sitting on the log. Mikey gave Logan the cattail torch as we left, but there's no holder out here, so he dug a hole in the ground with his fingers and stuck the torch inside. The flame illuminates us clearly from the knees down. I can see the dirt caked in his shoelaces, but his face is nothing but hazy lines and different shades of darkness.

Yes! I want to shout with every ounce of my being. *Don't leave me. Don't leave me the very day I finally let my guard down. Don't leave me here without anyone to love. Fate's already ripped away my mom and my sister. Don't you go, too.*

Just a few hours ago, I might have said these words. I might have allowed myself to beg. But not now. Not when the darkness between us might as well be solid. I want to reach out, see the creases in his forehead with my fingers, but I can't. The invisible wall between us keeps out more than my sight.

"Your future's back in Eden City," I mumble, trying to convince myself I believe what I'm saying. Trying not to be so damn-the-Fates selfish. "You're meant to be a gold-star swimmer."

"You don't understand." His heel moves up and down with so much force that bits of dirt fly off his shoe. "The swimming was always Mikey's goal for me. Never mine. I only do it for fun. I don't need the awards or accolades."

For a moment, hope flares in me, shiny and bright. The extent of my selfishness makes me dizzy with disgust, but I can't help myself. Even as I loathe myself for trying, the words pour out of me, searching, reaching, grasping for another solution. One that will keep Logan here with me—and save Harmony, too. "If you stayed, how would we communicate with Harmony?"

"We could send messages the old-fashioned way," he says. "We could leave notes for the Underground at the meeting point, and they could fulfill the supply order that way."

And just like that, my hope is snuffed out by the weight of logic. "That's not very practical. Think how long it took for us to travel here. Maybe it's faster on the way back, traveling with the current, but still, you're looking at a trip of three days just to leave one note. How often does Mikey send a message?"

"Two, maybe three times a week," he admits. "But we could take turns. Set up a rotation system, the way we do with the hot water. We could make it work."

I smile sadly. "You're really going to ask an entire community to sacrifice so that we can be together?"

His heel stops moving. "When you put it like that, it does seem a little selfish."

"A lot selfish."

We fall silent. Earlier today, he decided to stay. He asked me not to argue with him. He asked me... The word gets stuck in my chest, and it's almost too painful to think. He asked me to be his girlfriend.

And now, we're nothing. Two people who could've meant something to each other, in another world, in another time.

I shift my body to face him. A gnarled knot on the log jabs me in the thigh, but I stay where I am, trying to separate his face from the shadows. "You know the guilt you felt over not stopping your brother's arrest?" I ask softly. "Maybe this is your chance to make it up to him."

Abruptly, he leaps to his feet and strides to the torch. The fire glows around his body, engulfing him in flames. "I'll never be able to make it up to him."

"Why not? You were just a kid. There was nothing you could've done. Surely you can see that now."

He turns, and his face emerges in the light of the fire. I see in his expression the ravages of a hundred sleepless nights. Years of self-recrimination. "You know what? I should go back to Eden City. I should do exactly what Mikey says, what Mikey wants. And even then, I'll still owe him more than I can repay in a single lifetime." He presses his fingers into the corners of his eyes. "I told you more than I've ever told anybody. But I didn't tell you the whole truth."

I still. "What are you talking about?"

He takes a deep breath. The air stirs the fire, and the flames reach their fingers into the sky. "I was on the racquetball court that day, with Mikey and his friends. They were bigger than me, better than me. I kept getting tossed to the side like a brown paper bag. So I made the ball float high above our heads, spinning and bouncing, tracing figure eights. I thought the others would be impressed. Instead, they backed away from me and Mikey and ran to tell the teachers."

My mind whirls. "You mean you were the one who made the ball float?"

"Yeah. Telekinesis is my preliminary ability, not Mikey's. He was just covering for me. TechRA came to arrest him, and I stood there and let him take the blame." His lip quivers. "Don't you see? It's my fault he's here. Because of me, he lost everything."

Words have fled me. The only thing left is the knowledge that runs from his eyes, flowing into the lines of his forehead and the clench in his jaw.

"I'm sure Mikey's forgiven you," I say, but the words blow away like fallen leaves in the breeze.

"That doesn't matter. Because I haven't forgiven myself. And that's why I have to go back," he says, his voice filled with resolve. "I see that now. I don't know what I was thinking. There's no way I can stay. No way I'm going to ruin my brother's life any more than I already have."

I should be happy. This is what I wanted. This is what I was trying to convince him to do. And yet, I feel a hundred times worse than I did before.

31

The shore is an empty stretch of mud and grass that slopes into the cloudy water. I search the river's surface for the reflection of the moon. It would reassure me to see twin moons, round and unblemished, one holding court in the sky and the other one shimmering below it.

But the water is too choppy and dices up any reflection into a million pieces. My heart aches. How can Logan leave me? How can we accept Mikey's answer without searching for another solution? I thought we had something special. I thought what we had you don't find every day.

I bend down and pick up a flat stone. Pulling my hand back, I launch the rock onto the river, trying to skip it along the water. But the current is too strong and swallows the rock whole.

Thousands of questions hover in the air. I can pluck any of them from the sky, but one pushes its way to the front, demanding an answer.

Do I love him?

Yes, my heart screams. I've always loved him. Always.

No, my mind retaliates, determined to keep that wall in place. I don't love him. I can't. Logan and I have just reconnected. We have so much more to learn about each other. I don't even know what love means anymore.

I thought I loved Jessa. From the time my sister scrunched her wrinkled red face at me, her tiny fists pummeling the air, I loved her. Her hand wrapped around my finger, squeezing with uncanny strength, and I swore I would never let any harm come to her.

I was wrong. I thought love trumped everything. But now I know there's something in this world stronger than love. Something out there that can make me decide to take my sister's life. This force made me weigh everything—the birthmark like a splotch of paint at her waist, the way she alternates bites from two halves of a sandwich, her cat-like whimpers when she has a nightmare—and choose death over love.

I pick up another rock, tossing it from one hand to the other. A fine dusting of dirt coats my hands, and the rock slips through my fingers and lands on the ground.

If I can't understand something as simple as loving my sister, how am I supposed to know what it means to love a boy? And with Logan leaving in two days, is it even worth trying to figure out?

Dawn encroaches and the darkness fades. The diffuse light turns into actual sunshine. I dry the tears from my face, get dressed, and make my way back to the river. The fishermen are clustered by the shore, yelling and cheering. Spotting Brayden's lanky frame, I walk to the group. "What's going on?"

Brayden turns to me. He's sewn strips of cloth to his ball cap to shield his neck from the sun. "A race." He gestures to the river. Two figures slice through the waves, their powerful upper bodies rising above the water like dolphins. The cloudless blue sky shimmers overhead, and a flock of birds flies low over the river, as if they, too, hope for a view of the swimmers.

"Pride, honor, and a ration of deer jerky are at stake. Before Logan got here, see, Don was king of the water. The first time I met him, he asked me to call him Poseidon. Get it? Posei-Don." He rolls his eyes. "I told him I'd call him 'poser.' I guess he got sick of everyone talking about Logan's speed in the water, 'cause he challenged our friend to a race. They're swimming ten laps to the crab traps and back, dragging in a load each time. Whoever finishes first wins."

I squint at the water. Is that Logan's head? The figures are too far away, so I can't be sure. "Who's winning?"

"Who do you think?" He grins. "My man Logan! It's not even close. He's already beating Don by over two laps."

Well, of course he is. He's not a future gold-star swimmer for nothing. I always knew Logan was good in the water. But I didn't know he was *this* good. Even if his future memory didn't prove his potential by showing him in the final heat, he would make the national team on his own merit. He's that talented.

He has a brilliant future ahead of him in civilization. His memory says so, and if I needed any other proof, it's right in front of me. He'll have prestige and power. He'll be a celebrity with a lifestyle to match.

My knees feel like the tallow Angela uses to light the lamps. This is why Mikey wants him to return. Not only is he essential to Harmony, but this is the future that would be taken away from him if he stayed.

A swimmer approaches the shore, a net billowing in the current beside him, and I no longer have any doubt about his identity. Who else could look so beautiful in the water? Strong, steady, sure—like a sea creature that blossoms to full potential in his natural habitat.

Mikey's right. It's not about whether or not we can find another way to communicate with the Underground. This isn't the kind of talent to be wasted in Harmony. The most he can be here is a really good fisherman. Back in civilization, he could be somebody important. He could single-handedly save Harmony by stocking the backpacks. He could have the entire nation cheering him on to a gold-star win.

I place a hand on my forehead, as the ground tries to rise up to meet me.

"Are you okay?" Brayden's freckles swim in front of my face.

"Just dizzy." I stumble, and he wraps his arm around me, holding me up.

The real danger here is my selfish nature. I wanted to hold him in Harmony, in the middle of nowhere, and I almost begged him to stay. The thought of losing him slices through me. And yet, it's not about me.

The dizziness passes, and I look up. Brayden's face hovers inches from mine. The excitement in his eyes has faded, replaced by an unusual seriousness. He's read my thoughts.

"It's the right thing to do," he says softly. "He's going to be a star, Callie."

I nod, brushing the tears off my cheeks. For once, I see the advantage of a friend who can read my mind. Brayden knows how I feel, and I didn't have to say a word.

Impulsively, I lean forward and kiss his cheek. "Thank you. For understanding me."

Brayden blushes. "I didn't mean to read your mind, but I was worried."

"I'm glad you did."

The crowd erupts in applause and Logan pulls himself out of the river. He tosses the last net into the pile, and the fishermen converge on him, pumping his hand and slapping his back. Logan steps right through them and walks toward us.

"Great job, man. That was amazing!" Brayden extends his hand to Logan, his arm still slung around my shoulders.

Logan takes his hand, but he doesn't smile, doesn't respond. His lips march across his face as straight as a ruler. He just won a race. He should be skipping across water. Instead, he looks like his cat just died and was served up in one of Angela's stews.

Brayden sneaks a look at me, and I shrug. I've never seen Logan like this either. His bad mood fills the silence, creeping into the nook between my shoulder and Brayden's hand.

A half dozen uncomfortable beats later, Brayden

snatches his arm away. "Oh, well, I'd better get going. Catch you later, at dinner, maybe?" Without waiting for a response, he hurries to the supply shed. Can't blame him. If it were anyone else, I'd run away, too.

I face Logan. Water beads on his bare chest, and his muscles look even bigger than usual after the workout. "You were…" I search for the right word. Effortless? Inspiring? Sensational? "Right. Someone as talented as you belongs back in civilization."

His upper lip curls, and for an instant he looks just like his brother. "I don't want to talk about my talent right now."

"What do you want to talk about?"

He opens his mouth, but a gust of wind batters us, stealing his words before they can be said. He gives me a tortured look—one that gathers up my insides and runs them through a meat grinder—and walks away.

I watch him go. Heat pricks my eyes, but I refuse to cry. I don't know what just happened. I don't know why he left. But tears are like the water that drips in a cave. They may seem like nothing at the time, but over the years, the hurt builds up and turns you as hard as the stalactites in a cave.

I only have one more day with him, and I will not waste it on a misunderstanding.

"Logan, wait." I run after him, and when he turns, I don't worry about putting myself out there. I don't care about embarrassment or pride. I fling myself into his arms because that's where I belong, whether or not he's here tomorrow. "Talk to me, please. Why are you acting like this?"

His arms wrap around me, thank the Fates. The river on his skin soaks through my clothes, and the plant bracelet on his wrist presses into my back.

He doesn't say anything, and it's almost enough just to be in his embrace. It's almost enough that the icicle walls have melted between us, almost enough that I can put my head on his chest and sync our vital signs.

But it's *not* enough. Because I care about this boy when he's at his best and when he's at his worst. If he's hurting, I want to know why.

"You didn't talk to me for five years," I say. "And we lost forever that time we could've had. I can't bear it if we lose today, too."

He buries his face against my neck, his breath tangling in the maze of my hair. "I'm an idiot."

"Only when you won't talk to me."

His lips vibrate against my skin. I don't know if he's laughing or kissing me. I don't think I care.

"When I came out of the water, I saw you with Brayden," he says in a low voice. "And I didn't even care about winning. All I wanted to do was rip his head off."

"I'm not interested in Brayden."

"Not yet. But when I'm gone, all these guys will be after you." He pulls back. His mouth tugs down at the corners. He looks as lost as Jessa the day she misplaced her purple dog, Princess. As sad as I was the night I staked out our driveway and my father never came home.

"One day, you'll choose someone," he says. "And it won't be me."

"Oh, Logan." I lunge into him. I'd turn our arms into manacles if I could. Electro-cuff us together for the rest of eternity. But I can't. "I hate this situation so much. But this is how it has to be. You belong in civilization, and I belong here. We have to find a way to live with it."

He nestles his chin on my head and we fit together perfectly, like two pieces of a jigsaw puzzle. Perfectly, like two halves of a broken heart.

"What if we can't?" he whispers.

I don't have an answer.

My life was shattered in an instant, with a single memory sent from the future. Since I came to Harmony, I've been trying to put myself back together. Gathering the pieces. Laying the foundation for my new life, the one I was supposed to build with Logan. But just as I let myself feel at home in Harmony, my true home was taken from me.

And now the boy I love is leaving, and I'm right back where I started—with a million questions and not one good answer.

32

The sun has moved down the sky. If I hold my hand to my face, it's about a thumb's length above the trees, which means I have another hour to kill before Logan finishes prepping for his trip back to Eden City.

I wander into the square, Logan's absence a solid shadow. I've got to get used to this. Pretty soon that's the best company I can expect.

The feather of a bird floats by on the wind, and I grab it from the air. The feather is ripped, torn in fluffs that drift away, trying to resurrect itself into something new. Trying to carve an alternate path out of its dead-end flight. Trying to break free of the life dictated by Fate.

The thought ties anchors to my feet. I'm like the feather, too. Battered and mangled, wanting to change my fate, but not knowing how.

I'm in danger of drowning in the dry and dusty dirt when I see Laurel walking toward the log cabin, a bunch of wildflowers dragging on the ground behind her. Me with my tattered feather, her with her wilted flowers. Aren't we a sorry pair.

"Laurel, these poor flowers." I pick them up and blow the grime from the petals. "Let me get you some water."

I scoop up water from the barrel and plunk the flowers into the aluminum can, tucking the feather next to them. They fit nicely together. The can has more important functions than to serve as a vase, but maybe the flowers will perk up after a few minutes, even if I don't have much hope for the feather.

"I tried to give them to Zed." Her voice is as dull as a mud puddle. "He wasn't interested in the flowers. And even less interested in me."

"It's not you. He's afraid of his—"

"Future memory, I know," she says bitterly. "But he's already come all the way to Harmony to avoid it. Is he going to let it rule his life here, too? What kind of life do you have if you're afraid of your memory at every turn? That's no life at all."

I swallow hard. I pull out the feather and stick it back in again.

"I've known him for two years," she says. "In that time, I've seen nothing but a sweet, gentle man, trying to make up for sins he has yet to commit." She grips the aluminum can. "I'm not scared, Callie. I have full trust in him. He has complete control of his actions—not his future self, not some memory, but him. He either refuses to hear me or he's too scared to believe."

She bends her head over the can, watering the flowers with her tears. After a moment, she plucks out a yellow flower and hands it to me. "I heard about Logan. I'm sorry."

I take the flower and bring it to my nose. It smells sticky, like an overly sweet dessert. I can't imagine anything other than bees being attracted by the scent.

"How come he's going back?" she asks.

"He's needed to stock the backpacks," I say, trying to sound crisp. But my voice wilts like Laurel's wildflowers, and unlike the blooms, no amount of watering will perk it back up. "And well…he's not like the rest of us. No one was ever after him, so he doesn't belong here."

I choke over the words. A lot of things shouldn't have happened. Logan shouldn't have come here. I shouldn't have fallen for him. Doesn't mean you can take them back, no matter how hard you try.

"If you ever need to talk, let me know," she says. "We can be brokenhearted together."

I give her back the flower and, after a moment of hesitation, take the feather out of the can. "Sounds fun."

She squeezes my arm and heads into the log cabin. I continue through the square. Dinner time approaches, but I'm not ready to face the crowd yet.

I head to the clearing. Trailing my hand over the log, I dip my fingers into the grooves and skim them over the knots. I lay the feather inside the hollowed out space of the log. This is where it belongs, because this is the place where he told me he was leaving me forever.

But the trees have not absorbed that memory. When the leaves flutter, they do not crackle to the tune of severed hearts. They tell a story instead, of moist dirt and busy squirrels, of dry pine needles holding on stubbornly through the ice of winter.

The clearing's blocked on three sides by pine trees. I lie on the ground behind the log, my head aligned with the feather, turning the dead tree into a fourth wall. I miss Jessa. More than Marisa, more than my mom, I miss my little sister.

She would know what to say right now. That's what I need. Her cool hands on my hot cheeks. Her simple words, which hold more truth than a room full of future memories.

Ever since I've discovered my abilities as a Receiver, I've been opening my mind constantly to check for new memories. Looking for a way to help Jessa.

But this time, as I let the physical elements of my world melt away, I'm not trying to help my sister. I'm hoping she can comfort me.

Breathing deeply, I think of the blank spaces below a certain column. The gaping holes of a fish net. Angela's open heart as she weeps for a child that may never be born.

The rush is familiar now, and welcome. Then something fills me up as if it were coming home. Here it is. The memory. Open.

I am holding a racquet loosely around its rubber-grip handle. Black shiny walls reflect the sleek sports cap holding the hair off my face, and a large blue square is painted on the hardwood floor. Something knocks thunk, thunk, thunk against the wall.

I'm at school during the Fitness Core, standing on a

racquetball court.

The air is hot, as if it's soaked up the sweat of all the people who've ever played here. A ball ricochets off the reflective wall and whizzes past me.

"What are you doing?" Olivia Dresden's braids swish across her face as she spins on her foot. Her sports cap is on the hardwood floor, probably discarded as soon as she walked onto the court. "Hit the ball."

"We can't start the game," I say. Across from us, the two corners of the square are empty. "The July Fifteen girls aren't here."

"Oh, the twins aren't coming to school today," Olivia says smugly. "Or ever again."

The ball rolls off the wall and bumps into my foot. I pick it up. "Why not?"

"My mommy says all twins are the property of FuMA now. She says their brains have the same ge…ge…" She wrinkles her nose, trying to think of the right word. "Genetic makeup. So even though they're two people, it's like they're one person."

I frown, bouncing the ball with my racquet. "You're lying."

"Am not." Olivia puts her hands on her hips. "That's how the scientists figure out future memory. By looking at twin brains. You're just mad your mommy isn't head of FuMA, and you don't know anything. One day, everyone will listen to what I say, and you'll still be nothing." She snatches my ball out of the air. "I don't even know why I'm talking to you."

She sweeps up her sports cap and stalks off the square. The glass door of the court slams so loudly my ears rattle.

open my eyes. I'm back at the clearing, and the sun has ducked below the horizon. An insect crawls up my arm, and my entire back feels damp from the moisture in the ground.

My stomach ties into a knot. First universal screening and now twins. When will this madness end?

"There you are!" Like an apparition, Logan appears and steps over the log. "I've been looking for you everywhere."

I grab his hands and he pulls me off the ground. He's leaving in a few short hours, but I can't think about that. I'll have the rest of my life to mourn his absence. So I do something I've never done before. I forget about our past. I forget about our future. I focus fully and entirely on us, right now.

I sit on the log facing him and tell him about the memory I received.

As I talk, the Chairwoman's words echo in my mind. *The First Incident is rapidly approaching. Now you see why we have to do it. Now you see why we have to do it. Now you see why we have to do it.*

I suck in a breath. "If the scientists don't currently know how to send memories, the First Incident must be the first time a memory is sent to the past. And if it's rapidly approaching, then TechRA needs to figure out how to send a memory by that date. Because if they don't…if they don't…"

"Future memory as a technology may disappear from us altogether."

I frown. "Is that even possible? So many of us have already received our future memories. Where did all those memories come from?"

"Of course it's possible," he says. "It's the same reason you can change a future memory that's already been sent, even though FuMA wants everyone to think you can't. Time isn't a closed loop. A parallel world is created the moment a memory is sent to the past—a new world where anything can happen."

I jump to my feet, trying to wrap my mind around his words. If Logan's right, then there is no paradox. And if I'm right, then the very existence of future memory is at stake. That would explain everything. Why TechRA is so desperate. Why they're arresting psychics left and right.

Because their research isn't a bunch of experiments for the sake of science. This research might affect our entire way of life.

He stands and walks to me. "You're shaking."

"What have we've gotten ourselves into?" I whisper.

He takes my face in his hands. "You're safe here, Callie. Jessa's safe. That's what's important."

"For now," I say despairingly. "Until her hair grows down to her shoulders. Until they get around to testing her during the universal screening."

"Yes, but now is all we have. Now is what's important."

"I wish now could last forever," I mumble into his shirt.

He tilts my chin up and kisses me. And I wish that could last forever, too.

33

"I guess this is it," Logan says. After we left the clearing, we went back to the village square and had one last dinner. One last evening, with one last crowd. And now Harmony sleeps, but he asked me to meet him for one last walk. One last time.

Through the jagged shadows of the leaves, the moon glows against the night sky. It's as though a hole has been split in the cosmos and a splash of light from another place trickles into our world.

"Yeah," I say, looking at the moon. If only we could be up there, in the light, instead of inches deep in mud and muck, everything might be okay.

I knew this moment would be hard. But I don't think Mikey expected it. As soon as the bones were cleared off the table, he stood, flinched, and walked away. But not before I saw the sheen of moisture in his eyes. "How's Mikey doing?"

"He's going with me as far as the cliffs so he can make

sure I get back to civilization safely." Logan rubs a hand over his face. "He was crying when I got back to the hut." He shakes his head, as if he can't believe what he's saying. "I've never seen him cry before. Not even when TechRA took him away."

"He's upset. He doesn't want to see you go."

"I thought he wanted me to leave."

"He wants what's best for you and his people." I can't believe I'm defending Mikey, when I want to fall to my knees and curse him to Limbo and back. But now that we're about to lose the boy most important to us both, I finally understand him. "I promise you, if it were only about him, Mikey would never let you go. He loves you."

I love you, too, I want to say. I want to say a million things, share with him a million thoughts, confide in him a million stories. Because Logan's right. This is it. I'll never have this chance again.

But so many words swell in my heart that they get jammed in my throat. So what comes out is: nothing.

We continue to walk around and around the village, ducking under tree branches, hopping over roots. In the daytime, the woods are tricky to navigate. At night, they're downright treacherous. But we don't stop. We keep on as if our forward motion can make time stand still. As if by stopping, resting, acknowledging a place, we will also have to acknowledge real life.

Logan is leaving tomorrow. As soon as the sun rises, he'll pack his rations and go, retracing our steps back to civilization.

And then I'll never see him again.

"Callie." Logan turns to me. His head blocks the moon,

so even the glimmer of his cheekbone disappears into the night. "I don't want to see you tomorrow."

"Okay." We've stopped moving, so this is it. Reality. I should take off my plant bracelet. I should give it back to him. But I don't. Even if I have to lose him, I want to hold onto this memory.

"I mean, I don't want to say good-bye in front of everybody. I want to say good-bye here, when it's just the two of us. I want to look back on this moment and remember how it feels to be the only two people in the world."

That's what I want, too. Tomorrow I will start my new life, a life without him. Tomorrow I will try to forget my love. Tomorrow I will need to be strong. I don't want to see him tomorrow, either.

Cold fingertips brush against my arms. I step blindly in his direction and slip on a loose rock. He catches me, like he always does. Like he never will again. My lips seek his in the darkness, brushing against his jaw. The stubble scratches me. I turn, so I can feel more of the abrasion against my cheek, and his mouth captures mine.

The kiss tastes like dewdrops and a baby's tears and the mist in a foggy night. It feels like dandelion fluff and tree sap and the sting of a bee.

It lasts an eternity, but it's over too soon. I regret the kiss, for I will never, ever forget it.

"I will always remember you, Callie."

Good-bye, Logan. Good-bye.

When I get back to the hut, Angela's feeding a fire in the indoor pit. I join her on the ground and warm my hands at the flame.

"You're still awake?" I ask.

"I was waiting for you." She pokes the fire with a long stick. "How are you?"

"I'm alive. And breathing."

"Sometimes that's about all we can ask."

Sweat forms on my neck, even though cool air presses against my back. The fire crackles and hisses, and threads of gray dance around us before floating to the roof and escaping through the hole. I wish I could disappear right along with the smoke.

"You must've heard." Angela's voice pulls me from my thoughts. "Mikey asked me to marry him."

I look up. "That's wonderful."

"I said no."

Scooting over, I pick up her hand. It hangs limply against my fingers, as if the bones inside have turned to liquid. "You love each other. Why won't you marry him?"

"You know why." She squeezes her eyes tight, but tears seep out the corners anyway. "He yearns for children, and that's something I can never give him."

I let go of her hand and stand up, stepping away from the fire. I'm suddenly too warm, and I whip off my long-sleeved shirt, revealing the simple white tank underneath. "He's here, Angela. Right here, right in front of you. It's not like he's going back to civilization."

I rub my chest through the thin cotton material. *Stop it.* Just because my heart's broken doesn't mean I have to fling the shards at Angela.

Crouching down, I rest my cheek on my knee. "You've already changed the course of your future by coming here. Your memory might not come true. You could be so happy, Angela. Your little girl could grow up here, completely safe. You could see her midnight eyes widen at a flapping fish. You could braid wildflowers into her spider-soft hair."

She shakes her head, terror gripping every line of her face. "I won't take that risk. Not for me. Or my baby." Her words are resolute. Final.

I want to argue with her, but I can't.

I'd like to live in a world where love conquers all. But maybe we gave up that privilege when the Technology Boom changed our society. Maybe when we built a world based on images of the future, we bargained away our dreams. We traded in the passion of our souls, the passion that burns on hope and desire and possibility. And all we got in return was security. Goals already achieved. A life already lived. And in my case and Zed's and Angela's, a nightmare come to life.

Maybe we would've been better off if those memories had never been sent. Maybe we could learn to breathe again if we could only forget tomorrow.

The pine needles crunch as Angela tosses and turns. Her breath comes erratically. Sometimes, she gulps air as if there's a shortage of oxygen. Other times, I don't hear her breathe at all, and I'm tempted to cross the room and check her pulse. Finally, she settles, but sleep continues to elude me.

I reach for Jessa. If I see her, it will be like a security blanket to chase away the monsters. A good night kiss to ensure sweet dreams. I'll see her, and then I'll be able to sleep.

I open my mind, and it's easier than ever. I don't even get through one image when the rush of something fills me. I reach for my sister. I reach for the memory.

I am being dragged. Metal bites into my wrist, and the heels of my shoes dig into the ground. A high-pitched scream splits open the air. It takes me a second to understand it's coming from me.

Someone yanks me around and I fall, pitching into a coarse navy uniform. An hourglass insignia is etched onto the pocket. I'm being arrested by FuMA.

I wrench my head around. My mother stands in the doorway of our house, her hand reaching for me and grasping air. An open school bag lies in the hallway, and a holographic projection of my family shines from the desk screen . My mother. Jessa. Callie.

That's when I realize what I'm screaming.

"Callie! They've got me. Come save me. Please, Callie. I need you. I need you. I neeeeeeed yoooooooou!"

I open my eyes. My cheek rubs against the buckskin, and my throat feels raw, like I've been screaming loudly.

Except I haven't been yelling. I'm back in Angela's hut, and that was Jessa screaming.

I was wrong. Oh dear Fate, I was so wrong. I thought there was time. I thought Jessa wouldn't be arrested until her hair reached her shoulders. But FuMA has her. I'm too late.

She needs me. *My little sister needs me.* Picking up the buckskin and wrapping it around my shoulders, I step outside the hut. Millions of stars sparkle in the sky, and I think of that night in the woods, right after we left civilization, when I was convinced Jessa and I were connected through the stars.

Well, we do have a connection. Just not the one I envisioned.

I hear you, Jessa. I fling the thought out to the night. *I hear you, and you don't have to worry. I'm going to help you.*

How? All of a sudden, the stars seem to close in on me, trapping me in a cage of diamond-hard points. How will I help her? She's there and I'm here. We live in two different worlds.

It's better this way. I'm more dangerous to her than FuMA. They only want to study her. A future version of myself will kill her. Why tempt Fate by returning to Eden City?

The old arguments rise, but even as the words echo in my head, something feels different. No nausea wells up inside me. No crushing despair pushes down on my shoulders.

This is no way to live—cowering in Harmony, spooked by the future at every turn. Look at Angela. Look at Zed.

They're so paralyzed by a future that hasn't happened, they can't even allow love into their lives.

Fate can go to Limbo and back. I might tempt her by returning to civilization. But that doesn't mean I have to give in.

My lungs fill with the cold night air, and the stars snap back into place. I know who I am. Logan's showed me the girl I could be. It took coming here, away from everything I've ever known, to figure that out. I'm not a killer. That future Callie who plunged a needle into her sister's heart? That's not me. I don't know what her justification was, but no reason is good enough to do what she did.

This is my choice. My decision. I will not hurt my sister. And I'm not going to let anybody—not FuMA, not the future, not even Fate—tell me differently.

Gripping the buckskin around my shoulders, I walk into the night, across the village square toward Mikey's hut.

My sister needs me, and I know what I have to do. I'm going back to Eden City. I'm saving my sister, even if I have to conquer Fate in order to do it.

34

The cliff face rises in a vertical wall, pocked with a thousand crevices, ridges, and unsightly bumps. "Give me more rope!" Logan yells.

From the ground, I belay a few feet of rope, as he scrabbles up the wall like a crab. His foot slips, and a cloud of pebbles and dust cascades down the cliff.

My heart stops. An instant later he regains his balance and finds another foothold, and my heart starts beating again. I'm trying to be brave, I really am. But I didn't argue with Mikey until I lost my voice just so I could watch his brother plummet to his death.

That's why we have equipment, Logan explained. To stop a fall in midair. In theory, we will only fall twice the distance to the last "protection," which is what Logan called the metal wedges he jams into the rock as he climbs.

I let more rope out, ignoring the friction searing my palms. The sun's a full hand's length above the trees now, but I shiver when the wind blows against my damp clothes.

Early this morning, we rowed down the river in the boat, with the current instead of against it, traveling in a matter of hours the distance we covered in our two-day journey out. I've never felt anything like it—the wind rushing over my hair, the water from Logan's oars spraying my face. Best of all, we flew across the water as if we were gliding on air, as if Logan's vigorous rowing might catapult us straight into another realm.

I returned to earth long enough to pay attention to Logan's technique. If all goes accordingly, it will be me steering the boat in a of couple days, with Jessa as my passenger. And that, unfortunately, is the extent of my plan. Break into FuMA. Rescue Jessa. Row down the river. Here's hoping the rest of the details fall into place when the time comes.

Above me, Logan stretches, grabs, and leaps. He's three quarters of the way up the cliff face. Is it my imagination, or are his arms shaking?

I grip the rope and plant my feet. Beads of sweat break out on my forehead. This is exactly what Mikey was afraid of. This is why we argued for so long. If Mikey had come in my place, there would be no question whether he was strong enough or skilled enough to anchor his brother. But Logan claimed I could do it. He insisted that he trusted me.

I blink, and my throat closes up. How much do I owe him, when all is said and done? It's one thing to offer moral support. Another thing entirely to put his life on the line.

An insect buzzes around me, landing on my slick fore-head. I blow upwards, dislodging the fly without taking my eyes off Logan's diminishing form.

"You can do it," I chant under my breath. "You can do it. You can do it."

And then, a few minutes later he does. His feet claw up the rocks, kicking more dust into the air as his body disappears into the glare of sunlight. A short while later, he pokes his head over the edge and waves.

It's my turn.

My arms ache. My thighs burn. And I'm not even halfway there.

I find two steady footholds and hug the wall, gasping for breath. Sweat streams down my body. The air smells dry and dusty. It feels as if I'm inhaling tiny rock particles.

Somewhere above me, Logan's belaying the rope. Every inch he gives brings me closer to him. Every foot I climb also brings me closer to saying good-bye.

"Fine," Mikey had relented, fixing me with his stare. "You can take my place. But on two conditions."

I shot a quick glance at Logan. We'd been sitting on the woven mats for what seemed like hours, and tingles marched up and down my calves. "What?"

"First, if you find anyone in civilization who's changed her future—not partially or halfway, but someone who's managed to stop her entire future from happening—bring her back to Harmony. I want to prove to Angela it can be done. I'd like to convince her it's safe for us to at least adopt a child. Maybe even Ryder. He needs parents, and he and Angela already have a strong bond. I want her to feel like she has options."

I nodded. "Of course. And the second?"

Mikey looked from me to his brother. "I need both of you to promise me that once you get over the cliff, you'll go your separate ways. Logan has nothing to do with you or your mission once you get back to Eden City. Is that clear?"

I wanted to leap up and scream. No. We just rescinded our good-byes. You can't rip us apart again.

But our reunion was always temporary. Nothing's changed. Logan was never mine to hold.

"I promise," I said.

And then Logan, after a pointed look from his brother: "I promise."

It was the inverse of a marriage ceremony, with Mikey as the judge. Our vows to stay apart.

Pushing the memory away, I leap and grab the next handhold, bringing my face even with a metal wedge. Working it with one hand, I yank up, and the wedge slides out smoothly, even though it's virtually impossible to pull down. Hooking the protection on my harness, I climb toward the next one.

One limb at a time. Hand, foot, push, other foot, other hand. Rest. Repeat. It's excruciating work, but the closer I get to the ledge, the more my mind drifts to my last few days with Logan. The way he looked as he held out the venison for me to eat. The calluses on his palm as it brushed along my skin. The feel of his lips when he kissed me for the first time. I want to roll these details up in a memory and send them to myself, over and over again.

They say you can get better at anything with practice. I

don't think I'll ever be any good at leaving Logan.

I jam my fingers into a crevice, and a fingernail rips off. It's my fourth one today, and this one breaks a little too close to the skin, so that blood wells up along the tear. But it doesn't matter because I'm pulling my waist over the ledge, and it squeezes the breath out of me. Logan hooks his hands under my arms and pulls me up.

I'm back in Eden City.

"Well," I say. "I guess this is it."

The words taste bland in my mouth, as if they've been said before. And they have. Not on this patch of dirt that ends in midair. Not with a roaring river on one side and a thicket of woods on the other. But they've been said, between the two of us, a short while ago. Even the new scenery cannot convince me I want to relive that moment ever again.

"Let's not say good-bye." I gesture at the stretch of trees and rocks that slope away from us. "Let's turn our backs to each other and walk down the hill in opposite directions."

He adjusts the backpack on his shoulders. "Do you know where you're going?"

"Sure. Go down this path and I'll be in the woods behind the FuMA building." I lick my lips. "I'm not going in tonight. I need to rest and plan. And I'd like to see my mother."

"So you're going home?"

"Thinking about it."

He grimaces. "They might be watching your house. They've probably been staking it out ever since we broke out of detainment."

The wind skims along the earth, blowing leaves and twigs over the cliff. The sun has fallen behind the trees, and it feels like we're standing on the precipice between two worlds. A strong wind, or a single choice, can blow us to either side.

I take a step down the hill. I choose not to leave my future to a frivolous breeze. "Okay. I won't go home. But don't worry about me. I'll find some place to spend the night."

"At least let me walk down with you," he says.

It would be so easy. I could agree, and once we're down the slope, I could beg him to come with me. *Just a little while longer*, I would say. *Mikey would never have to know. I need you.*

But I will not make this harder than it already is.

I put my hand on Logan's cheek. "You've done so much for me." My fingers begin to tremble. I pull my hand down and curl it into a fist. "Let me do something for you."

Without another glance, I turn and walk away. I hear his footsteps behind me, and I start running. The slope magnifies my speed, and I'm falling, skidding, sliding down the hill.

Branches crisscross over my head like a jumble of firewood. It's getting darker by the minute, and the dense cover of trees blocks what little light there is. Winding my arm around a tree trunk, I come to a stop, panting. Is Logan still following me? I look up the hill. Nothing but shadows and leaves rattling in an invisible breeze.

My fingers tighten on the bark. Don't be ridiculous. There is nothing creepy about the woods. They've been my home for days and nothing bigger than a squirrel has ever popped out to scare me.

Taking a deep breath, I force myself to start moving again. I spot a fallen branch and yank it out of the bushes. See, this is just like the woods around Harmony. I poke the stick into the ground and hoist myself over a rock. The scent of pine surrounds me, and small creatures scurry in the nearby bushes. Nothing to worry about.

I hop over a log, and two things happen at once.

My foot gets caught in a rock, pitching me onto the ground, and a red and black dog bounds toward me, barking at the top of his lungs.

His ears droop, and the skin around his face sags like the loose skin of an extremely old person.

My heart jumps into my throat. It's a bloodhound, the same kind of dog that tracked me through the forest on my seventeenth birthday. The kind that can follow a scent that's days, maybe even weeks, old.

I'm right back where I started. FuMA's got me once again.

35

The bloodhound pants six inches away. Drops of saliva glisten on his tongue and his stale, damp breath wafts around me.

My heart drums so fast the beats almost overlap. Do dogs eat people? And if not, will he take a bite out of me anyway?

I push down against rock and begin to crab-walk away from the bloodhound. My ankle screams, but the dog doesn't care. Broken bones are easier to gnaw.

The bloodhound advances, and I choke back a sob. This is it. All of my running, and I've come full circle to the morning of my seventeenth birthday. I'm going back to Limbo.

All of a sudden, an object floats through the air, hovering in the space between the bloodhound and me. What on earth? It's a stick, a broken branch, really, with dead leaves still clinging to the wood.

The stick twitches back and forth in front of the

bloodhound's nose. When it has the dog's attention, the stick shoots through the air away from me, and the hound scampers after it.

I blink. Since when do sticks have minds of their own?

"Are you okay?" Gentle hands skim over my body, checking for injuries.

I turn, and every muscle sags in relief. "Logan! You came back."

"I never left." His fingers land on my ankle, and I suck in a hiss of pain.

"Was that you with the stick?" I ask between gritted teeth. It's the first display of his telekinesis I've seen.

"Yeah. We're lucky he likes to play fetch," he says. "Can you stand? We've got to get out of here."

I grip his arm and pull myself up, but my ankle throbs the moment I put weight on it. "I think I've sprained it."

Twigs snap and the leaves rustle. I whip my head around just in time to see the bloodhound crash through the brush again. But this time, he's got a human in tow.

He doesn't look like a ComA official. Instead of a uniform, the man wears water-resistant pants and a black mesh shirt. White whiskers sprout beneath heavy jowls, and his nose is shiny red, as if he's rubbed it raw with a tissue.

But he's carrying a Taser. It has a short barrel and metal plating. And it's pointed right at us.

The man looks us over, taking in our scratched-up arms and my injured ankle.

The Taser swings. I jump, landing right on the sprain. My vision wavers with the pain, but I don't dare cry out in case the sound makes his trigger finger jerk.

"You kids better come with me." He lowers the Taser, but his feet are set shoulder-width apart. He's not moving until we do.

"Um." Logan winds his arm around my back, supporting me. "She can't really walk."

"Then carry her."

Logan and I confer with our eyes. I don't want to go with this man, but the Taser limits our options. Logan bends down, cradling an arm beneath my knees and another under my shoulders. A moment later, I'm in the air.

The bloodhound takes off, barking. The man gestures for Logan to follow the dog, and then I'm bouncing through the woods.

"You comfortable?" Logan whispers. His neck pulses next to my cheek, and he twists his body left and then right to shield me from the worst of the brambles.

"Hanging in there," I say.

He smiles a little at my joke, and we fall silent as we move through the forest, the questions stirring the air between us. Who is this guy? And where is he taking us?

Presently, we come to a squat building next to a large plot of cleared land surrounded by a chain link fence.

"Inside," the man growls.

Logan lowers me to my feet and helps me hobble over the threshold. A utilitarian sofa with triangular cushions is covered with dog hair, while a pair of indoor shoes waits by the entry. An old-fasioned glider made of wood sits in the center of the room. The bloodhound leaps onto the chair, shaking it so violently it almost tips over.

"Have a seat," the man says as he changes into his

indoor shoes. "Let's have a look at that ankle."

My eyes widen. He's going to treat my injury…before tasing me? Or does this mean he plans to let us go?

I sit on the sofa. The man digs his fingers into a small jar of salve and smears it on my ankle. "This stuff is like magic. You'll be walking in no time." He peers at me and then blinks. "Betsy here didn't scare you, did she?"

The bloodhound barks, jumping off the glider and trotting over to her owner.

I cough. "Her name is Betsy? Did you know she's a dead ringer for a ComA hound?"

"She should be." The man screws the lid on the salve and gets to his feet. "I'm the one who breeds them."

Logan and I exchange a glance. "You work for ComA?" he asks.

"I'm not one of them, if that's what you're wondering," the man says. "My name's Potts, and I sell ComA my hounds. No more, no less. I don't snitch to them, and they don't do me any favors."

Betsy wanders over to a plant and begins nosing through the soil. Potts snaps his fingers and she dashes back to his side again.

"I've seen them patrolling around the city, every night for the last week or so. Looking for vagrants trying to get around without using their IDs. You wouldn't know anything about that, would you?"

"No, sir," Logan stutters. "My girlfriend and me, we were hiking in the woods, and we kinda got lost."

"Hmmm." Potts rubs his face. His hands leave behind a sticky residue in his whiskers. "Isn't it a school day?"

"We skipped," I say. "We're about to turn seventeen,

and we wanted one last day together before we get our memories."

Logan slides his hand around my back. My heart drops. I forgot about the tattoo on his wrist, right under his plant bracelet. One glimpse of the hourglass and Potts will know I'm lying. As casually as I can, I shift forward, shielding his wrist with my body.

"That's very interesting." Potts settles his large body onto the glider. "Because you see, I've been hearing rumors that some people might be disappearing off the grid. Running off to live in some community hidden in the woods. Don't know if it's true or not, but I've got to tell you, ComA's been awfully interested."

"That's just a tale," Logan blurts out. "Like that community in the mountains. I've heard talk about it for years, but it doesn't really exist."

Potts narrows his eyes. "Are you so sure about that, young man?"

"Well, yeah," Logan says. "Why would ComA allow a hidden community to exist all these years, without doing anything about it, if there was any truth to the rumors?"

"Maybe because this community was never ruled by the ComA government. Maybe these mountain people have been living together, in their way of life, even before the Boom. They want nothing to do with us and our technological ways, so maybe ComA sees no cause to get rid of them." Potts folds his hands over his belly.

For a moment, all I hear is the swish-swish-swish of the glider. And then Potts clears his throat. "On the other hand, I hear this wilderness community might be formed by people running away from TechRA. Psychics that are very interesting to them, particularly now. So I'd say the situation's a little different, wouldn't you?"

Logan and I exchange a look. Betsy's roaming around the room again, and the glider continues swishing. If Potts doesn't mean us any harm, maybe this is our cue to leave.

I clear my throat. "Thank you for your hospitality, sir, but we need to get going. Our parents will worry."

"Is that so?" Something flickers across Potts's face. He gets out of the chair, snapping his fingers for Betsy to follow. "Wait here a minute. I have something for you."

Whistling a cheerful tune, he leaves the room, the bloodhound bounding after him.

As soon as they're out of sight, I turn to Logan. "Did you hear that? They know about Harmony."

"They don't know. They suspect, but they don't know anything for sure."

"It's not such a big leap from suspecting to investigating. I know the hologram projection keeps out casual intruders. But how good is it if they make a targeted search?"

He chews the inside of his cheek. "I'll get a message to the Underground. They've got contingency plans for situations like this."

The slats of the wood floor creak, and we fall silent. A moment later, Potts returns to the room, holding a long stick with a small pillow tied to the end. "This is my walking stick, but it'll have to do."

"What is it?" I ask.

"Your crutch."

I blink at the unexpected kindness. Instead of my executioner, Potts has turned into an ally. "Thank you, sir."

Waving off my words, he sees us to the door. "You'd

best scoot along. The patrols may be back, and I wouldn't want them to mistake you for those vagrants." He pauses, and that something flickers again. "But if you ever need to find me again…you know where I live."

We move back into the dense cluster of trees, me hobbling and Logan ambling beside me. Potts's house disappears from sight, and the only bark closing in on us grows on the trees. Now that we're back in the woods, I assume we'll revert to the original plan. Any minute now, Logan and I will go our separate ways.

I tuck the padded part of the crutch more firmly under my arm. "He was nice."

"I'm guessing he's an Underground sympathizer," he says. "Not quite one of us, on account of his ties with ComA. But I bet he knows a lot more than he's letting on. Good thing we ran into him and not one of the patrols."

We totter along a few more yards. "How's that crutch treating you?" he asks.

"Not bad."

"It'll start jabbing you in a few minutes, and then you'll be cursing up a storm."

I swallow. As long as I live, I don't think I'll ever forget the dimples in his cheeks. Those grass-green eyes. "What you can't hear won't hurt you."

"Why wouldn't I hear? I'll be right next to you."

My hand slips on the crutch. "Logan, you promised your brother you would sever all contact with me as soon as we reached civilization. We're here now, and this—" I point the stick from me to him. "This counts as involvement."

"Keep hopping, Callie. We can fight while we walk."

I wobble forward. Already, the strain is making me short of breath. "I'm not trying to fight with you. I just don't want you to disappoint Mikey."

"I don't want that either, but there are a few things to consider. Number one, you've sprained your ankle. You can't take public transportation because you can't scan your ID. And my unit is a whole lot closer than yours. Mikey's going to have to live with the situation."

A tangle of exposed roots lies across my path. I grip Logan's arm to keep from falling. It's hard to argue when I so clearly need him.

"Callie…" He guides me over the roots. "You really think I'm going to leave you here, with a sprained ankle, knowing ComA's patrolling the city?"

Of course not. He's too honorable to desert me when I'm injured, no matter what he promised his brother. "No."

His eyes drill into me, and I shiver at the intensity reflected in them. "Then you'll have to put up with me for a few more hours."

Logan's unit is closer than mine, but to get there, it takes two hours of shuffling on my crutch and riding on his back. At least we can stick to the woods. His residential building is made of gray stone and shoots into the sky, but it's on the edge of the city and backs up to the forest.

We ignore the front entrance. Although it's been a week since I broke out of Limbo, I'm sure there's still an alert on my ID. So we head to the fire escape at the back of the building, and I hobble up five flights of stairs.

By the time we reach his balcony, sweat has soaked through my T-shirt and washed the dirt from my face. I'm not sure which look is preferable—caked mud or oily sweat—but Logan's not looking at me anyhow. He's staring at the back door to his unit. I'm sure he's not seeing the dusty gray stone that could use a good washing. He probably doesn't even notice the reflective patio furniture, which doubles as solar panels to convert every drop of sunshine into energy.

He sees what I wish *I* was seeing: home.

"You ready to go inside?" I ask.

He stirs and gestures at the warm glow spilling out of the open window. "Someone's in the eating room. Mom's usually in the leisure room by now, waiting for my dad to get back from work. She must have company."

I stiffen. "Does she usually have friends over?"

"No."

A light mist begins to fall, and the sun dips behind the horizon. We crouch behind the solar-paneled chairs, so that we are semi-sheltered from the rain. Logan's forehead is creased with lines, and we stay there for what seems like forever, looking at each other.

"Your mom will come out to cover the furniture," I finally say. "Then we can find out if it's safe to go in."

"Good thinking."

So we huddle and wait. The rain falls faster and harder. The darkness rolls in like a thundercloud, but Logan's mom still doesn't come out.

"She must be really involved with her conversation,"

he says. "It's probably someone from the Underground."

"What if it's not?"

"Who else would it be?"

"Maybe a ComA official is interrogating her, and he won't let her out of her seat to cover the chairs."

All of a sudden the window swings closed with a thud. My pulse shoots into double time. "Okay, that's it. Let's get out of here." I stand up and begin to squeeze behind the table.

He grabs my arm. "Wait a minute. This is my house. My mom's inside."

"Your mom's noticed the rain, Logan. And she doesn't care about her solar furniture. Something's wrong. We need to leave, now."

But it's too late. The back door opens and a thin beam of light jumps all over the balcony before landing on us. "Who's there?" a woman's voice asks.

I shake my head, but Logan squeezes my arm and steps around the table. "It's me, Mom. Who are you with?"

That's when I notice there are two shadows by the door. I squint, but before I can make out any details, the beam jerks away from us, and the first figure runs out to embrace Logan. The second figure bends down and picks up the flashlight. As the light swings upward, I glimpse a messy brown bun.

My breath catches. Could it be? But how? As I stand rooted to the spot, the beam hones in on my face. A woman cries out. Next thing I know, I am enveloped in arms that smell like vanilla and disinfectant and spring.

My mother.

36

The rain pelts us, but I don't care. I'm in my mother's arms again. A minute passes, or an hour, and I finally work up the strength to loosen my hold. "What are you doing here?"

"I could ask you the same question." The lines in my mother's face seem to have multiplied since I've been gone, and the bun in her hair droops from the weight of the rain. But she's still beautiful. So beautiful.

She loops her arm through mine and guides me toward the house. "I suspect your answer will be longer than mine, so I'll go first. I met Hester when your father and I first got married, but we've lost touch over the years. When FuMA informed me you had broken out of Limbo, I got in touch with the Underground and learned that Hester's son was responsible for your rescue."

We reach the doorway and escape from the rain. "Since they took Jessa, I've been hanging out here, hoping to hear some news through Hester's telepathy with Mikey.

The transmission's been spotty, but Hester was able to glean enough to know you were with them in Harmony."

A million questions bubble up. So they arrested Jessa? Did it happen like my vision? How long has my mother known about the Underground? Did she get the message I sent? What does she know about Harmony?

I open my mouth to ask, but Logan's mother cuts me off. "You poor children." Hester tucks her son's hand firmly in her own. "Let's get you cleaned up and fed. Everything makes more sense after a hot shower and full stomach."

"But—"

"In due time, Callie." Mom pushes the bangs off my forehead, like she's done a thousand times before. "We have all night to catch up. You're home now."

Ten minutes later, I'm assaulted by drops in every direction. An overhead shower sprinkles rain on my head. Vertical rows of nozzles squirt water on every inch of my body. A fountain even spurts from the floor, to give my feet personal attention. One button mixes soap with the water. Another adds a moisturizing scent of my choice. A third replaces the water with heated air to dry the droplets from my body.

I've never thought twice about the showers in civilization. But now they seem luxurious. Excessive even. I would give it all up for a bucket of hot water.

I put on clean socks, clean sweatpants, and a clean T-shirt. The steam from my shower fogs up the mirror, and I stare at the glass while my reflection slowly comes into focus. I look the same. Sure, my skin's darker. The flesh on my face hugs my bones a little more tightly, but the girl looking back at me is largely the same. How can that be, when so much has happened? When I feel so different inside?

Suddenly, I want to smash my hand against the mirror and watch the cracks ripple out from underneath my fist. I can't stand seeing the girl I used to be. So young. So clueless. Waiting for my future memory to tell me what to do, how to act, what to feel. I actually thought the memory would bring me my happily ever after. I couldn't have been more wrong.

I fling open the bathroom door. A rush of cool air envelops me, and I smell the sweet tang of tomato coming from the eating room. The two mothers, ordering up a late-night meal for their children. Nothing could be more innocent. But there are secrets here. Things my mother's not telling me. So it's time for answers.

I limp into the eating room, my stomach growling in response to the smells of garlic, tomato, and basil. Hester looks up from the Meal Assembler and points at the table. "Sit. Your food will be ready in thirty seconds."

My mother takes my arm, helping me to the table. As soon as I sit down, Hester sets a steaming plate of spaghetti squash in front of me. I can already taste the crisp strands of squash, smothered in rich, bubbling sauce. They may be manufactured, rather than handmade, but I'm tempted to scoop up the food with my fingers and cram it straight into my mouth.

Then I notice Logan, already at the table. And even though he has a clean set of silverware and a plate of food, he's sitting there patiently. Waiting for me.

"You look nice," he says.

His damp hair sticks up in spikes, and he's wearing flannel pajamas. All of a sudden I'm hungry for something else entirely.

Blushing, I sneak a glance at my mother. She's preparing mugs of peppermint tea, and if she notices the matching plant bracelets on our wrists, she doesn't mention them. "So do you," I say.

Hester swoops down on me with a set of silverware. "Eat. The food will get cold."

She doesn't have to ask twice. Logan and I dig in, and for the next few minutes, the only sounds are the clink of the forks and the crunch of the squash.

When we finish, my mother picks up my injured foot and settles it onto her lap. Potts's salve has worn off. Where my ankle used to be sits a goose egg the shade of an eggplant.

"What did you do?" she asks.

"Twisted it on a rock." I try to pull away. "It'll be fine, Mom. It's starting to feel better already."

She holds on to my foot. "I've been so helpless to do anything for you. At least let me wrap your ankle."

I nod. As she nurses the injury, Logan and I tell our mothers everything. From jumping off the glass and steel building, to the huts in Harmony, to Mikey's relationship with Angela. From my newfound psychic abilities to my plans to rescue Jessa.

As we talk, my mother seems to withdraw into herself. She smears a gel over my ankle and wraps it with a bandage with built-in ultrasound therapy. When there's nothing left to be done, she sits quietly, hands folded in front of her.

"Mom?" I ask, my ankle buzzing soothingly. "What did Jessa's hair look like, when they arrested her?"

She blinks, as if she's not sure why it matters. "She's been begging for extensions. All the other girls in her unit had them. Last week, I relented."

I exchange a look with Logan. Extensions! I hadn't thought of that. The teens in Eden City change their appearance almost daily, but I assumed it had yet to hit the T-minus eleven class. I assumed wrong.

"Now, can you answer a question for me?" my mother asks. "I just don't understand. Why were you even arrested in the first place?"

I look out the window. The raindrops splatter against the glass and chase each other down the pane. The bandage has numbed my ankle. Too bad the same can't be said for my heart.

I've been dreading this moment ever since I got my future memory. If I'm being honest, I might have even left civilization, in some small part, to avoid telling my mother what I did.

Hester stands and gestures for her son to do the same. "Let's give Callie and her mother some privacy. Your father will be back from work soon, and he'll want to speak with you."

Logan takes a step toward me, as if he wants to shield me from what's coming. But he can't help me. No one can. This is my mother, and what I'm about to confess is only the truth.

Hester prods her son. He looks at me one last time

and then follows his mother from the room.

We're alone now. There's spaghetti sauce on my shirt. A small insect buzzes around the lit-up walls, and the leaky faucet drips in the sink.

I take a deep breath. "I don't know how to say this. So I'm just going to tell you what I saw."

Staring at the floor, I recount every detail of my future memory—the shoe print on the ground, the trail of soil leading to a broken plant, the teddy bear with the red ribbon. And then, there's only one thing left. I look into my mother's face, knowing she will never see me the same way again. Knowing I'm about to tell her the one thing that can make her unconditional love conditional.

"I stab the needle into her heart, Mom. In my future memory, I kill Jessa."

Her eyes widen. In that moment she looks so much like the Jessa of my memory, an instant before she died, that I feel the needle as a physical pain stabbing my own heart.

"I'm sorry, Mom."

She doesn't say anything. She won't look at me. She stares at the air vent as if she's counting the particles of dust lining the edges.

I move closer, and the bandage slips on my ankle. "Look at me. Please."

She jerks, but when her eyes land on me, they're vacant. It's even worse than I imagined. I thought she would yell, throw things, cry, not look at me as if I didn't exist. As if I were already dead to her.

"Do you hate me?" I whisper.

This rouses her. "How can I hate you for something

you haven't done?"

"But what if the memory comes true?" I swallow hard. "What if I kill Jessa? Will you hate me then?"

My mother sighs. "I don't know, baby. If I'm being honest…I can't guess how I would feel in that situation. I'm sorry."

"That's okay." I stare at my reflection wavering in my tea. "If I kill her, I'll hate myself, too."

"Hey," she says. "It hasn't happened yet, so let's not worry about it, okay?"

"So you think I can change my future?"

"I know you can."

"How?" I ask. "How do you know?"

My mother picks up the mug and swirls the tea around. "I've seen it happen. I know someone in the Underground who managed to change her future."

Something snaps. Too many emotions whirl inside me. Too much guilt, too much remorse. In an instant, the heaviness turns to rage. I spring to my feet, ignoring the pain in my ankle. I snatch the mug from my mother's hands and fling it into the sink. This is my life. And she never bothered to fill me in about any of it. "How come you never told me about the Underground? Didn't you think I deserved to know?"

She blinks. "It was too dangerous."

"Dangerous! And it's not dangerous for me to walk around without a clue?" My hands are shaking now, rattling at my sides like bags of bones. "Mom, I never prepped Jessa on how to answer their test questions. I didn't even know you could. Apparently, the Underground's got whole libraries of prep materials. So you see? It's my fault she's locked up at FuMA."

"Oh, Callie. That's not what happened."

I lace my hands together, but they continue to vibrate. "I saw FuMA take her away kicking and screaming. Are you saying that didn't happen?"

"No. They picked her up a few days ago, just like you saw. But not because of some test." She rubs a hand across the back of her neck. "The reason your sister was arrested is because she's your father's daughter."

37

Time stands still. The insect stops flitting, the water pauses mid-drip from the faucet. My heart hangs in a vacuum between beats. And then I hear the vibration of the bandage around my ankle again.

"What did you say?" I whisper. "Did you say Jessa and I have the same father?"

My mother touches my face. "She looks just like you. I thought you'd guessed. I thought that's why you pestered me so much about your father coming home."

I push her hand away. No. I'm not letting her off that easy. "You lied to me. You told me Jessa had a different father, and I believed you."

She winces, as if I'm throwing pebbles at her instead of accusations. "I had to tell you something. You wouldn't stop asking questions. You wouldn't drop the subject. What was I supposed to do?"

"Tell me the truth!" I dig my fingernails into my palms. "Do you know how much I wanted my father? I thought if I was good enough, if I behaved perfectly and followed all the rules at school, he would come back to us. But he didn't." I open my palms. Little crescents decorate my skin like a henna tattoo. "Now you tell me he was here after all. Didn't he want to see me, at least once? Didn't he care how I turned out?"

"Oh, dear heart," my mother says. "Your father loved you so much. He would be so proud to see how you've grown up."

"So why didn't he come see me?"

"He couldn't." My mother lowers her hand as if to pick up her mug, but I've already thrown it into the sink. "You know your father was a scientist. In particular, he studied the displacement of physical bodies in space."

I make a face. I've always known my father's profession, and it's never bothered me. But that was before I was locked in Limbo. Before Bellows treated my brain like his own personal experiment.

"Callie, he was a lab rat himself," my mother says, as if she can hear what I'm thinking. "That's what I meant about FuMA taking Jessa. They're so desperate to find the Key they've started detaining the offspring of every person with known psychic ability."

Bellows's words about my father echo in my mind. *The information is classified. If your mother didn't tell you, I cannot divulge it.*

Nausea rocks my stomach. I thought the scientist was lying. I thought he was just trying to upset me.

"What was Dad's psychic ability?" My voice is low, like it's trying to hug the floor. "Could he send memories, like Jessa?"

"No. He could teleport his body from one place to another. He thought by studying himself, he could figure out how to move his body into a different time altogether."

"You mean time travel."

"Yes." My mother jostles my mug, and tea splashes onto the table. She pushes her fingers through the liquid. "When the first future memories arrived, the scientific community was beside itself. They felt it proved that time travel was possible. What are future memories, after all, but memories sent back in time? Your father became obsessed with the idea. He felt his psychic ability made him uniquely qualified to study this field. He was convinced he would pioneer a new frontier of science."

She takes a shuddering breath. "So he decided to send his body to another time. I begged him not to go. The scientific knowledge wasn't there. We couldn't ensure he would come back safely. But he said the price of knowledge is risk."

The pain around her mouth is so deep I shiver. This is Mom. She's not supposed to look so lost, so helpless. She's supposed to hold our family together. Except we're not a family anymore. We've been ripped apart, flung to different corners of the world. There's nothing left for her to hold.

"I'm sure you can guess what happened," she says. "He sent himself to a different time, and he never came back."

"But he must have come back, at least once. Because of Jessa."

My mother shakes her head. "No. I never saw him again after that day."

"But then how…?"

She sighs, intertwining her fingers together. I think she's going to brush me off again, like she has so many times before. But she doesn't. "You know how I always said I never got a future memory?"

I nod.

"Well, I lied. I did receive one, but it wasn't good. FuMA had no way of tracking the memories back then, so no one even knew I'd gotten one. I thought I had a shot at changing it. I distanced myself from friends, stopped associating with the Underground. All in hopes of altering my future."

My heart begins to pound. "Did it work?"

"Yes. In a fashion. That person I knew who changed her future? I was talking about me." The shadow of a smile crosses her face. "But I wasn't entirely successful. A version of my memory came true a few days ago."

I'm pretty sure I don't want to hear this. Whatever her memory is, I'm pretty sure it will devastate me, like all the other bad memories I've heard. But ignorance is no longer an option.

"What was it?" I whisper.

"I was standing in the doorway of our house, reaching out my hand, but grasping nothing, screaming at the top of my lungs with no sound coming out. I watched as FuMA came and took my babies away. My twin daughters. Seventeen years old." She cups my chin, tilting my face from side to side. "Both with this face."

The chill begins in my stomach and spreads outward to each of my organs. Lungs. Heart. Brain. "I don't understand."

"I thought I could circumvent the future," she says. "They took you away because somebody somewhere received a prophecy that the Key to unlocking future memory lies in a pair of twins." Her voice drops to a whisper. "So I tried to cheat Fate. I thought if I didn't have twins, FuMA couldn't take my babies away."

I can hardly breathe. "What did you do, Mom?"

"You and Jessa shared the same womb. I had her fertilized embryo removed and stored until I thought it was safe, six years ago. I thought enough time had passed." Her shoulders move, as helpless as a kite blowing in the wind. "I guess I was wrong."

38

I limp into Mikey's old room, where I'll be sleeping for the night. He's been gone five years, but a row of medals still hangs on the wall. The air has the strong chemical smell of furniture varnish, and his shelf overflows with old-school textbooks from before the Boom. Textbooks made out of actual paper, rather than the digitized kind.

Logan waits for me on the twin bed.

Twin. As in, two embryos in the same womb. As in, me and Jessa. My mind's still spinning. No wonder we look so much alike. No wonder we've always been so close.

I bite my lip to keep my emotions under control.

"Does my mom know you're in here?" I ask.

He grins. "She said I could have an hour with you, and then you needed your sleep. She also said I'd better keep my hands to myself, or she'd banish me to another dimension."

"She could probably do it, too."

"I know." He reaches out and touches my plant bracelet,

and for a moment, he's the only thing that matters. His hair has dried, but the little spikes remain. The cozy material of his pajamas invites me to snuggle into his arms and stay forever.

Except I can't. Tomorrow, I'll go to FuMA and rescue my sister. We'll go back to Harmony, and he'll stay here in civilization, continuing his old life.

The pressure builds behind my eyes. Blinking rapidly, I turn and study the awards decorating the walls. "These are science fair medals," I say, trying to keep the tremors out of my voice.

"Yeah. Mikey's always been consumed by the idea of time travel for physical bodies. You know, black holes, Gödel funnels, that kind of thing."

Just like my father. A wave of sadness hits me. Before it can overwhelm me, I take a textbook off the shelf and page through it. Little strips of paper flutter to the floor, and handwritten notes march across the margins. I read one of the notations and frown. Instead of a student's elementary thoughts, as I expected, the page contains complicated equations, theorems, and proofs.

"How old was your brother when he was arrested?"

"Same age we are now. Why?"

I hand him the open textbook. "I never learned any of this stuff in school. Did you?"

Logan squints at the equations. "I told you, he was kind of a science geek."

I pick up another textbook and flip through it. More notes in the same handwriting. More equations I don't understand. I look through another, and it's the same. And then another. Soon, the entire shelf of textbooks is scattered around my feet.

He grabs my hands. "What's going on? What are you doing?"

The rough skin of his palms rubs against my knuckles. "Did you ever think that Mikey wasn't meant to run? Maybe he was supposed to stay in civilization and become a great scientist. Maybe he would've gone on to discover the Key, and maybe without him, they'll never find an answer to future memory."

"I suppose it's possible." He continues to hold my hands. "But so are a million other scenarios. What difference does it make?"

I pull out of his grasp and collapse on the bed. "Because if that's not it, and there's nothing stopping the scientists from discovering the Key…" I crumple the comforter in my fists. "Then I think I know why my future self kills my sister."

Logan doesn't say anything for an entire minute. He sits on the bed and rests his elbows on his thighs. "Go on."

Taking a deep breath, I mimic his position, going through the logic in my head. I know I'm right. I have to be. It's the first scenario I've come up with that makes any sense.

"FuMA has started arresting sets of twins to study. And I found out Jessa and I were supposed to be twins."

I tell Logan about my mom's memory and how she removed my sister's embryo and implanted it again six years ago. "And then there's my future memory. I know I kill my sister, but I don't know why." I shake my head. "I've been going over this again and again. Whatever the reason is, it's got to be big. I know myself, and I don't care which future version of me is out there, I'm not going to kill my sister because I'm upset or to spare her a little pain. It's got to be bigger than that." My sweatpants are fraying at the cuffs, and I grab one of the longer threads and pull. "It's got to be something that affects all of humanity."

I take a deep breath. "So what's the one thing our world's built around? What is FuMA so anxious to discover they've been disregarding civil liberties left and right?"

"Future memory," he says.

"Exactly." I wipe my palms across my thighs. "I think Jessa's the Key the scientists have been searching for. She has such a unique ability. She can send whole memories into my mind, not just telepathic messages like you and Mikey. It's not such a stretch to think she's the one."

"Oh, wow." He flops down on the bed and looks up at the ceiling, where the teenage Mikey had rigged up a light show of the galaxy. "So you think you kill Jessa to prevent future memory from being discovered? Why would you do that?"

"Something bad must happen in the future." I lie down next to him. "Future memory must somehow be responsible for something so devastating, a future me decided she'd rather kill Jessa than live in that world."

He turns his head, and our eyes meet, six inches apart. I hadn't planned on telling him this next part, but no matter what happens tomorrow, I want him to know I tried my best to do the right thing.

"Logan, I'm going to rescue my sister tomorrow. But before I do, I'm going to look for some answers. I need to find out what happens in the future. I'll never find any peace otherwise."

"How are you going to do that?"

"I'm not sure," I admit. "But Chairwoman Dresden said the information came from a precognitive. Not like Jessa's ability to see a couple of minutes into the future. But a real precog who can see years, if not decades from now. I have to assume the precog's one of their subjects in the lab. I'll start there and figure it out."

He lifts his hand to trace the bones in my face. My eyebrows, cheekbones, jaw. "Let's say you do find your answer. What if it makes you change your mind? What if you decide to kill her after all?"

I cover his hand with mine. "You once told me knowing my future doesn't take away my free will. I guess I'll have to trust myself."

He sits up abruptly. My cheek burns from the absence of his touch. This is it. The moment he wishes me best of luck. Whichever future I choose, it has nothing to do with him anymore.

But instead of standing and putting more distance between us, he stares at his feet in the dim light.

I bite my lip. I'm not going to cry. I'll accept his well wishes and thank him. He's the most decent boy I've ever known. The most decent boy I will ever know.

"I want to help you tomorrow," he finally says.

I shake my head. "Logan, don't—"

"If you can take on FuMA, if you're willing to go against your very destiny, then surely I can go against my brother's wishes."

"It's not about what you can do. It's about what you want."

He picks up my hand and runs his thumb along my

palm. "I never told you why I came after you. After we said good-bye in the woods, after you tore through the trees like something was chasing you."

That's right. He and the floating stick had miraculously shown up, just when I thought Betsy was about to take a bite out of me. "Why?" I whisper.

"Sometime in the future, in this world or a different one, my future self was wise enough to send me a message. He was telling me, this is what's important. Go after it. And for a while, I ignored him. I let guilt cloud my decisions. I submerged what I wanted under other people's desires." He presses his lips over my knuckles. We stay like that for a moment, his mouth warm on my skin. "But I'm not going to do that anymore. I'm not leaving you, Callie."

"What about the backpacks?" I ask, hardly daring to breathe.

"We'll figure it out. If I have to, I'll make the trip to the meeting point every few days to leave messages for the Underground. I'll return to Harmony, give you a kiss, and go right back again, if that's what it takes." His eyes are intent on mine, and I couldn't look away, even if I tried. "That's how important you are. It took you walking away to fully understand what my future self was trying to say. I love you, Callie. I think I was always meant to love you. My future memory hasn't come true yet, and I want it to. I want you by my side for the rest of my life."

I fly into his arms. "Oh, Logan. I love you, too. So much."

I should argue with him. I should try to convince him to stay. But if there's anything I've learned in the past couple days, it's that we can't live our lives in fear of the future. We have to make the right decision, for today, and trust that tomorrow will work itself out.

He kisses me, and it's everything I've ever needed. Gloves for my fingers when winter roars. Dried fruit in a tin when starvation creeps. Hope in a world that's fallen apart. It's a kiss from Logan. My Logan.

I didn't realize until now just how much I've been holding back. Knowing that Logan and I were destined to be apart, I had put up a wall. In that moment, with that kiss, Logan breaks through. Down crashes the glass and steel. This kiss feels unlike any before it, because, for the first time, I'm able to truly give myself to him. There are no future memories or backpacks keeping us apart. I feel Logan's love like I've never allowed myself to feel it. And when he pulls away from the kiss, my body cries for more. A lifetime's worth. No matter how often he kisses me, I'll never stop wanting. Never stop needing. Never stop loving.

Later, when my body settles onto solid ground, I cuddle into his chest and listen to his heart. I try to match our heartbeats, but mine dances all over the place, while his marches steady and strong.

"I'm going with you tomorrow." He traces his fingers across my face, as if daring me to disagree. "If you can fight the future, then I can let go of the past."

My heart leaps. I hug him tightly, and the buttons on his pajamas jab me in the chest. I'm still terrified of tomorrow, but with Logan by my side, what could possibly go wrong?

39

"Wake up, Callie. You're going to be late."

I groan and roll over. I'm about to go back to sleep, and then I remember.

Flinging the pillow off my face, I sit up and squint at my mother. Sunshine floods into the room through the open blinds, and for a moment I can't see anything but the blur of a figure. Then my eyes adjust and I see hair slicked back in a neat bun and a white button-down tucked into navy slacks. My mother holds my silver jumpsuit in one hand and a long auburn wig in the other.

"I forgot for a moment," I say. "I thought you were waking me up for school."

"I wish I were." Mom plops the wig on my head, tugging it this way and that. "Good. I knew it would fit perfectly."

I grab a fistful of the wig. It's slick, like extremely fine strands of plastic instead of hair, and a few shades darker than my own. "Where did you get this?"

She sits on my bed and motions for me to turn around. Once I do, she braids the wig with quick, sure movements. "When your father sent himself back in time, he took off his clothes and shaved all the hair from his body. The scientists thought it would be easier to push a body through spacetime if it left the non-essentials behind."

She winds an elastic band around the end of my braid, and I turn back around. In the glare of the sun, my mother looks old. Her skin has always been tissue-paper soft, but now I see a million tiny creases in the lines around her mouth.

"Your father used to tell me it didn't matter where his body was in spacetime. He and I would always be together because we were the same person." Mom picks up a makeup kit and gets to work on my face.

"When he didn't come back, I shaved my own head," she says. "It made me feel closer to him. I wore this wig around for months, and you never even noticed."

"Oh, Mom." I push her hands aside and wrap my arms around her. "Come with me and Jessa, back to Harmony. There's room in the boat for all of us, and then we can be together again."

For a moment, she hugs me back, so tightly there's no room for any air inside my lungs. And then she sighs, and the breath whistles along my neck. "I can't, baby."

"Why not? There are whole families living together in Harmony. We can make a new start, for all of us."

My mother pulls back and cups my face in her hands. "You've always been such a good sister to Jessa. I could always count on you to take care of her. I know you'll continue to do that."

"No." I shake my head. "Don't say that. We need you, Mom. I don't know what I'm doing. I need you."

"I'm sorry, Callie. I can't leave Eden City." The words are halting and slow, dragged from her mouth like an electro-cuffed prisoner. It's as though she's fighting against something inside her, and she can't be sure which side will prevail. She picks up a little brush and begins to blacken my eyebrows, her hands shaking. "I'm acting like an anchor for your father. He needs to focus on a particular person, in a particular location, if he is to find his way back to this time. If I leave Eden City, he'll be lost in spacetime forever."

"But he may already be lost," I whisper.

"Yes. He probably is." She pauses again, as though struggling with a demon inside her. A demon I can't see.

And then she drops the makeup and grabs both my hands. "Your father's an excuse. I love you and Jessa more than gravity itself. I would rip spacetime apart to stay with you both. You know that." Her eyes pierce me with the intensity of a laser. "But she said if I loved you, I had to let you go. She said this was the best way to protect you."

"Who said that, Mom? Why?"

"I can't explain, but this is the way it has to be. Nothing you say or do will change my mind." Her voice vibrates like it's on a string, like it might break if I pluck at it one more time. "Someday, in the future, you'll understand. But I can't answer your questions right now, so please, don't ask them. Please, trust me, just this once."

I want to scream, NO! Tell me now.

But I've put her through so much heartache these past few weeks. Whatever happens today, there will be more pain in the days ahead. I can see it in the tremor of my mother's fingers, in the pale skin that's become even more translucent with worry. She's made her decision, and now she'll have to live with it.

If I can make this moment a little more bearable for her, then I'll do it. I'll drop my questions. And so I nod, and that simple gesture seems to unlock a chain around her heart. Her spine straightens, and she even manages a small smile.

We're silent as she shades my cheekbones and high-lights my forehead, changing the contours of my face.

"There," she says a few minutes later. "If you weren't my daughter, I would never recognize you." She packs away the makeup tools. "I have to go. The Russells have contacted some of their friends from the Underground, who are going to help you. They'll give you the details, okay?"

I nod again. It's all I seem capable of at the moment.

My mother checks her watch. "I'll meet you in the sanitation room in about two hours. We won't have much time to talk then." She places her hands on my shoulders and kisses the air by both my cheeks. "Dear heart?"

I clear my throat, looking for my voice. "Yes, Mom?"

Her fingers tighten on my shoulders. "I trust you to do the right thing today."

My cheek presses against hard, cold metal, and fifty pounds of linens flatten me against the bottom of the cart. Logan is next to me somewhere in the darkness.

I think that's his stomach my feet are poking, and that might be his arm encircling my knees.

We rode in on a delivery van, packed inside an oversize cube of new linens. The cube was dumped on a conveyor belt. From there, it was untied and transferred to a laundry cart by a bot. The bot is now pushing the cart toward the building's sanitation room, where the sheets will be laundered before being put on the beds of the lab subjects.

Supposedly, there's plenty of oxygen within the folds of these sheets. I breathe through my nose. Bad idea. The chemical stench of freshly manufactured cloth makes the breakfast rise in my throat.

Switching to shallow, open-mouthed breaths, I try to keep a mental map of our path. But the cart constantly jerks and halts. I lose track of the turns and just lie there, feeling every bump of the cart against my bones.

Finally we stop, and I hear my mom's voice. "Quick. You can come out now."

Logan and I claw our way to the surface and climb out a moment before the cart is lifted by mechanical arms. Its contents are dumped onto another conveyor belt, which leads into the sanitation machine. The linens will come out the other end washed, dried, and neatly folded.

My mother presses a few buttons on a keyball, and the bot spins and leaves the room. I hear the hiss of boiling hot jets, and the lit-up walls flicker. The sanitation machine takes up an entire wall of the room, and a row of empty carts lines another.

"Your Underground contact will meet you here," my mother says. "I can't stay, but you can hide in one of those empty carts until he arrives."

She touches up my makeup and then hands me the kit. "This makeup would last through a war as long as you don't forget to freshen it every few hours." She straightens my wig, her fingers lingering briefly on the fake strands of hair. "Remember what I said."

"Always." I reach up and give her one last hug.

She turns to Logan. "Be careful. Take care of my daughter."

She looks back at me, a gaze that sears itself into my memory forever, and then she is gone. It all happens so fast, I almost don't have time to feel the pressure building in my chest.

Logan and I climb into one of the empty carts, settling our spines against the metal frame.

"Were you able to get in touch with the Underground?" I ask. "To tell them what we learned from Potts?"

"Yeah. My mom called her contact on the board last night." He takes my hand, tracing the lifeline along my palm. "As I suspected, they were already aware of the situation. They sent a messenger to Harmony to tell Mikey."

"What are they going to do?"

"Move," he says. "They'll wait for you and Jessa to get back, and then they'll pick up camp and leave. Instead of finding another location, they'll roam around for a while, until we can be sure ComA's no longer looking."

Just as he finishes talking, the door slams shut. My heart pounds against my chest, but the whirling of the sanitation machine drowns it out. Logan puts a finger to his lips and motions upward, to indicate we should take a look.

Rising to my knees, I peek over the edge. A uniformed

guard stands near the entrance, scanning the room. I can't see his face, but his hair is the prettiest color I've ever seen. Deep russet red threaded with bits of gold. Without thinking, I stand straight up.

He whips his head around, and I'm looking into the startled face of William, the guard who lied for me.

"October Twenty-Eight." William staggers backward, his eyes wide. "What are you doing back here?"

I'm surprised he recognized me with the heavy makeup, but my face has probably been haunting his dreams at night. The girl who almost made him lose his job.

"So this is why you helped me," I say, making the connection for the first time. "Because you're part of the Underground."

He jerks his head up and down.

Logan climbs out of the cart and helps me out. "You know each other?"

"William administered my memory. When he saw what it was, he gave me the chance to escape." I turn to the guard. "This is Logan. He broke me out of detainment."

"I was glad to hear you'd gotten away," William says. "I had no idea they were going to try to dig out your true memory. I swear, if I had known, I would've warned you."

"How'd you find out?" I ask.

"My girlfriend, MK." His face reddens. "I don't like to talk to her about FuMA business, for obvious reasons. But she knew I had administered your memory, so she told me what happened."

I suddenly remember something he told me when we first met. His girlfriend will be the leader of FuMA in thirty years. That's how he got his job. MK isn't just Chairwoman Dresden's assistant. She's being groomed for the top position.

William's walking a dangerous line here, between his girlfriend and the Underground. Between his love and his beliefs. Can I trust him? Suddenly, I'm not sure. I suspect he knows more, understands more than he's letting on.

But I don't have much of a choice. The Underground has faith in him, and he's our only contact. It will have to be good enough.

"Are you going to help us?" I ask William.

He tilts his head, studying me. "You're not here to kill your sister, are you?"

"No! I'm here to rescue her."

He chews his lip, as if wondering whether to believe me. Clearly the suspicion goes both ways. "Where do you want to go?" he asks.

"I'm looking for a subject in the labs. A precognitive. Can you get us to a computer where we can access the records?"

"I can do that," he says. "Let's go."

We follow William down a busy hallway. I try not to fidget, but my hands keep returning to my wig. Touching, smoothing, pulling the braid onto my shoulder. *I'm a schoolgirl. Minding my own business. Following a FuMA guard for an approved purpose.* I say these words over and over to myself, but they do nothing to slow the jackhammer of my heart.

William leads us into an area filled with rows of cubicles. "This is the administrative area."

I peer at the room closest to me. Sheets of clear plastic serve as walls, and stuffed inside each box is a wrap-around desk, a bookcase, and a filing cabinet. Potted plants and flowers cover every available surface.

"Seems a little cramped," I say

"You get used to it," William says. "The plastic dividers keep outside noise to a minimum. And FuMA allows us to bring as many plants as we want."

We walk down several aisles. The plastic dividers begin to change, becoming more opaque as we move deeper into the area, until they turn solid white.

"These offices belong to the more senior administrators," William says. "The information they handle is more sensitive; hence, the actual walls."

We reach an office in a remote hallway, opposite a set of double doors, and William goes inside. A curly-haired woman sits at her desk, surrounded by plants. At the guard's appearance, the woman gets up without a word and leaves the room.

"Andrea's a sympathizer, but she doesn't want to be involved in any way. We have fifteen minutes before she comes back." He stands before her desk screen, his hands moving busily over the keyball. "Okay. We're in. What do you need?"

I want to find the precognitive, but I can't forget my first priority. I lick my lips and glance at Logan. He squeezes my shoulder reassuringly.

"Can you look up my sister?" I ask. "Jessa Stone."

William types in her name, and a few seconds later, a 3-D projection of her file pops into the air.

Name: Jessa Stone

Room No.: 522

Preliminary ability: precognition

Primary ability: telepathy

She's here. Somewhere in this building, within my reach. Seeing the words on the screen knocks the breath out of me, as if Jessa herself has launched into my arms for a full body hug.

Room 522. Of course. *A golden placard with snail-like swirls bears the number 522.*

I shiver. Ever since I pulled myself over the cliff, I've felt the long fingers of Fate pressing into the small of my back, urging me forward. The feeling was subtle and easy to ignore, a low vibration that wasn't present in any physical way. I felt it in the same way I could feel Mikey's telepathic messages to Logan swirling in the air.

That sensation flares to life now. My future memory's coming true. Bit by tiny bit.

I don't know how long I stand there shivering, and then Logan rubs my arms through the silver mesh of my jumpsuit.

"Can we search the database by ability?" he asks. "Look for 'precognition' under 'primary ability.'"

Willliam presses a few keys. "No records listed."

I tug Logan's arm around me. Now that he's wearing his school uniform, he smells like chlorine once again.

"Are you sure?"

William squints at the projection. "I've got thirty-eight records with precognition as the preliminary ability. But you only wanted primary ability, right?"

"Yeah."

We try a few more search parameters. I even flip through the thirty-eight records, but nothing stands out.

I look at the potted plants on the shelves. Spider plants, cactii, bamboo. Many more whose names I don't know. Sword-like leaves, flowery spikes, wooden stems. I've heard somewhere vegetation is supposed to help us breathe. But these plants loom over me. They look like they're about to topple down and smother me.

"Now what?"

"We go get your sister?" Logan asks.

Looking back at the desk screen, I know he's right. It's time to find Jessa. What was I thinking? This whole idea is ridiculous. Why did I think I could waltz in and find the precog?

I open my mouth to agree when I hear a high-pitched scream. The wail pierces through the solid walls and makes me want to double over and grab my knees.

Worst of all, I think I recognize the voice. It sounds just like Sully.

40

"What is that?" Logan whispers.

The cry dies and we hear the scuffle of feet and then the hard, responding slap of flesh hitting flesh. The wail begins again.

William rubs the back of his neck. "You know how they take the inmates out of Limbo after they fulfill their memory?"

"This is where they go?" I ask. It can't be her. It can't. She was never supposed to leave Limbo. She's probably in her cell, looking at the roses I made out of leaves. There's no way she's here.

Crouching down, I crawl over to the door and crack it open. Two uniformed guards are dragging an electro-cuffed girl down the hallway. She wears a short-sleeved yellow jumpsuit, and horizontal scars mark up her arms. Her head is bent forward, but I know her profile as well as an eye through the wall.

I fall backward and the door closes with a soft click. I

feel like I'm in the river again, spinning crazily and going nowhere. Which way is up?

Logan pulls me into his arms. I look into his eyes and blink. A hundred blinks later, he comes into focus.

"Why is she here?" I whisper.

"I told you," William says. "She's fulfilled her memory, and she's being taken out of Limbo."

I round on the guard. "There's been a mistake. Her brain scans showed she wasn't aggressive. Her ripples shouldn't affect anybody. She never wanted to fulfill her memory. Didn't want to kill that man. She even cut up her arms so she wouldn't be raped…"

"No. There's been no mistake."

His voice is flat, his words final. No room for argument.

I struggle to recalibrate my world with this knowledge. Sully isn't safe in her cell in Limbo. She was raped by a stranger and then forced to kill him. By the agency that's supposed to be protecting us all.

Tears close up my throat. Something went wrong. Something made them decide she was aggressive, after all.

I let out a shaky breath. "Where are they taking her? What's going to happen?"

William shakes his head, not looking at me. "They're going to the Processing Room, since she's leaving Limbo. But I'm not sure what will happen."

I get in his face. "That girl had the cell next to mine, William. She was my friend. So talk to me. What will they do to her?"

Sweat beads on his brow, plastering his hair to his forehead. "Honest to Fate, I don't know. This isn't my department."

"Then take me to the Processing Room," I say.

"You can't barge in. They'll arrest you and throw you back into Limbo."

I shake my head. I ran to Harmony when I got out of Limbo. I cut myself off from civilization because I thought it was safer that way. But life went on without me. Jessa got arrested, and Sully was made to fulfill her memory. I can't wear blinders when it comes to the people I care about. Not anymore. Not when there's something I can do to help them.

"I'm not planning on interfering," I say. At least not yet. "I need to see what happens. Think how you would feel if they had someone who meant something to you. Your mom or your girlfriend. Wouldn't you want to see, too?" I put my hand on his shoulder. "Sully was an eye in the wall, but she was there. When I had nobody else, she gave me hope. Please, William, take me to the Processing Room."

He looks at the hand on his shoulder. And then he sighs. "Fine. I think I know another way in."

A few minutes later, he's perched on a stepladder in the corner of a laboratory. Countless machines sit on tables in nests of wires, surrounding a reclining chair on a platform. The smell of acid permeates the air, and long shelves hold everything from glass slides to circuit boards.

William punches the ceiling and a panel lifts off the metal grid. Dust floats down over us, and he pushes the panel aside. With one fluid movement, he pulls himself into the crawl space above.

"You're next," Logan says to me. "I'll give you a boost."

Taking a deep breath, I place my good foot into his interlaced fingers. Pain shoots through my other ankle. Gritting my teeth, I grab the edge of the ceiling, and then I'm up.

I choke on the air. Long, thin pipes run over my head, and I slither on my stomach down the box-like tunnel. William's sneakered feet squeak against the metal, and I sense rather than hear Logan behind me. We crawl forward about ten yards. Then, I hear the sound of another panel being lifted. Moments later, William disappears down the hole. He catches me as I drop, setting me soundlessly on the floor. A few seconds later, Logan follows.

We're in a closet. Light seeps through the crack at the bottom of the door. As my eyes get used to the darkness, I make out bottles of pills crowding each other on the shelves, along with gauze and test tubes and metal tongs.

I rub my ankle, but there's no time to think of the pain. Footsteps and low voices drift through the closet door. At least Sully isn't wailing anymore.

I open the door a couple of inches, keeping as low as possible. Logan's chin brushes against my head as he positions himself above me.

Sully is strapped to a reclining chair, and a gag covers her mouth. The chair looks like the one in Bellows's lab. What are they going to do? They already have her future memory. Now that she's fulfilled it in real life, will they make her relive that memory, the one that actually happened, over and over again?

I shudder. Bellows would do it, too. He'll give her the

fumes. Make her relive the rape every day for the rest of her life.

Sully looks from one guard to the other. Even from the distance, I can read her story. *Look at me. Haven't I been punished enough? I'm the victim here. They made me into a criminal. If anyone should be punished, it should be them. Not me. All I ever did was receive a bad memory from the future. Look at me.*

But her story is lost on the guards. The two of them bend over something on a side table, their gloved hands busy, not even glancing in her direction.

But I see you, Sully. And I'm so sorry this had to happen. I didn't know. I thought you were safe. But you don't have to worry. I'll get you out of here and we'll forget our memories ever existed.

One of the guards steps into my line of sight. I shift my gaze, and it lands on the side table. On a locked glass case with a rack of syringes inside.

My heart stops. One needle with clear liquid swimming in the barrel; another needle with red. The syringes are small and cylindrical. And identical to the one I used to kill my sister.

The guard has another syringe in his hand—a syringe with clear liquid.

"No," I whisper. "Oh, please, no."

But it's too late. Even as I watch, the guard steps forward and slams the needle into Sully's heart.

Her body bucks a few times. And then it is still.

41

scream. I scream over and over until my head explodes.
Again and again until my chest caves in.

But no sound comes out. I try to take a breath but
can't draw any air. A hand covers my mouth. Logan's
hand. Smothering me and keeping the screams inside.

I wrench away and collapse on the floor; I hug the
linoleum tiles as if they can anchor me to this world. I
don't know how long I lie there. Long enough for William
to open the closet door and announce, "They're gone."
Long enough for Logan's cool hands to turn sweaty
against my shoulder. Long enough to wonder if I can stay
here forever.

Logan's hand moves to my neck, dislodging the wig
from my head. "I'm so sorry, Callie."

I pull the wig off and drop it into my lap. The fake hair
flops against my legs like a dead animal. "How can this be
her sentence after getting out of Limbo? How?"

"Once she fulfilled her memory, the ripples are taken

care of." William stares at the empty reclining chair. "FuMA has no other use for her…alive."

Leaping to my feet, I cross the room and shove him as hard as I can. He tumbles into the chair.

"You knew, didn't you?" I grip the collar of his shirt and dig my nails into his skin. When he flinches, I push my nails deeper. "You knew they were going to kill her, but you didn't say anything. If you'd warned me, maybe we could've done something. Maybe we could've saved her."

He meets my eyes. "What would you have done? Would you have exposed yourself to give her the antidote?"

I freeze. "There's an antidote? Where?"

He gestures toward the locked glass case. "In case the administrator accidentally gets injected."

Two needles remain. One clear and one red.

Once upon a time, Sully told me a story about a girl named Jules, who was supposed to attempt murder against her father. She was dragged into the fulfillment room by a detainment guard. A scientist followed, with two rows of needles. A few minutes later, they all walked out, seemingly unhurt.

She killed him with one needle and revived him with the next.

The red needle is the antidote.

I look around wildly and snatch the floating keyball off its magnetic stand. With all my strength, I smash it over the locked case. Shards of glass fly everywhere. Paying no attention, I reach between the jagged edges and pluck up the red syringe. "What are you waiting for? Let's go."

"Callie." William shakes his head. "It's too late."

The needle begins to vibrate in my hand. "What are

you talking about? We can still find her body. We can save her."

"In order to work, the antidote needs to be injected within a minute of the poison. It's been at least ten minutes since they took her body away. I'm sorry."

I stare at him. "No. There's got to be a way."

"Callie. She's gone."

My gaze drops to the red liquid swimming in the barrel. Red like the leaf that falls into a little girl's hand. Red like the blood that no longer pumps through Sully's body. "So much for not knowing anything because it's not your department." Sobs wrack my body. I fling the needle to the ground and bury my face in my hands.

Warm arms encircle me, and I know without looking that it's Logan. "It's done," he whispers in my hair. "You can't change it. We need to think about your sister. You've got to keep it together if we're going to rescue her."

"No." It's suddenly so clear to me. So terribly, horribly clear.

A stillness flows through me. It takes all my worries and silences them, picks up my emotions and numbs them. All of a sudden, I understand how a girl can look into her sister's eyes and kill. Everything is turned off except for the task at hand. The solitary goal that must be accomplished.

"We can't rescue her yet. If they can kill Sully over a bad memory, what else are they capable of?" My hands no longer shake. The tears have dried on my face. And if any pieces of my shattered heart remain, they cower from my sight. "Don't you see? I can't turn my back on this now. I owe it to Sully to see it through. I was meant to find this precog. I was meant to see a future so awful I'm willing to do anything to prevent it. I won't act on it the way my future self does, but this part of my destiny, I need to fulfill."

"Okay." Logan nods, and I know I have his support, no matter what. He glances at William. "Are you still with us?"

William drags his eyes from the seam of the chair. "I risked my life giving you that extra minute to escape. I risk my life every day helping the Underground. And yet you still blame me for your friend's death. For all of their deaths."

He had a role. But so did I. I had a split second of realization before the guard plunged the needle into Sully's heart. A split second where I could've burst from the closet, knocked the needle out of his hand. I should've figured out the red needle was an antidote from Jules's story.

But I didn't. I stayed in the closet and cried. That's something I'll endure for the rest of my life.

"I do blame you," I say. "But I also blame me. And do you know who I really blame? The guards and Chairwoman Dresden and FuMA and future memory itself."

William nods, as if he knows I can't absolve him of his guilt. No one can. It's something we each need to work through on our own.

There's one more lead I have yet to follow. William won't like it, but we've gone way past anyone's comfort level.

"I need you to take me to Chairwoman Dresden's office," I say to him. "When MK assisted Bellows in giving me the fumes, she had a bear in her backpack. A white bear, with a red ribbon. The same bear that was in my future memory. She, and by extension the Chairwoman, are connected to Jessa. I'm going to find out how, and you're going to help me."

He slowly gets to his feet. "I don't like to involve my girlfriend in Underground business."

"I don't care." My voice shakes, and I point to the chair. "A girl died right here. An innocent victim. I'm to blame, and you're to blame. So you have to help me."

He takes a shuddering breath and nods. "In light of…what's happened…I'll do it. I'll get you into the Chairwoman's office. But you have to follow my lead, okay?"

Logan and I both nod.

We are almost out the door when Logan turns back. Picking his way through the glass, he retrieves the red needle from the ground and the clear needle from the case.

My pulse jumps. "What are you doing?"

He checks to make sure the safety caps are on and then puts both barrels into a medical kit he finds on the table. "If we take these needles, they can't be used on anybody else."

"Yes, but…" I swallow hard. "Logan, that's the needle I used. In my memory."

He tucks the medical kit under his arm. "You have complete control over your decisions, Callie. You won't use it unless you choose to."

That's exactly what I'm worried about.

42

MK stands behind a pure white desk of stacked concentric circles. Her desk screen, a thick pane of glass that goes all the way around her, is the biggest I've ever seen. A massive door of etched glass looms across from her, and the metal walls curve up to meet at a ringed skylight in the center of the ceiling.

Our footsteps tap against the white marble floors, and she looks up from the dozen or so files open on her desk screen. "Will." The shine of her eyes rivals the sheen of her hair. "What are you doing here?"

"I missed you, MK." Glancing down the long hallway, he drops a kiss on her temple.

I hover behind Logan's shoulder. With my reapplied makeup and the wig, we figured MK wouldn't remember me if she doesn't look too closely at my face.

"I thought I'd help you out." He gestures at us. "I've got a couple of interns from a local high school, and I thought maybe they could watch Olivia so you could get some work done."

At her name, a little girl sticks up her head from behind the cubicle, where she must've been sitting on the floor. I immediately recognize the pudgy cheeks and precisely-cut fringe of black bangs. Olivia Dresden. Chairwoman Dresden's daughter.

"That would be so helpful." MK drums the desk screen with her fingers. "The Chairwoman wants these files organized by the end of the day, and I'm at my wit's end."

"I don't know why she doesn't get a child-minder," William says. "It's a bit ridiculous, really."

"She doesn't like having outsiders poke into her business." MK ruffles the little girl's bangs. "And Olivia here is a breeze to watch, aren't you, dear heart?"

Olivia nods. "MK, I need to tell my mommy about my nightmare."

"Sure thing, but your mommy's in meetings all afternoon, remember? So as soon as she gets out, I'll let her know." She turns back to William. "Have you heard the news? TechRA thinks they've found her. Our Key to future memory."

I draw a sharp breath and shoot a look at Logan. His muscles bunch, as if he's about to swim a race.

"It's my classmate from school," Olivia pipes up. "I thought we'd be able to play together, since she's living here now, but MK says Jessa's too busy taking tests."

My knees buckle. I would've hit the floor, but Logan wraps an arm around my waist, holding me up.

"Hush, Olivia," MK says. "We don't know anything for sure. The scans of her brain are like nothing we've ever seen, but the scientists need to study her neural activity while she's in the process of transmitting a message to her Receiver. Problem is, she's not cooperating."

William leans his hip against the desk. "How do you even know she has a Receiver?"

"Her scan shows all the signs of a Sender," MK says. "And when there's a Sender, there's got to be a Receiver. One is useless without the other."

"Wild." A disarming smile spreads across William's face. "Well, I'll leave the politics to you bureaucrats. I'm nothing but a lowly guard, you know."

"Oh, Will. You could never be lowly." They melt into gooey smiles.

I was right. My sister actually is the Key. In a way, I'm not surprised. This whole day feels like a puzzle clicking into place, piece by piece. It's not déjà vu, but something similar. Rather than having experienced this moment before, I feel the compulsion to live it.

It's Fate's fingertips at the small of my back. I have to come to the Chairwoman's office. I have to listen to William talk to MK. I have to find this precog. Because somewhere, in some future world, I already did.

William straightens up. "Maybe the interns can entertain Olivia in Chairwoman Dresden's office. That way, they'll be out of your hair."

MK hesitates. "I don't know. She doesn't usually allow outsiders in there."

"It's up to you, of course. I thought it might be easier to focus, if they were out of your way."

She gnaws on her lip. "You're probably right. I suppose it wouldn't do any harm. Olivia plays in there all the time, and I'll be right out here." She sighs and presses William's hand. "You're so good to me."

William smiles, but I can see the pulse throbbing at his temple. His jaw is clenched so tightly his bones protrude against the skin. It's killing him to lie to MK.

I steel my heart and turn away. Too bad. It killed Sully to be a part of this system. This is the way it has to be.

William pushes open the etched glass door, and I catch his arm. "Thank you," I say, hoping he understands the words are more than a formality.

He blinks, and he can't hide his resentment. Against me and himself. "I'll be in my office if you need me. You can ask MK how to get there."

And then he is gone.

Olivia immediately starts running in circles around the office. Behind the glass and steel desk, on top of the white leather couches, narrowly missing her knee on the mirrored coffee table.

I'm not sure what I expected. The white bear, waving its red ribbon from the top of the Chairwoman's desk? But the answer must be here, somewhere in this room. The bear connects my sister to MK. And the Chairwoman herself must have documents on the precognitive.

Logan heads straight to the desk screen, jerking his head to indicate the blur of movement is my responsibility.

Floor-to-ceiling windows span the outside wall. I suck in my breath as Olivia speeds past. If I don't slow her down, she might crash right through the glass. On her next circuit around the office, I snag her arm. "Olivia, do you want to stop and talk to me?"

Strands of hair tumble from her twin braids, and her chest heaves up and down. "I know who you are."

"Well, yes." I guess my disguise is no match for a hyper-observant six year old. "I'm Jessa's sister. You've probably seen me picking her up at the T-minus eleven classroom."

"No, that's not it. I've seen you in my dreams." She takes off running again and hops over Logan's feet where he kneels in front of the desk, looking for a work-around to the desk screen. She screeches to a halt in front of me. "What's he doing?"

"Nothing. Do you want to play a game? Or sing a song?"

Olivia looks over her shoulder. Logan's all the way under the desk now, examining the underside of the screen. "I had a nightmare at school today," she says. "I need to tell my mom about it."

"You fell asleep? Are you tired now? You could take a nap on the couch, if you wanted."

She rolls her eyes. "No, I didn't fall asleep. You don't have to be asleep to receive dreams, stupid!"

She dashes away again. Figure eights this time. Around the desk, behind the table. I watch her, the skin at my neck prickling.

"Olivia." When she stops again, I crouch down so I can look into her face. Her round cheeks are flushed, and she squints at me as though she might need laser correction. "You're not actually talking about dreams, are you?"

"My mommy says I should call them that, so people don't get suspicious."

My mouth is suddenly dry, and I lick my lips. "Suspicious of what?"

The loose hair flops around her face. "My mommy says I'm not supposed to talk about it. But I've seen you. You're nice. You try to help me, in the future."

"Olivia, when you say dreams, are you actually talking about visions? Visions from the future?"

She peeks at me. Something in my features must reassure her because she nods, slowly.

I let out a breath. My heart's thundering so loudly I'm surprised it doesn't send vibrations across the room. "Logan," I call. "Can you come here, please?"

"What is it?" He crosses the room and squats down next to me. "The Underground scientists have developed a back door to these desk screens," he murmurs in my ear. "I'm almost in."

"Forget about that for a moment." I turn back to Olivia. "We're looking for a precog. Someone who can see years and years into the future. Do you know anyone like that?"

She picks at a hole in the knee of her jumpsuit. "I don't like that word. It sounds like a bot, when really, a precog is just a person, like anybody else."

"Well, of course, a precognitive is a person," I say. "A person who can help others, by preparing them for the future, or warning them about what might happen."

She stands abruptly. "It's so boring being the only kid here. I thought if I gave Jessa a teddy bear, she would come play with me. But I haven't seen her. Maybe my mom forgot to send it."

My mouth drops open. "That was you? You sent Jessa

the teddy bear?"

"Yeah. MK gave me the bear, but I already had one." Her lower lip sticks out. "I thought Jessa would come by for a visit, but she hasn't."

Regaining my composure, I lean forward. "I'm sure she would play with you if she could." I rub her shoulders, like I might do with my sister. "I'm trying to help her, Olivia. But I can't do that unless I find this precognitive. Something bad happens in the future, and I need to find out what it is. Do you understand?"

She nods. Her narrow shoulders rise with her next breath. "I'm the precog. And this bad thing you're looking for? I think it's my nightmare."

I rock back onto the marble. I can't believe it. We found her. The source of the prophecy, the information being fed to an entire team of scientists. It was the Chairwoman's daughter all along. A six-year-old girl. And we found her.

Logan's hands close over my arms. I can't tell if he's supporting me or holding himself up. "Can you tell us about your nightmare?" he asks Olivia.

She shakes her head. "Too hard to explain. You'll have to watch it yourself, the way my mom does."

"How do we do that?" I ask.

"On the same machines they use to read your future memory."

We wrench open the glass door. MK has her hands on her hips, studying the open files projected above her desk screen. Looking up, she blows a strand of hair off her forehead. "Just think how worse off I would be if you weren't here right now. How's it going in there?"

"Not bad," Logan says. "We were hoping we could take Olivia on a walk. To visit William, maybe? It's getting a little rowdy in there."

"Yeah, I can hear the thumps." She laughs. "I suppose that should be fine. Make sure you stay in the building, though, and have her back in an hour."

He thanks MK, and then we're on our way. As soon as we get to William's office, we'll hook Olivia up to the scanner. The machine will read the images in her mind, and I'll see her vision of the future. If my theory is correct, I'll finally know why a future Callie decided to kill her sister.

If, if, if. Nothing's definite, and yet, the muscles in my neck and shoulders turn to stone. This is the answer. I can feel it.

The halls are mostly empty. Olivia skips ahead of us, her braids unraveling a little more with each bounce. The few people we see give her indulgent smiles, letting us pass without question.

"No wonder the Chairwoman doesn't have a child-minder," I murmur to Logan. "She doesn't want anyone to find out."

Olivia starts racing down the hallway. "Hurry up!" she calls over her shoulder. "We're almost there!"

"Olivia, be care—"

A uniformed employee comes around the corner, carrying a potted plant. Olivia slams into him, knocking him to the ground. The pot flies out of his hand, smashes into the wall, and breaks into a million pieces.

The ceramic remains scatter across the floor. A trail of soil leads like breadcrumbs to the broken plant stalk.

The cool wind of Fate blows against my spine. I've seen this image before.

Logan helps Olivia to her feet and apologizes to the man.

The man frowns, his mustache twitching. "I don't have time to deal with this. I'm late for a meeting."

"Don't worry, sir," Logan says. "We're interns here. We'll call a bot to clean it up."

Grumbling about out-of-control kids and their irresponsible child-minders, the man strides down the hall. I wait until he's out of earshot, and then I turn to Logan.

"That broken pot was in my memory," I whisper. "It looked just like that. The trail of soil, the broad green leaves. My memory's coming true."

All of a sudden, I'm not sure I've made the right decision. Maybe I don't need to know the future. Why am I tempting Fate? Maybe I should just grab Jessa and run.

Logan takes my hand and repeats my words back to me. "Knowing the future doesn't take away your free will. Only you can decide what you will do." He grips my hand. "We've come so far, Callie. Let's finish this."

I look at him, the person who's been by my side almost this entire journey. "I'm scared."

"Me, too," he says.

43

It's the same room. Same chair with cylindrical cushions, humming machines, tray of meditation aids. Same shiny black tiles, although the dust has been swept to the side and forgotten, like a pile of mouse droppings. Same glass walls, but the white sheets providing the illusion of privacy have been pulled down.

I focus on these minor differences, but it's no use. I can't catch my breath, and every fiber in my body screams *run*!

Instead, I grab the glass bottle from the tray and twist off the stopper. The spicy scent of peppermint clears my nose. I think of a morning, not too long ago. Sitting around the eating table with my family, drinking peppermint tea. Jessa warms her hands in the steam rising from her mug, while my mother closes her eyes, lost in dreams of the past.

The memory washes over me, and I inhale deeply. My heart slows to a steadier rate. Maybe these meditation aids work, after all.

William adjusts the metal headpiece on Olivia's head. She's sitting on the recliner, her ankles crossed as if she's done this a hundred times. And maybe she has.

"Brings back memories, doesn't it?" he says to me, leaning over and tightening Olivia's chin strap.

I roll my eyes at his deliberate double meaning. "Ha ha."

"My mommy always lights me a candle," Olivia says. "I like to play with the flame."

William raises his eyebrow, as if not sure he should be giving fire to a little girl. "If that's what gets you into the proper state of mind, by all means…" Shrugging, he sets up a candle on a bedside table and wheels it over Olivia's lap. "Open your mind and let the vision come to you. If you need anything, we'll be right next door."

He beckons to me, and I follow him to his office in the adjacent room, where Logan's waiting. Since there's no white sheet, we can see Olivia through the glass walls. I wave at her, but she's busy trying to pinch the flame between her fingers.

William plugs wires into a desk screen. Instead of flat and horizontal, the screen is vertical and curves all the way around, so that it resembles an oversize donut. Logan's already found his way inside.

"How did you get in there?" I ask.

"Just duck under," Logan says. "Careful you don't hit your head."

I join him inside the machine. All around me, white lights dance, chasing each other like fireflies across the black screen.

"What is this?" I ask.

"Olivia's mind figuring out where to land." William ducks under the machine and pops up next to us. "When the vision comes to her, these lights will form images so we can live it with her."

"Live it?" Logan reaches out to touch a light, and his fingers bump into the screen. "Don't you mean watch?"

"You'll see what I mean." William passes out headpieces and motions for us to put them on. "The vision will translate across all five senses. You'll feel like you're experiencing the vision yourself. You'll see it through Olivia's perspective."

The lights begin to vibrate, drifting together to form a solid mass.

"Here it comes," William whispers. "Hold on tight."

My hands are wrapped around black bars. Thick, bloody scratches travel down my arms, and the smell of urine and feces chokes the air. Teenage girls in dirty school uniforms press all around me.

At the end of the cell, a brunette roars and leaps onto a redhead's back, grabbing her hair and yanking until it detaches in clumps. Another girl in the corner sings at the top of her lungs. Her head lolls around in a pile of feces, streaking her once blonde hair with brown.

Suddenly I hear short, staccato raps against the concrete floor. We all fall silent, even the singing girl. Two people appear at the end of the hallway. They converse briefly, and then the tall one walks toward us. I see a navy uniform and silver hair cut closely to a well-shaped head. Her face is more lined, but the features are unmistakable. Chairwoman

Dresden.

I stand on wobbly legs and grip the bars even tighter. "Mom," I say. "You have to call off the execution."

She scans past me a few times, as if she doesn't recognize who I am. She finally meets my gaze and winces. "I told you, Olivia. You knew the price of receiving a mediocre memory, but you wouldn't listen, would you?"

"My future self sent me a happy memory," I say. "In it, I held my newborn baby and felt at peace with the world."

"It was mediocre! You of all people should've known what was coming." A muscle ticks at the corner of her mouth. "It was your vision of the future that showed us what we could become. A race of superhumans." She wraps her hands over mine, on the bars. "I know you've got talent, Olivia. You're my daughter, aren't you? Why didn't your future self send a better memory? You could've chosen any memory. One that showed off your superlative skills as a violinist. One that illustrated your mathematical genius. Why did you send this one?"

I straighten my spine. "I don't know why she did it, Mom. Maybe my future self thought it wasn't right to execute ninety-nine percent of the population on the basis of their memories. Maybe she knew this was the only way to get you to listen. To show you there's more to humanity than pure talent. There's also happiness. And love."

Her fingers fall away. "Not in this world, I'm afraid. We can't allow any mediocre genes to contaminate the breeding pool. The execution has been set. You and the other Mediocres will serve your sentence in two hours."

She turns and walks away, her heels clicking against the floor, toward the person I now assume is her assistant.

"*Mom!*" *I call after her.* "*You can't do this. I'm your daughter. Your daughter!*"

"*No.*" *Her voice carries down the long hallway, and I can't see her face anymore. The only thing I can make out is her navy uniform.* "*No daughter of mine is mediocre.*"

44

The image breaks apart, and white lights buzz against the black screen. I'm breathing, but the air turns to lead when it enters my mouth. My heart pounds, but the beats scatter like insects in the night.

So this is why. I finally have my answer. I finally know why my future self kills Jessa.

The donut screen whirls around me. I'm in the center, but I'm no eye of the storm. I'm spinning fastest of all, so fast I'm about to collapse. But then Logan grabs my arms, holding me up.

I glimpse myself in the reflection of his irises. The girl he's always seen, but the one I wasn't sure existed until now.

A high-pitched cry punctures the air, followed by a heavy crash.

"Olivia," William says. As one, he and Logan rip off their headpieces and duck under the machine.

A moment later, I hear her hysterical babbling: "I

didn't know…it was worse than before…why did Mommy say I wasn't her daughter…why were all the Mediocres killed…"

"Shhh," Logan says. "It's going to be okay. Shhh."

Moving in slow motion, I take off my headpiece and fall to my knees. Future memory will cause this, the systematic execution of the mediocre. But it doesn't have to be this way. I can prevent it all if future memory is never discovered. It can be stopped if I kill my sister.

I take a shaky breath. It was always my decision. Nobody forced my hand. Fate never pre-empted my will. My sister or ninety-nine percent of the population. The death of a single girl or genocide.

I close my eyes. My hand finds its way to my mouth. I bite, but my mind doesn't register the pain. It's too full of those girls in the prison cell. The fighting ones and the listless ones. The one rolling in her own feces and the teenage Olivia. Another cell and another, all full of seventeen-year-old girls and boys. Executed day after day until mediocrity is snuffed out. Until all that's left is a society of superhumans.

How can I let that happen? How can I kill my own sister?

A thick wetness coats my tongue. I take my hand from my mouth and see teeth marks puncturing skin. Blood. I look wildly around the room and land on the medical kit with the syringes inside.

I glance into the next room. Olivia's head is cradled in Logan's lap, and he's stroking her hair. William is picking up the machine that's been knocked to the floor.

It's my decision. But really, when it comes down to it,

what choice do I have?

I take the needles from the medical kit—both the clear and the red—and stuff them in my pocket. I leave the room and hear Logan call out after me. I don't look back.

I walk down the hall. It has green linoleum floors, with computer screens embedded in the tile. The lighted walls shine so brightly I can make out a partial shoe print on the ground. The acrid smell of antiseptic burns my nose.

I curl my fingers into a fist to staunch the flow of blood, but red drops litter the floor. I turn a corner and skirt around the shattered remains of a ceramic pot. A trail of soil leads like breadcrumbs to a broken plant stalk and loose green leaves.

I walk down an identical hallway. And then another. And another.

Finally, I stop in front of a door. A golden placard, with snail spirals decorating each corner, bears the numbers 522. I take a deep breath, but no matter how much air I draw, I can't seem to get enough.

There's nowhere left to run. No one left to save me from this moment. This is my future, and I'm living it.

I go inside. The sun shines through the window, the first window I have seen for hours. A teddy bear with a red bow sits on the sill.

So the Chairwoman sent Olivia's present, after all. The madwoman has a heart. A bubble of laughter rises in my throat. Underneath the despotic lunacy is a woman with consideration. A tyrant who tickles. A killer who cries.

The laughter bursts from my mouth like crazy, frothing foam, and then it shuts off as I take in the rest of the scene.

Everything is hospital white. White walls, white blinds, white bed sheets.

In the middle of the sheets lies Jessa. Oh, she is so young. So innocent. My bones turn to liquid, and I sink to my knees by the bed.

Her chestnut hair billows around her head, tangled and unbraided. Wires protrude from her body like they are Medusa's snakes, winding every which way before ending in one of several machines.

"Callie! You came!" My sister's lips curve in a smile.

It takes me three tries to force the words through my parched lips. "Of course I came." I pick up her slender hand. It fits in my palm the way a sparrow belongs in her nest. "How are they treating you?"

Jessa wrinkles her nose. "The food is gross. And they never let me play outside."

A lifetime of memories flit through my mind. Newborn Jessa rooting in the air like a baby bird searching for food. Toddler Jessa crying for me to kiss the boo-boo on her knee. My sister as she was last month, wiping the tears from my face.

I stand up. It's always been my choice. Knowing the future doesn't take away my free will. I have complete control over my actions. This is my decision. Mine. Not FuMA's, not the future's, not even Fate's.

"When you leave, you can play as much as you'd like." I move the wires off her chest and place my hand squarely over her heart. "I love you, Jessa. You know that, don't you?"

She nods. Her heart thumps evenly against my palm, the strong, steady beat of the complete trust a child has for an older sibling.

Tears drip down my face. This is an impossible choice. Impossible. But I have to make it.

I'm so sorry, Jessa. Words can't describe how sorry I am. You are more than my sister. You are my twin, my half, my soul.

You are the candle that shines when all power is extinguished. The proof that love exists when life is snuffed out.

When all my layers are stripped away, when everything I know is turned inside out, all I have left is this.

My love for you.

It's the only thing they can't touch.

"Forgive me," I whisper, although I will never, ever forgive myself.

I reach into my pocket and take out the needles.

The door clatters open, and Logan bursts into the room. His gaze zeroes in on the syringes. "No, Callie. Don't do this. Don't—"

It's too late. I smash the red needle to the floor, destroying the antidote. And then I whip my arm through the air, plunging the clear needle straight into my own heart. The liquid empties into my body.

He crosses the room in three strides and catches me as I sway forward. "What have you done? Oh dear Fate, what have you done?"

I reach up to touch his cheek, but already I'm too weak and my hand stops halfway there. He lowers his face to meet my fingers. I feel the bristles on his jaw and the hot, wet salt of his tears.

"This is the only way." My voice trembles, as if it knows

these are the last words I'll ever say. "The only way to save Jessa. The only way to save the future."

She's the Sender. I'm the Receiver. One is useless without the other. If there is no Receiver, Jessa can't send her memories. They won't be able to excavate her mind. They won't discover future memory.

The girls in the prison will be safe. My sister will be safe. Everyone will be safe.

Except me.

I turn to my sister one last time and look straight into the face of an angel. The round curve of her cheek catches the glow of the light, and her hair falls around eyes so luminous they could've been plucked from the stars.

I love you, I mouth inside my head.

I look up at Logan, and my last thought is: *despite everything, I'm so glad I took Jessa to the park on October Twenty-seventh.*

And then everything goes black.

EPILOGUE

I float through an endless dark night. My consciousness tries to grab hold of a thought, it tries to make the thought concrete and present and real, but then it lets go again, and I continue to drift. Am I dead? Will I continue to float for an eternity? The questions fade as soon as they appear, before I can even begin to formulate answers.

There is a voice sometimes, so sweet and young. I can't make out the words, or if I can, they slip away as soon as I comprehend their meaning. There is love in this voice, unconditional love that pierces all the way through the haze, so that for a moment, I am substantial and whole. For a moment, I almost remember.

Then there's another voice, low and achingly familiar. How can it be so familiar, when it is so different from my own? How can it resonate so deeply, as if it lives inside me, when I don't know to whom the voice belongs? There is love here, too, but a different kind. This love fills me and makes every fiber of my existence mourn. How can I cry, when I don't have eyes? How can I despair, when I don't know what I've lost?

Questions, always questions, eternal questions, floating in and around my consciousness. But never any answers. Either because I can't think of them, or when I do, it is too late.

I don't know how long I drift. Five minutes or fifty years. An eternity or a second. I feel like I'll float forever, but then something flashes across my consciousness. Something searing and acute and aware. A vision. No, slivers of visions, snapshots of memories, tumbling one after the other, faster and faster, pressing at my mind, making me remember.

A young girl with a purple dog. My arm whipping through the air. The brush of a boy's lips. A tattered feather floating in the air.

I can't be dead, not when my heart aches this much. Not when I live the memories this clearly. Not when I feel the little girl's touch. Not when I hear the boy pleading with me to come back to him.

I will, I want to tell them. I'll come back as soon as I can.

As soon as I figure out how to open my eyes.

end of book one

ACKNOWLEDGMENTS

I've wanted to be a published author ever since I was six years old, and I've been lucky to have so many people support me on this journey.

Thank you to my unparalleled agent, Beth Miller, for being a true partner in this business.

My heartfelt thanks to Liz Pelletier, my editor and publisher, and one of the most brilliant women I've ever met, for believing in this book. Thank you to the entire team at Entangled, and in particular, Heather Riccio, Meredith Johnson, and Stacy Abrams for your hard work. Special thanks, as well, to Debbie Suzuki, Melissa Montovani, Jessica Turner, and Ellie McMahon. You are all amazing. Thanks to L.J. Anderson for the gorgeous cover, and thank you to Rebecca Mancini for the foreign-rights magic. Thank you, as well, to my film agent, Lucy Stille.

The following writers have critiqued for me, but more importantly, have given me their friendship. Thank you to

Kimberly MacCarron and Vanessa Barneveld, for always being here; Meg Kassel and Stephanie Winklehake, for sharing your passions and dreams; Denny Bryce and Holly Bodger, for never being more than a text message away; Danielle Meitiv, for your scientific expertise; Stephanie Buchanan, for reading countless drafts; and Kerri Carpenter, for the accountability. Thank you to Romily Bernard, Natalie Richards, Cecily White, Michelle Monkou, Masha Levinson, and Darcy Woods. You are not just writing friends; you are the best friends a girl could have.

Thank you to the late Karen Johnston. Karen, you were one of the earliest cheerleaders for this book, and your belief in me has left a footprint in my heart.

I am so grateful to my writing communities for giving me a home: the Waterworld Mermaids, Honestly YA, the Writing Experiment, the Firebirds, the DoomsDaisies, the Dreamweavers, the Dauntless, and the Washington Romance Writers.

Thank you to my favorite beta reader, Kaitlin Khorashadi.

Over the years, I have been fortunate to have teachers who have encouraged me to pursue my writing, in particular Jeanie Astbury, Professor Phil Fisher, and Professor Kenji Yoshino. I am grateful to Frankie Jones Danly, for her early support and guidance. Thank you to Kim Brayton, for writing my first book with me.

Thank you to my dearest friends who have believed in me for two decades: Anita, Sheila, Aziel, Kai, J.D., Francis, Josh, Nick, Steph, Peter, Gaby, Alex, Larry, Nicole, Julia, and Monique. Thanks to my newer friends, who are just as dear -- Jeanne Johnston, for always listening, and the talented Elizabeth Chomas, for my author photos.

I am exceedingly blessed to have such a loving family. From the bottom of my heart, thank you to my dad, Naronk, and the rest of the Hompluems: Uraiwan, Pan, Dana, and Lana. Thank you to the Dunns: Donald, Catherine, Chantal, Franck, Quentin, and Natasha. Thank you, P. Noi, and thank you, Karen. Thank you, as well, to A-ma and my Thai family, the Techavachara clan. Your support means everything to me.

Thank you to Aksara, Atikan, and Adisai. For you, I would fight the future and Fate itself.

And finally, thank you to Antoine. You believed in me even when I didn't. Even if the future told you otherwise, you would still believe in me.

THE BOOK OF IVY

BY AMY ENGEL

What would you kill for?

After a brutal nuclear war, the United States was left decimated. A small group of survivors eventually banded together. My name is Ivy Westfall, and my mission is simple: to kill the president's son—my soon-to-be husband—and return the Westfall family to power. But Bishop Lattimer isn't the cruel, heartless boy my family warned me to expect. But there is no escape from my fate. Bishop *must* die. And I must be the one to kill him…

PERFECTED

BY KATE JARVIK BIRCH

Ever since the government passed legislation allowing people to be genetically engineered and raised as pets, the rich and powerful can own beautiful girls like sixteen-year-old Ella as companions. But when Ella moves in with her new masters and discovers the glamorous life she's been promised isn't at all what it seems, she's forced to choose between a pampered existence full of gorgeous gowns and veiled threats, or seizing her chance at freedom with the boy she's come to love, risking both of their lives in a daring escape no one will ever forget.

THE BODY INSTITUTE

BY CAROL RIGGS

Thanks to cutting-edge technology, Morgan Dey is a top teen Reducer at The Body Institute. She temporarily lives in someone else's body and gets them in shape so they're slimmer and healthier. But there are a few catches. Morgan can never remember anything while in her "Loaner" body, including flirt-texting with the super-cute Reducer she just met or the uneasy feeling that the director of The Body Institute is hiding something. Still, it's all worth it in the name of science. Until the glitches start. Now she'll have to decide if being a Reducer is worth the cost of her body *and* soul…